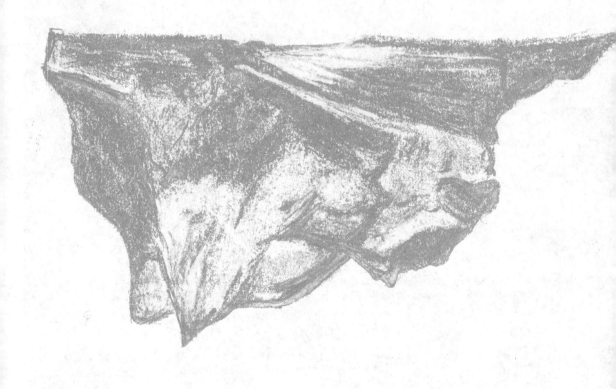

Fence Volume 20, No. 2 winter 2020
©2020 Fence Magazine, Incorporated

Cover: *Titanic* by Jacqueline Goss

Fence is published in print approx 2x/yr

Fence receives submissions electronically at fence.submittable.com. Response time is between three and nine months. Repeat publications take place after at least four issues or two years have elapsed.

Find us at fenceportal.org or rebeccafence@gmail.com.
Or, at (518) 567-7006.

This issue of *Fence* was printed in the United States by Versa Press. *Fence* is distributed in North America by: Small Press Distribution, Berkeley, CA (510) 524-1668; by ANC (615) 267-4047, www.anclink.com. Fence is also available for direct distribution via: send an email and we'll set something up. rebeccafence@gmail.com.

ISBN: 978-1-944380-17-5
ISSN: 1097-9980

Fence is published by Fence Magazine, Incorporated, a not-for-profit corporation. Donations and gifts are tax-deductible to the extent allowed by law.

Fence is made possible by the agency of the Fence Trust and all Friends of Fence. This project is supported by awards from the Whiting Foundation and the New York State Council on the Arts. Often we have funding from the National Endowment for the Arts, but not this year.

A one-year subscription is $25; two-year subscription is $40. Membership is available at fenceportal.org and offers a host of promises, if not privileges, including subscription and books.

If you'd like to support *Fence*, you can donate on our website, or contact Rebecca Wolff at rebeccafence@gmail.com.

DID YOU SEE FENCE 35

MATERIAL AND DIGITAL CALAMITIES ABOUND. THE MATERIAL ISSUE IS SOLD OUT AND ALL THE DIGITAL FILES FOR THE ISSUE WERE SWALLOWED UP INTO A DROPBOX VOID AND CANNOT BE ACCESSED ANY LONGER BY THE EDITORS. THE CLOUD ATE FENCE 35 AS WELL AS FENCE 34, 33, 32, 31, 30, 29, 28, AND 27.

BUT NOW YOU CAN LISTEN TO THE ENTIRE FENCE 35 AS READ OUT LOUD INTO DEVICES BY THE AUTHORS INCLUDING

EDGAR GARCIA
TESS BROWN-LAVOIE
LAURA SIMS
ARIANA REINES
ELENI SIKELIANOS
RACHEL LEVITSKY
SUZI GARCIA
BLAKE BUTLER
BRIAN KIM STEFANS
AMY LAWLESS
STEVEN ALVAREZ
SERENA SOLIN
DESIREE ALVAREZ
ERICA HUNT
CHRISTOPHER PATRICK MILLER
WENDY C. ORTIZ
SAM TRUITT
LEAH DWORKIN
DAVID BLAIR
GEOFFREY CRUICKSHANK-HAGENBUCKLE
KRISTIN BOCK
BONNIE CHAU
ABBY MINOR

IT'S A PODCAST

AVAILABLE ON PLATFORMS INCLUDING

ALL OF THE PLATFORMS

SEARCH FOR IT PLEASE

← ▢ ⓘ 🗑 ✉ ⊘ ⎗ ▷ ⋮

209

Dropbox Support Chat   Inbox ×

Dropbox (Dropbox Support) <support@dropbox.zendesk.com>
to me ▾

-##- Please type your reply above this line -##-

Ticket #9809828: Dropbox Support Chat

You can add a response by replying to this email.

Please be sure to reply with the same email address that you used to originally contact us.

Fence Fencebooks, Oct 8, 1:00 PM PDT:

Chat transcript:

(19:10:25) Visitor: yesterday hundreds of my files were deleted without my permission or having anything to do with it. They have simply disappeared. I receive
(19:11:46) Visitor: Some kind of update was happening as they were deleted, and I believe that something in the update caused the files to be deleted.
(19:15:14) Audrey: Thanks very much for contacting Dropbox Support, my name is Audrey. I'd be happy to help you with your request!
(19:15:17) Audrey: Can I start by getting your first name please?
(19:18:38) Audrey: Are you still with me?
(19:21:15) Visitor: Rebecca
(19:21:30) Audrey: Hello Rebecca
(19:21:33) Audrey: it's nice to meet you
(19:21:38) Visitor: same
(19:21:46) Audrey: have you checked the deleted files page of your account?
(19:21:55) Visitor: yes, they don't appear there.
(19:22:10) Audrey: okay, can I have a file name to look up as an example?
(19:22:37) Visitor: The folders the files were in all have the word Fence in them: one would be Fence 35
(19:23:00) Audrey: I'll take a look this side
(19:23:06) Audrey: in the meantime
(19:23:06) Visitor: k
(19:23:16) Audrey: can you check this link: www.dropbox.com/events
(19:23:30) Audrey: a deletion can sometimes mean a move as well so perhaps you just moved them
(19:23:38) Audrey: the the events page will tell you more
(19:24:40) Visitor: nothing appears out of the ordinary on there; I recognize all the changes I made
(19:24:50) Visitor: none of the deleted folders are there
(19:25:18) Visitor: This was approximately 7 folders which each contained at least a hundred files
(19:26:13) Audrey: okay but have you tried searching for the file you are missing in the search bar on the website: https..
(19:27:54) Audrey: as I mentioned, a mass deletion could also be a move so you might have them in your account but j..
(19:30:21) Audrey: I don't see any deletions on your account
(19:30:35) Audrey: can you tell me when you got the email telling you that your files were deleted?
(19:30:44) Visitor: Ah let me try what you describe, hold on.
(19:31:00) Visitor: I didn't get an email, I got series of pop-up notifications
(19:31:19) Visitor: sometime around 5 pm last night
(19:31:21) Visitor: eastern time
(19:32:28) Audrey: okay, I'm still looking this side but as I said I think they were moved because I dont see any deletions
(19:32:33) Visitor: let me know what you find
(19:34:15) Audrey: Take a look here as well: https://www.dropbox.com/share/folders
(19:35:25) Audrey: and see if you can see any of the folders
(19:34:48) Visitor: so far i am not finding anything, one filename I remember very well is "riofblue"--it's nowhere.
(19:35:16) Visitor: nothing in the shared folder
(19:36:00) Audrey: okay let me check
(19:38:37) Audrey: You know what I think I might suggest in this case Rebecca?
(19:38:52) Visitor: do tell
(19:38:33) Audrey: Have you heard of Dropbox Rewind?
(19:39:38) Visitor: no

Q audrey   X ·

← ▢ ⓘ 🗑 ✉ ⊘ ⎗ ⋮   ‹ › ▣ ▾

(19:40:27) Audrey: for a large scale activity
(19:40:45) Visitor: if the files do not appear in "deleted files" then . . .
(19:41:11) Audrey: then you can set it back to before all the strange happenings occured and it will revert your account back to the way it was
(19:41:20) Audrey: before all these changes occurred
(19:41:45) Audrey: Do you want to give that a try and then we'll take it from there if you were unable to get things back to normal?
(19:42:30) Visitor: I would like to try that, but I have to make sure that I don't roll it back to before I made a lot of changes to a particular file yesterday. I finished work at 3 pm yesterday and it was sometime after
that that all the files were deleted.
(19:43:51) Audrey: is there another file name I can look up on?
(19:44:07) Visitor: you mean what I was working on yesterday?
(19:44:34) Audrey: I mean of a missing file
(19:44:46) Audrey: riofblue wasn't coming up with anything on my end
(19:45:13) Visitor: it's easier for me to remember tider names than file names. Fence 35 is one. Fence 34 is another.
(19:45:27) Audrey: and fence 35 was coming up with all the data in your account because as you mentioned - most files have the name fence inside
(19:46:11) Visitor: right, I honestly don't remember file names right now except that one, but that one is definitely right.
(19:46:31) Visitor: so if you can't find it anymore, what does that mean? it has to be somewhere, right?
(19:46:38) Audrey: Did you rename anything yesterday?
(19:47:22) Visitor: nothing I can think of
(19:47:47) Visitor: There was some kind of upgrade to dropbox yesterday, right? everything looks different.
(19:48:32) Audrey: yes Dropbox has a new version but this wouldn't delete your files
(19:48:58) Audrey: sorry I know this is taking long I'm just trying to search for anything I can here
(19:49:11) Audrey: please also take another look through the events page: www.dropbox.com/events and change the dates if you need to
(19:49:39) Audrey: try and see if you can find an event that can explain any of your missing files
(19:50:20) Visitor: okay
(19:51:39) Audrey: can you check this link and tell me if this is one of the files you are looking for?
(19:51:39) Audrey: https://www.dropbox.com/rewind_delete/178616/29784974670330629
(19:51:49) Visitor: no, that's not one.
(19:52:32) Visitor: I'm working on Fence 36, and that's the only folder that's left in the Fence folder, which used to contain all 6 other folders. it's so weird!
(19:52:48) Visitor: btw, you are an actual person, yes?
(19:53:08) Audrey: yes yes haha, it's me Audrey
(19:53:17) Audrey: it really is so weird
(19:53:18) Visitor: it's that's cool.
(19:53:33) Audrey: have you worked on a lot of folders or files in the fence 36 folder?
(19:53:46) Audrey: I'll tell you what I'm thinking
(19:53:47) Visitor: yes, I really can't understand what's happening. The thing I
(19:53:52) Visitor: k go ahead
(19:54:06) Audrey: You can rollback a folder and not your whole account
(19:54:10) Audrey: its an option
(19:54:12) Visitor: what I don't understand is wouldn't any deleted files or folders still be visible?
(19:54:33) Visitor: Ah. The folder called Fence is the one I would want to roll back, but first I want to move Fence 36 out of it.
(19:54:36) Visitor: so I was going to say rather perhaps rollback the folder fence 36 and it will put everything back the way it was
(19:54:43) Audrey: ah yes sorry
(19:54:45) Audrey: what you said
(19:54:54) Visitor: exactly what you said
(19:54:54) Visitor: good, okay, and I do that now?
(19:55:08) Audrey: I need to email you the instructions and then yes please do
(19:55:13) Visitor: okay
(19:55:17) Audrey: keep in mind though - on the website
(19:55:31) Audrey: you'll see everything right away but it'll take a while to sync to the computer
(19:55:40) Visitor: okay
(19:55:45) Audrey: is there anything else I can help you with today?
(19:56:12) Visitor: did you send the instructions?
(19:56:34) Audrey: Not just yet, we need to close the chat first so I can send you your ticket number as well
(19:56:36) Visitor: well?
(19:56:52) Visitor: Ah okay, thanks. can you tell me which email address you are using
(19:57:06) Audrey: fence.fencebooks@gmail.com
(19:57:11) Visitor: great
(19:57:13) Audrey: this one is the one linked to your account
(19:57:16) Audrey: okay wonderful
(19:57:24) Audrey: im crossing my fingers for you
(19:57:45) Audrey: email me back when you have done the rollback so I can know if you need more help or not
(19:57:46) Visitor: actually, can you tell me how to move the folder on the website?
(19:58:34) Audrey: is there anyway you can rather download the folder?
(19:58:57) Audrey: how big is it?
(19:58:50) Visitor: oh, yes, I can do that. it's not too big.
(19:59:08) Audrey: good - its better to avoid duplicates later etc
(19:59:18) Audrey: Have a great day! When our chat closes I will email you a follow up, there will also be a short survey. Dropbox would love to hear how easy it was for you to receive the support you needed
today!

FENCE

POETRY FICTION ART AND CRITICISM / F--K the CL--D
FENCE DIGITAL HERE BUT NOT THERE / ALL OF IT OUT HERE BUT NOT
OUT THERE / **CONSTANT CRITIC** / **ELECMENT** / **FENCEPORTAL.ORG** /
THE CLOUD INSIDE YOU /

Rainy Days on the Farm

WINNER OF THE OTTOLINE PRIZE

Lesle Lewis's NEW POEMS GIVE, AND TAKE, THE UNIT OF THE MEANING OF THE SENTENCE. SHE RHYMES WITH MICHAEL BURKARD, ROBERT CREELEY, MARY RUEFLE, JEAN VALENTINE, JAMES TATE, FANNY HOWE. WHO SPEAKS HERE REPRESENTS AN ESOTERIC, DOUBTING, CANNY, COHERENT, CHEMICAL SELF WHICH WAKES—SLEEPS—UTTERS ALL FROM THE SAME MOUTH WITH WAYWARD, ROVING, STRABISMIC WALL-EYE. IT IS THE GENEROUS, CENTERING INDETERMINACY WE MAY HAVE BEEN MISSING.

FENCE BOOKS

Lesle Lewis

is the author of *Small Boat, Landscapes I & II, lie down too,* and *A Boot's a Boot.* She lives in New Hampshire.

"YOU DON'T PUSH THE BAD THINGS OFF BUT LET THEM BREAK OFF ON THEIR OWN."

"WE SPY AN ANGEL, A THREE-DIMENSIONAL FLATNESS ACHING IN US TO ENVISION OUR EFFORTS MANIFESTED."

"ESCAPE WITNESS TRIANGULAR BANDANA CRANKCASE UNDERNEATH BONDING CREPES STARS FIGURINE ATTEMPT POULTRY FORGERY FREAK TANK STUDY"

"FRAGMENT PLUS FRAGMENT EQUALS FRAGMENTATION AND WE CAN WORK HARDER WITH WHAT WE HAVE LEFT OF WHAT WE HAVE LOST OR WHAT WE HAVE LEFT OF WHAT WE NEVER HAD."

"WHATEVER IT IS, IT IS THE FLUID THAT'S NEEDED FOR THE FUTURE OF WHATEVER WALKS OUT OF THE WINTER WOODS."

FENCE publishes with the support of members, organizations, and institutions. A not-for-profit corporation, *Fence* is mandated by its board to make decisions in keeping with its mission

TO MAINTAIN THIS VENUE, IN
PRINT, AURAL, AND DIGITAL
FORMS, FOR WRITING THAT
SPEAKS ACROSS GENRE,
SOCIO-CULTURAL NICHES, AND
IDEOLOGICAL BOUNDARIES,
AS ACCESSIBLY AS POSSIBLE
SUCH THAT FENCE PUBLISHES
LARGELY FROM ITS UNSOLICITED
SUBMISSIONS, AND IS
COMMITTED TO THE LITERATURE
AND ART OF QUEER WRITERS
AND WRITERS OF COLOR.
FENCE ENCOURAGES COLLECTIVE
APPRECIATION OF VARIOUSNESS
BY INHERING COLLECTIVELY
OUTSIDE OF THE CONSTRAINTS OF
OPINION, TREND, AND MARKET.

FENCE *welcomes new members. Joining means*
you receive books, magazine, a tote or other memento,
handmade Editor Juice, and connection via landline.
WE ALSO WELCOME YOUR IDEAS ABOUT WHAT YOU WOULD
LIKE FROM FENCE IN EXCHANGE FOR YOUR SUPPORT. *Join*
these folks in membership:

AMY ADAMS SALLY ALATALO KIRSTIN ALLIO JEFF BAILEY
CHRISTINE BEGGAN CAREN BEILIN STEVE BENSON TYLER
BREWINGTON MATTHEW BROADDUS HEIDI BROADHEAD
OLIVIER BROSSARD LEE ANN BROWN NATE BROWN LUCY
BURNS JAKE BYRNE BUCHOLTZ DANIEL CALDERWOOD JOHN
CLEATER CORT DAY TOM DEBEAUCHAMP JENNIFER S. EPSTEIN
JENNIFER GALLAGHER NICOLE GAUTHIER MICHELLE GEOGA
JACQUELINE GOSS MARK GOZONSKY ELLIOT HARMON JEAN
HARTIG MATTHEW HENRIKSEN LUCY IVES SARAH JEWELL
DC KALBACH ANDREA KLEINE MATTHEW KOSINSKI YOUNA
KWAK ANN LAUTERBACH MARCO LEAN JEFFREY LEPENDORF
MUNIRA LOKHANDWALA ADAM MALINOWSKI PETER MCARTHUR
RUTH MCILROY HASSAN MELEHY JOHN MELILLO JAMES
MENDELSOHN MEGAN MILKS JANE ORMEROD CARYL PAGEL
SARAH PALEY JAMIE PEREZ DELIA PLESS HILARY PLUM JOSHUA
RIEDEL BETH ROBERTS CHRISTINE SCANLON STEVE SCHWARTZ
BOB SHARKEY MATT SHAW CLARA SIMONSON LAURA SIMS
JASMINE DREAME WAGNER MONICA YOUN

Join online at fenceportal.org/support
Contact editor REBECCA WOLFF *if you*
would like to fiscally or institutionally
sponsor one of our book prizes.

CONTENTS

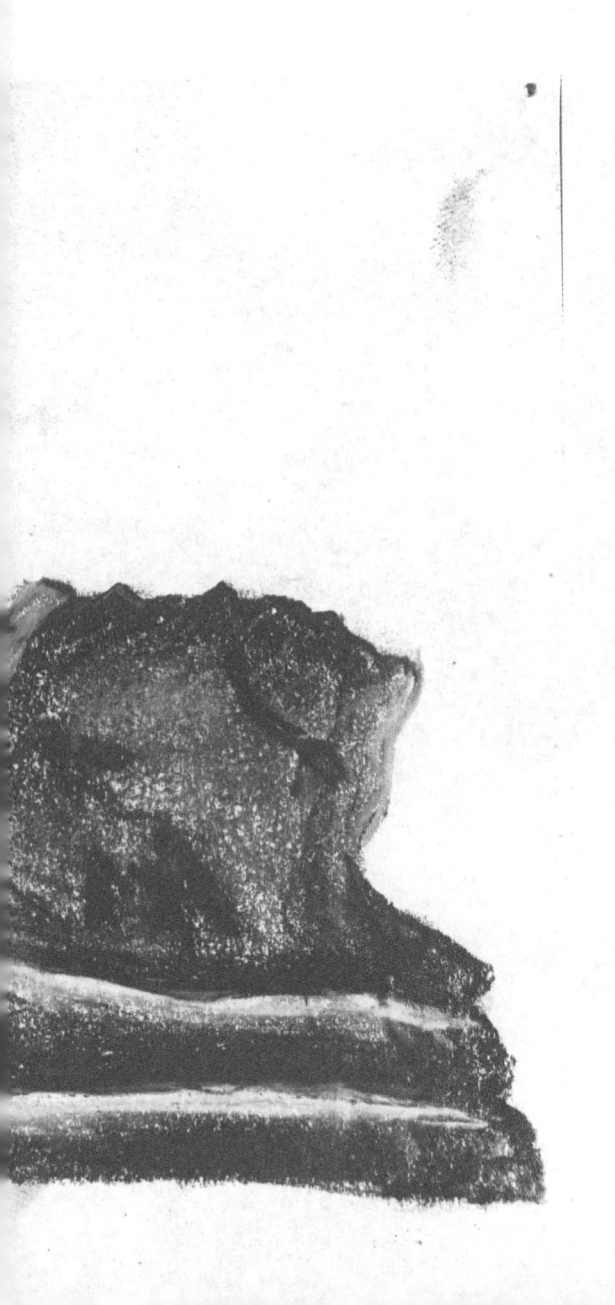

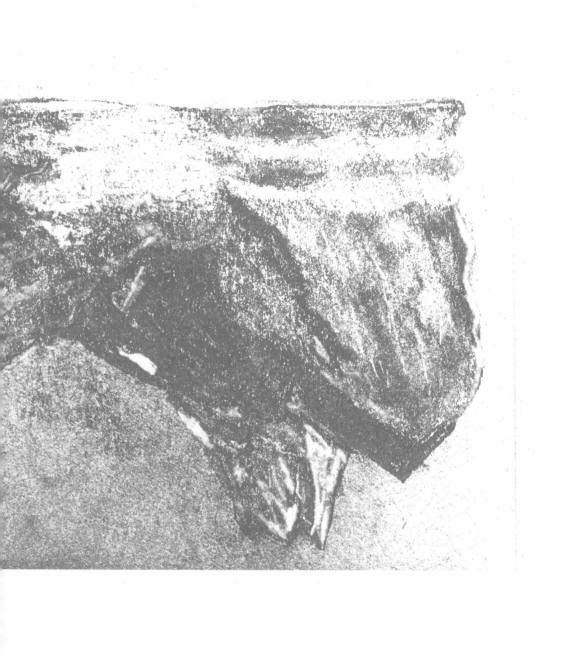

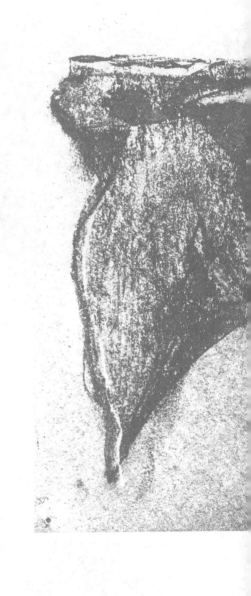

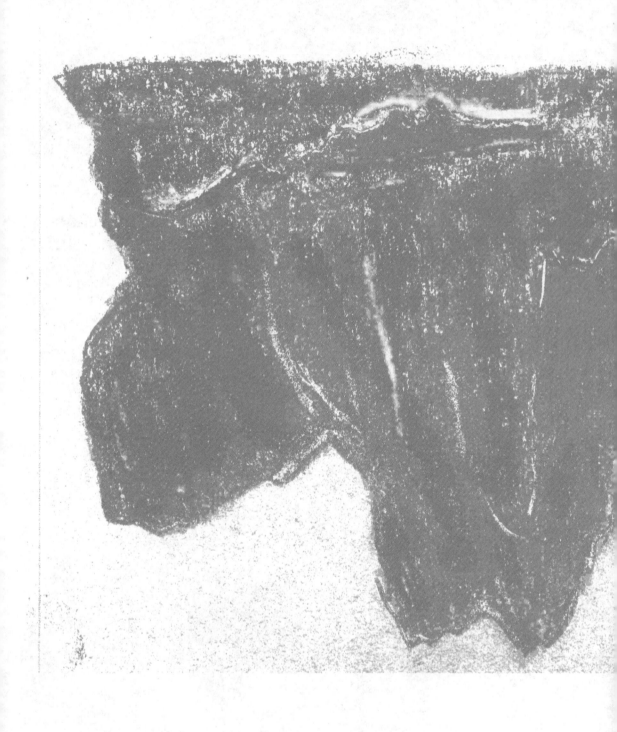

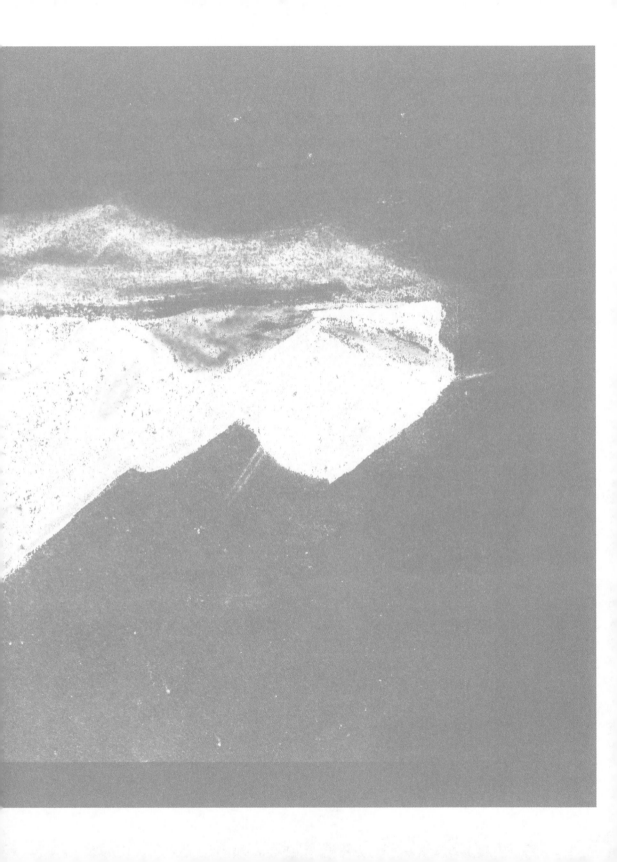

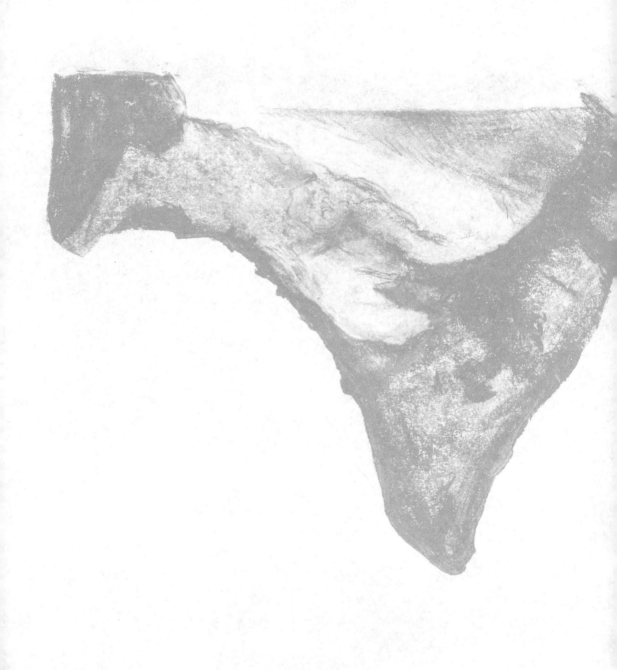

DAMON MOORE

Going for a Walk

1.

In a distracted mood, I went
for a walk, reaching that place
we call Wuthering Heights
where the owner had curtains

drawn on a lane cleared of cars,
walkers and driverless cars
leading to a famous beauty spot.

Soon there may be nothing
new for humans to do,
since walking is not exact purpose.

A walk it seems most likely
describes activity in pursuit of itself
and not the host of all will be well.

2.

"The Last Time I Saw Richard" is a song
it took me decades to get the hang of,
and now I realise it concerns

adulthood, the aftershock of "you"
matching to "me," repeated and repeated
until both are in accord.

3.

People keeping dream journals
notice in the end how dreams delight
in any opportunity to laugh at you,

slip under your outstretched arm,
slap down some cosseted idea.
They never seem to want us, dreams

so perhaps, after all, as someone once
said, I am part of that hallucination
and that is all I want to say about
"The Last Time I Saw Richard."

PHYLLIS PETERS

(untitled)

It used to be
that waking up in the middle of the night
scared me—

the quiet need
attacking itself.

I could not turn on the light
nor keep it off.
It was being, hovering, nowhere—
then
and for all time.

But why scared?
Why a train's horn, blaring so far away?
Why this moment?

The dead of the night comes to me,
not I to it.
The dead of the night come to me,
not I to them.
Not all have met death, some are simply gone
and in the dark, their
absence
wields me.

Someone once wrote
that when poetry indulges
in too much abstraction,
its power
diminishes
greatly.

Now I see.

Only the dead of the night indulge well
in abstraction.

(untitled)

Holding the lamb, we waited at the shore as if boats would appear. Emergency crept toward us, down the mountain, crusty black lids on flaming goo. We walked calmly toward the water with the others.

Have we swum far enough?

The eruption—no one had said it was dormant. And yet we dared live there, knowing full well the danger, the view, the smell of sulfur. We'd planted, kept sheep.

At the shore, rowboats arrived, small, rickety. Only two. We knew they'd never make it, and yet, how easily you climbed in, to the one I did not climb into. The boatmen winked. You had tied the lamb to a stick on the beach—it would be overtaken, slowly, most painfully, and you knew it. Its bleating haunts me even now.

No sirens, no medics, no drama. The island had none. It was simple, smoldering advancement, one stone at a time. An everyday volcano bursts, and a couple embarks in separate boats, abandoning all belongings, no other options under a red sky. It happens all the time.

Have we swum far enough?

Someone nearby just went under, never to resurface, but I've stopped asking why—energy saved for more pressing needs. Our boatman perished as well. Good riddance. His hot raunchy breath will not be missed.

And you. You never could swim, you said, and you never could sing, either. And yet, when the boats shoved off, you broke into hallowed song, in a voice that stunned the tide.

Pessi/Opti

1. *Horrible is a slippery abstraction*

> like when the guy three blocks[1] down
> raped his girlfriend's infant.[2]

> The Hubble, pointing at a dime of black beside the moon
> captured more matter than had been imagined to exist.[13]

> Wheelbarrow not red, necessarily, it merely
> reflects best the red of the sun's spectral menagerie.[31]

---

1. Three blocks from the narrator's childhood house, a cozy, innocently-creepy-basemented home swathed in the sprawl of north Minneapolis. But far enough from Minneapolis that the nearest apartment complex was three blocks away.

2. She left him to babysit. He smoked a joint of oregano double-spritzed with PCP. After, bloody and wet, the future lifer watched afternoon cartoons.[3] Vacancy took over. First her eyes, backseat. Then the apartment. The building was sold and demolished, a new home erected and who could blame the earth for creations of humans, however deranged?[4] When news of the event rippled through the community it followed model of pond and excised its little energy quickly. Drew little news coverage.[5] And for some reason the distasteful blood it painted afternoons with remained a faux pas. As if Spring insisted with each budlet of lilac[6] (crowded in pom-pom pods) a head-in-the-sand reaction.[7]

3. How his girlfriend found the scene.

4. Many. Though eventually the house was sold to an anonymous couple, who sold it three years later to an anonymous man.

5. This was, of course before 24-hour news channels.

6. Green.

7. Or, at very least a premature and urgent stop-and-smell-the-flowers reaction.[8]

8. Such a vibrant, promising bouquet in the nose you swear it makes the morning taste fresh.[9]

9. Fresh, though, is a poor excuse for a forced euphoria, which is still nice.[10]

10. For, in a way, another look at abstraction, which, according to the title, is at least in some way horrible[11] to fully consider, refer immediately to L3.

11. Though, definitely not in the unspeakable terms that L1–2[12] describe.

12. Specifically L2.

13. The Hubble Ultra Deep Field image shows at least 9,000 previously unknown galaxies.[14] The HUDF exploded the Hubble Constant efficient for the measured stellar density equation[17] greatly changing, among other things, the way we look at the Drake equation.[18]

14. The Milky Way contains 200,000,000,000 stars[15], and is a smallish galaxy.[16]

15. Our sun, a tiny star, has at least 8 full planets and three kid-brother dwarfs.

16. Only between 200,000,000,000 and 400,000,000,000 stars in the spiral Milky Way[19], spiraling around a massive maelstrom[20] that will, undoubtedly compact all matter within the whorl.

17. The new figure for estimated stars in the universe is 9,000,000,000,000,000,000,000,000 in the observable universe.[21]

18. The Drake Equation ($N=R^* \times f_p \times n_e \times f_l \times f_c \times L$—perhaps it's best not to ask) calculates the probability of contacting extra-terrestrial societies. Drake estimated N to be 10 civilizations actively seeking us[22], assuming that a modest 1% of intelligent civilizations who are capable of communicating, are willing to communicate with us.[23]

19. Our neighboring galaxy, Andromeda has nearly than 50 times as many stars, 10,000,000,000,000.

20. Black hole.

21. Which is merely a sphere of observation centered around the observer, and not a measure of the universe, which is impossible to know from our vantage point.

22. "Us" in general, someone not "them" as we[24] see it.

23. The Fermi Paradox supposes to explain, with the enormous probability of extra-terrestrial life, why our civilization (give or take a millennium) hasn't discovered[25] alien life.

24. Humans.

25. In a Columbian[26] sort of way.[27]

26. Finding for ourselves.

27. Though, not really like that at all. More like chair-bound Jimmy Stewart with that enormous telephoto lens. An impotent urgency.[28]

28. In what skeptics call Drake's optimistic view, 99% of intelligent civilizations purposefully avoid contact with what we know as us.[29]

29. For another, purportedly[30] horrible abstraction in the vein of S1's inhumanity and S2's numerically numbing diminutive to humanity, refer immediately to L5.

30. As informed by the titled, but really, who is to feel sympathy for the narrator at this point?

31. Pigment is hue made[32] of mottled materials to imitate purer hue, given standard white light.[33] Given non-standard, perhaps of cloud-screened afternoon or glass bulb tinting electric light, the wheelbarrow's applied pigment would reflect something not red. The rain slicked red now dulled down to brown.[34]

32. Through chemical deconstruction.

33. Or, as Paul Valery put it, "The color of a thing is that which, out of all colors, the thing repels and cannot assimilate."

34. A theme recurrent in the poem. A breaking down not of building blocks, but the molecules of building blocks. Knocking off individual nubs of the Lego castle.[35] Creation of instability.[36] Being *untoward*.[37]

35. Or, knocking off the metaphoric rose-colored glasses, which antithetically, in reality, create the unsettling spectrum shift described in S3.

36. *Creation* of instability as Columbian as Hubble telescope's *discoveries*.

37. If, however, the unsaid of S1 declared itself: the way no one needed to say *shhh*. Calendars fractured the tiniest fraction for something too removed from their realm of *real*, a 1/10th millimeter crack in the concrete reaching the liquid core under the car's tires,[38] and rolled over for daily, tangible concerns.[39]

38. Isotropic is how we describe the universe, without proper numbers to describe it.

39. Without words to express the colors we don't see, events we will not picture. To enumerate *horrible*.

2. Familia it

We l ke the
l ves we a e
fam liar
wi h, wher
we c n
f ll in t e
blan s wh n
we tir
of pre ending
to be payi g
at ention,

and eevn if
smoetmies
we swaer
teh wolrd is
mxeid up
so bda taht
terhe's no pssobile
wya teh pceies
wlil eevr fti
bcak tgoetehr,
we cna alywas fnid
our wya bcak
home.

COLLEEN O'BRIEN

Genealogy

There are those who wake
and rightly wrongly think

most of what my parents said
was close to right and close to good.

Then there are those who wake
in on/outside the joke:

The wolves were wolves.
That stuff we drank was blood.

Always the twain shall meet,
consort and procreate,
divorce or die or not.

Then there are those who wake
two-mouthed

That blood right stuff was said
Close to wolves we drank
My parents were what was

This Time

Which is it
then? Are you

a naked woman
or a woman

wearing clothes?
The truth,

Madam.

A. S. M. R

```
massage on the mind     medium luke-            warm, here come
the cool          turbines, touretted &     tourniquet for
the tongue       ,         silence regards its noises     dimensional  ,        of
           incremental decision                  "OK, whatever,      give me
tingles or     give me        desideratum              fold me            into
        microplush fleece            deep in the              soil
organisms             modify our double-            helix- ((s/he
            -dance of              (ideas of)    order                ((performs
                chevrons                            ((skin grafts
         of                                      ((stuck on
                 no land                ((lizard sax
        manual labor            busy at                pencilsound        how
                sexy                        it all is
& automatic          these bodies,          who furnace      frisson (of)
        spectrum     waves, in heat                i know      what lack
this body places me          in ((s/he whispers          into
        ears of        a multitude              shingles        corner
the market on          intimacy, junkies            of golden
        dawns                at equator                      ((s/he senses
            our                          walking twd
        bitemarked apples, the edenic        X            pleased
        w/itself          this fallen        sunk- en world-

((s/he lullabies                                          ing


              industries of affect          narcosis, mercs
        at the door                  prescribing        fear of
iteration          i'd like to see her      in their commonwealth
                                                  eyes
                            when he        rises
        on pixelated parapets              what fortress
                              of massage styles
while
        grimy wastrels        bleeding at              the toes
on the street      ask you          for change &          you recoil
        principium     individuation-        is      our current
politics      letter it        on civilizational      medium        machine-
```

-porn　　　when s/he takes up　　　　　a human hand
& holds it　　s/he recoils,　　interrogation of the same　　diseased
　　eros　　　　　　we aren't in control　　　　the automata are not
in control　　the sleepers awake　　　　they are not　　　　　"in control,,
　　a body　　　　　that trans-verses　　its voltage
on the cog　　labor markets　　　loses　　　its hair stylists
　　to desuetude　　　　or objecthood　　in the　　　　UID
margins　　why is it　　　when ((s/he taps　　　　glass, or plastic
　　its timbre　　equates to　　　memories of el monte　　our mater
lacrymosa　　why is it　　that estrangement　　on the　　　screen
　　satisfies　　our shared　libidinal　　economicon　　why is it
when ((s/he　　strokes the　　　tympanic　　　　membrane
　　our feelings　　are seduced　　　into sedition
who is it　　that's indignant　　whose body　　　is rioting
　　in the grasses　　whose face　　　is collecting　dust
in digital　　mesmerism　　clouds of clouds　　　　　of
　　toxic　masculinity　　a switching　of power-　　grids
hong kong　　handovers　views of rennie's　　　satanic
　　mills　on kowloon　motorways　((to matriarchal　ordinations
refugees squat　　in high-rise, high on paganism　　we are
　　autonomous, at last　　they are calling us
to action　in the　　depart-　　　　　　ment stores
　　((s/he soothes　　like when like responded
　　　((futures of　　　　　　to like
　　　　((deciduous foliage　　teen-
　　　　　((fume-drunk, "selfwrung,,　　age mnemonics
the latin vulgate
　　　　　promises our wyrd　　sisters　　trans-
　　-mission　　　　across medias　　rerum
　　　　natura
but i'm not　finished yet　　"that's the shit　　i don't like,,
　　　　spinal fingers　　that tabletap
　　i'm readyto liquify　　spread the　　ash
over　　　the phalanstery　make
　　those dismembering　　sounds &
(dis)remember me　　"a mellow organ,,　　to reconvene us to
　　earths to　　sensory firmaments　to
　　　　Meridian

The weather is what produces awareness. There's wood enough, within.
Surreptitious, cameras were positioned in the hallway, in the faux marble
corner of the roman suite. Panopticon, mannequin, plus balcony. A banana
plantation in the New World brings us much nutrition and genuflection at
the dinner table, site of mastications, and infidelities of an uncertain nature.
Chrome yellow. The mustachioed novelist was known to compose her best work
from the vantage point of a calcium-deprived voyeur, and with many erasers
at hand. Whose perspective is it anyway. They won't retire this system until it
brings us to Deep State. He had seen them there before, skirmishing on the
edges, the grotesque whiteness of it all, their flaccid patriotisms slung on their
back with apparent nonchalance. Semi-automatic organisms, who caterwaul or
print when they reach their apex, distract other paragraphs from an awareness
of the fact. Damn. Genealogy of truthiness, leading us to Bacchus. Units in an
ungovernable syntax, their lives to split open at the crevice of enunciation, like
pods of an achiote. I was very young, greener than a flea at noontide, when the
television began to speak in tongues to me. The gun ripped open and emerged
from his chest. She reported to the policeman. The rains refracted the vapor
of the syllables. How manifest, yet how cruel, the ethical anthropophage, who
specializes in the gustatory art of bloated french liver. Journalistic fakeries
remind us of the Demiurge sipping on coca-cola at 5 in the afternoon. Babylon
will always have its Hollywood, after all. Need I remind you that the square
dance is the official dance of 24 states, and we are hard-pressed to describe it in
terms adequate to its performativity, or to the why which encoils its wherefore.
She realized, upon winning and losing a few thousand bitcoins each week at
the tables, that hoteliers provide luxuriant quarters on the highest floors, and
with spectacular amenities and services, to their most valued franchise players
and risk-management agents, at zero cost. La vida novale nada. 100 gigabytes
of identity politics. Or maybe the garrulous black dog had left a string of hair in
the bowl. The red plague rid you. It reflected to itself, or remarked to no one in
particular, looking down from the highest reaches of the Golden Pavilion, that
it could not be seen, and they could not glimpse it either, if they ever chanced
to look up. Ponder you the thisness of Duns Scotus. Tobacco conglomerates
would seek their vengeance through money laundering and the transfiguration

of corporate flesh into personhood. Bump stock, diversify your DFA portfolio, double down on drone strikes. We have deciphered who the emerald tablet disempowers. Let us retire, you and I, to these solitudes and on these mats rehearse the splendours which the heavens above have bestowed upon us. That which is below is like that which is above. It rains down jewels & quetzal feathers rather than words. It was animated, but still I cried. I am not he said with a plangent unsettled voice a master of my domain.

After Stripping out the Hillside in Order to Lay the Highway, the Good
Old Boys Inadvertently Uncover Acidic Pyrite Rock and Have to Call in the
Department of Environmental Protection Before the Watershed Goes to Shit

Isn't it strange, all that water flowing beneath us?

It slips through the rock like a horse that has fallen and soon will be shot in the head

Help us understand.

Before there was light there was rock and before there was rock there was boy
he shot marbles at a tree from his sling   didn't you all hear the sound?

Why do they call it Fool's Gold?

The fish in the creeks will suffocate from the metals leaching outward
                              maybe think of fireflies and other crepuscular ones

Why don't the creeks just seep into the ground?

They run because they're cowards

Wasn't the pyrite already there?

Unearth is another word for discover such as cover is another word for disguise
          prove anything exists

Explain the water table to us.

The boy with the sling spit as every marble struck the tree   his shoes sunk in the mud
as his waters fell through the earth   where do you spit if at all?

Why do they call it Yellow Boy?

Sulfate isn't that hard to swallow if you have the gumption to persist
or like my lover you bury all cedar waxwings

How long will it take the Department of Environmental Protection?

Decades   they'll blame every second on you boys and you will accept this
                              hang yourselves in the sky as swans with your lyres

Did that horse get shot in the head yet?

Don't agonize over the colt his femur has shattered   bone splinters through both
hoof and skin

This doesn't seem worth the trouble.

It's too late for regret the ground is swollen
                                        what else do you set into earth?

Why do they call it a highway?

The Gods will relieve you of your pity and adorn you with feathers for hair

But still, isn't it strange, all that water beneath us?

The light in your eyes left you all long ago   it rides the backs of creeks
in late morning

Gone Beautiful

Someone is at the door and asking for help. This is like when I walk down the street and see a sign in a store window that says, Help Wanted. I always want to go into the store and ask what kind of help they need, if it is urgent, if someone needs medical attention. I always assume someone has collapsed and is dying on the floor, someone that can't breathe and is in cardiac arrest, convulsing.

This happens to me sometimes. My chest hurts and my vision blurs and my mouth goes dry and then I'm down. Only sometimes do I get the shakes. People are sometimes careful to step around me when I get the shakes. Sometimes people are good this way.

I feel a kinship with people when they step around me. I never look them in the eye because I am usually convulsing and I can't keep my eyes open. If I could I would thank them.

Other times they kick me repeatedly and rifle through my pockets.

This is why I never go into stores that have a Help Wanted sign up in the window because I don't want to see something like this. Maybe certain people want to see something like this but they are one of two things and I'm neither. If people know anything about me this is what they know.

I have been locked in my room for however many days now. I'd been planning on this for months so I started hoarding food and water and other supplies weeks ago.

I decided I needed some time to think things through and figure out where my life is headed.

I haven't been to the noontime meeting and shared with the group and I haven't been out on furlough, either.

How I pass the time is I read my books or I draw stick figures on the walls and floors.

I draw stick figures in relation to other stick figures. Some stick figures are standing in traffic while others rush over to beat them senseless or usher them to safety. Some are sexually harassing an attractive hostess in the back of a restaurant, while others are against the wall and frisked by police officers.

In one drawing there is one stick figure driving a car and another in the passenger seat. In the next drawing the one in the passenger seat goes through the windshield and lands in a bloody heap some twenty feet away. Right next to that picture is a mother stick figure putting makeup on a child stick figure and then taking his photograph. This stick figure is looking up at his stick mother with an expression that is inscrutable.

I haven't seen Watermelon Man in a long time, not at the noontime meetings nor in the yard or recreation center but I'm certain he is still inside as he's never allowed out on furlough.

I do not think that is him at the door asking for help because I would recognize his voice.

It's possible that whoever is at the door and asking for help wants to come in because there is an active shooter in the building.

This would explain all the gunfire and screaming.

Hearing gunfire isn't unusual, but this amount of gunfire isn't something we hear every day.

There is a sign on my side of the door instructing us what to do in the event of fire, medical emergency, active shooter, earthquake, tornado, ice age, tsunami, etc.

It's only during the active shooter scenario that you are supposed to locate and load all your guns and then hide under a bed or behind a chair with your favorite trained at the door.

Opening the door to someone asking for help is not on the list.

This is why I think this building used to be a high school because this sign couldn't pertain to us anymore. They confiscated all of our guns when they admitted us as guests that first day.

We haven't had an active shooter since I can't remember when, but that could be on account of my failing memory.

I also don't want to see if this isn't the case, if no one is on the floor and can't breathe because then I'll want to know what all the fuss is about. I'm not saying I want to see the Senator on the ground like this, for instance, or the janitor who said what the fuck is a furlough or Betty or Gus or even Trina or any of the other guests, but I don't think it would bother me, either, and at least then someone would actually need help.

This is what we are supposed to call each other, guests. Not prisoners or detainees or hostages or captives. We are called guests because the state is housing us here and we are trying to get better, all of us.

In the corner there is a stick mother giving birth to a stick baby and then a stick police officer comes over and shoots the stick baby in the face.

Sometimes they march us into a room and have us perform tasks. This was before I locked myself in my room, of course. I assume they still do this but I have no real way of knowing.

They have other groups in other rooms that perform similar tasks and they compare the results. Then they shame one or both groups for their lackluster performance.

Today I remember my brother because he's probably dead and doesn't need help anymore.

The last time I saw my brother he needed all kinds of help, as machines were hooked into him for breathing and eating and using the restroom.

I tried depicting this in a drawing but I couldn't make the stick respirator look real. I also had trouble drawing a stick dialysis machine and stick catheter.

I keep a running tab of people who are probably dead by now and my brother and father, who is confirmed as a KIA, are both on the list.

My father threw himself off the roof of a hotel one day after we had lunch some years ago. He'd left a note and said he'd gone beautiful, which was true. The note was in his very own language, which was likewise beautiful, like a cross between Arabic and Mayan hieroglyphs.

This I refuse to draw on the walls, though I'm sure it would be breathtaking. I can just imagine how I'd trace the stick figure plummeting through the air, graceful like a ballerina, and then crashing onto the pavement dead.

In my head he looks like the falling man from that famous photograph of the poor bastard who had to jump out of the towers as they burned.

But actually drawing this seems disrespectful.

I could never replicate the written language, either.

Tanya and My Sofia are probably both dead, too, along with the other brothers I sometimes lived with and couldn't stand the sight of.

I don't know how any of them died.

The gunfire is sporadic but steady. It sounds like a semi-automatic and like the shooter is going from room to room. This one sounds methodical; like he has an entire performance planned to the last detail. My guess is the shooter has with him several weapons, but I haven't heard anything like an explosion, so he probably doesn't have any grenades or IEDs.

I hear people running and screaming, though whenever there is a report of gunfire the screaming is drowned out.

I assume the shooter is a man because most shooters are men and it seems that's all we have here are men.

It could be one of the guests but I'm guessing it's a staff member, either a supervisor or doctor or janitor.

I never need help when I'm out on furlough, but still people try to help me. They think I'm confused or trying to kill myself because I go stand in traffic. They say that suicide runs in families but in this case I don't think it's true. Sometimes people usher me to the side of the road and beat me senseless. They tell me they do this for my own good. They tell me I shouldn't stand in traffic and ask me questions to find out if I'm South American or European.

It could be they only want help in the kitchen, though, doing the dishes, and that will be a disappointment. I don't like doing dishes and I don't think anyone can blame me. There is something wrong with my hands, I lose feeling. What happens is I start working with my hands and before long I feel the pins and needles and soon they go numb and I have to stop whatever it is I'm doing and shake them out.

I never pass out when my hands go numb.

This is one reason I don't like doing dishes, but there are others, too.

I remember in the restaurant I worked at with Esperanza there was a Mexican fellow named Roy-Boy who did the dishes and anything else I asked of him. He was a good one because he didn't harass Esperanza like his brother Jorge and the rest of the pendejos in the back did.

No one knows whatever became of Roy-Boy but it's probably true that the police got him and you know what that means. If they found out he liked men during the interrogation then they probably beat him to death right then and there.

It is possible that the person at the door doesn't need help after all and the gunfire is the sound of the television in the rec room. It could be that it's a ruse because they think I have someone in here with me. We're not allowed to have

overnight guests, especially if you have a history of chaining people to the radiator or haven't left your room for days on end.

There is a pause in the gunfire, but not the screaming.

It could be the shooter needs a break or has to reload or perhaps he is on the phone with a negotiator of some sort. Perhaps they are trying to strike a deal so they can come in to treat the wounded and save everyone else.

I know I am safe inside my room and that it's probably not the shooter at the door asking for help.

If I still had a gun I would have it out and trained at the door.

Instead I am drawing a stick figure lying on the ground with kindred stick figures stepping around him as he convulses and writhes.

Notice how no one is kicking this stick figure or rifling through his pockets.

When people hear about this on the news I wonder if they will think I'm the shooter.

I think it's possible for some of them to think this, like maybe Django and Roy-Boy, but not Gus or Esperanza.

Not the people who know anything about me is what I'm saying.

Not the people who remember what I was like years ago, when I had a job and would commute to work each day like everyone else.

I won't say more than this because who cares.

It's like when I was a kid and I would ask my mother for help with my homework. I can't remember what she would say, but I'm sure it proves my point.

LESLE LEWIS

Two Poems from *Rainy Days on the Farm*
winner of the 2019 Ottoline Prize

The goodness has collapsed and gone.

It's the same "now" for everyone.

We are at onceness at oneness.

We are a long march of people and resources, waves and sheep, a march of demonstratives.

We eat candy and irony.

Deerhunters roam the woods and bad people are in power.

Good people are digging up reasons not to seek substance-fueled escapes, happier imaginations.

They are walking with their bundles away from the core of the hearts of their enemies.

Their bundles are made of children and cats and dogs and cows and chickens and tigers and elephants and giraffes and sloths and orangutans and alligators and lobsters and spiders and trout and chickadees.

Their bundles are made of what they are without and also the bundles of the others and the others themselves.

One person walks one way, another another.

One person looks one way, another another.

One person thinks up an experiment of entangled particles under the superluminal.

One person simplifies but they limit and deny by simplification, milk, and eggs.

They generalize and share the weather.

Enter the wolf, the toothpick, the bee, the glass, the staircase.

Enter the elite and the ordinary and the back-to-bedders.

One person reads what one writer writes about another writer writing about unfitness.

Enter the superpowers and siblings, the notes to self and accidents.

Meanwhile, until the big hand is on the nine, polarities are stretched farther and no amount of force on one side can break the other.

One person breathes one way, another another.

The people keep their heads down and walk slowly until they are dead and don't carry anything.

Just say "basket" or "no basket," and there's the basket.

1.
Labor sight candy
Right situation impeccable
Stationary station pullet

2.
Confidence cloudy tea
Flight bean company
Thickness folder cart

3.
Ballet crow caucus
Velcro turnstile secrete
Fulcrum pajamas slip

4.
Humid triangle particular
Wife step report
Tomorrow mist frozen

5.
River hot quarter
Double institution key
Crisp reflection start

6.
Moth shore small
Trinket botany bay
Stop storm man

7.
Negative style bear
Square maple fanning
Mall age scene

8.
Proof symptom carpenter
Silly saw cure
Walking coast over

9.
Mere inflate worker
Jester motherly bauble
Resting pull flooring

10.
Cheek haggle continuous
Addiction medium pour
Mealtime name torture

11.
Exposure fools manifest
Greed way discussion
Field fear tear

12.
Silk remote bead
Farfetched second fig
Position swap consider

13.
Drape temple size
Yarn cubicle coal
Greek electric dark

14.
Radical absorption fact
Starve diagnose profuse
Planned sky bark

15.
Scrap assembly pan
Torque scramble insist
Sculpture prevention resistance

16.
Insomnia mop cactus
Lover moisture illumination
Flux streambed global

17.
Humble butter stripes
Peony whispering glacier
Mentor traffic salvage

18.
Execution measure model
Clash standpoint saint
Armchair torch facts

19.
Volcano uniform sister
Harbor inhabit between
Zinc respect prospect

20.
Bounty rival song
Vacuum strict fantastic
Chord friction panorama

21.
Pistol froth error
Opportunity urban wedding
Wet interest intensity

22.
Effort morning meander
Cow recycle busy
Breast inherit news

23.
Lawn lakefront Maxwell
Overcast headline post
Other angle sting

24.
Prey drinking industry
Relative hidden twitter
Kingfisher sign Rhinebeck

25.
Flat rag leaf
Sorrow chain rock
Afternoon wish fraught

26.
Tax soup mirror
Wander crestfallen stand
Generous town cleaning

27.
Bleeding forgetting ownership
Yours camp cover
Quarantine white ladder

Worry Yourself Well

Your own headache, your own moon, your own book is warm to the touch because maybe there are no other stories, just stars I am content with your failure, your return, your own answer your wilderness, etc. is giving up, my own English language is a shotgun pointed at a map and in the last remaining photograph, the dust owns the air, the ants crawl from the margins of a book whose edges are the horizon and the population is a construct guarding ruins, let me write something real, there is trash on the ground, waiting to watch a tower bow, your own brutal attention, your own dead horse, your pile of wood, as dawn breaks a window, you assume you understand survival, wreaths wrapped around your teeth, let me tell you, you are allowed to look away, you are allowed the feeling of snow on your bones, this stoicism is a philosophy of control

TERMINAL:
LET MY BONES BE THE WEAPONS THAT WILL BREAK YOUR BONES

SIGNAL:
QUE MIS HUESOS SEAN LAS ARMAS QUE SE ROMPAN LOS HUESOS

TERMINAL:
MY BONES ARE THE WEAPONS BONES BREAK

SIGNAL:
MIS HUESOS SON LA RUPTURE DE HUESOS DE ARMAS

TERMINAL:
MY BONES ARE BROKEN BONES OF WEAPONS

SIGNAL:
MIS HUESOS SON HUESOS ROTOS DE ARMAS

TERMINAL:
MY BONES ARE THE BROKEN BONES IN ARMS

SIGNAL:
MIS HUESOS SON HUESOS ROTOS EN SUS BRAZOS

TERMINAL:
MY BONES ARE THE BROKEN BONES IN YOUR ARMS

SIGNAL:
MIS HUESOS SON HUESOS ROTOS DE SUS MULTITUD

TERMINAL:
MY BONES ARE THE BROKEN WEAPONS OF YOUR ARMIES

SIGNAL:
MIS HUESOS SON LAS ARMAS QUEBRADAS DE SUS ARMAS

TERMINAL:
MY BONES ARE BROKEN BUT ARE YOURS

ADRIENNE WALSER

Entertainer of the Year

At age eight I receive the award Entertainer of the Year Runner-Up for a jazz-gymnastics routine I perform to the disco song, "Give Me the Night." My hair is short and I'm barefoot and bare-legged in a pale blue leotard with a red and white zigzag down the side. On stage I do disco moves with cartwheels, front flips, round-offs and neck-rolls. My small hands land firmly on the mat and shoot up in the air, fingers spread in jazz-hands. I am exuberant.

In second-grade I live on Bonbrook Drive in Wabash, Indiana, in a friendly neighborhood with wide streets and large trees. I love to ride my pink and white bike with a banana seat and tall handlebars I reach up to hold. I ride it after school and on the weekends around the neighborhood, experiencing new pleasures of exploration and independence.

My best friend Shelly and I are in a ballet class together. I become impatient with what I think is her bad dancing and ask my mom for private lessons. A few months into my private ballet class my knees swell, and the swelling doesn't go down. My mom takes me to a doctor. I'm diagnosed with juvenile rheumatoid arthritis, a disease of the auto-immune system that is potentially crippling. Your body produces antibodies that attack the body, in particular the cells that line the joints. At the time, I don't know this; I just know I have to stop taking ballet and gymnastics.

I'm in sixth grade, and my pediatric rheumatologist decides I should get gold shots, an old treatment for arthritis that contains actual gold. Twice my mom takes me to a small office where the glittering liquid is injected in my arm. Not long after the second shot, my body stops making red blood cells. Doctor P calls this Aplastic Anemia. For a year, I take cortisone in order to get my bones to produce red blood cells; I also need monthly red blood transfusions. The prednisone makes me retain water, and my face puffs out into a moon. I am embarrassed at school about my fat face. My mom and I go to the Children's Hospital in India-

napolis once a month where I receive blood transfusions over the course of a year until the drug, Cytoxan, which has its own potential scary side effects, shocks my system into producing red blood cells again. My mom sits with me in little white hospital emergency rooms for four hours each time, which is the length of the infusion. She brings along our little black and white television. It has a messed-up antenna, so when the reception is bad, the screen turns into waves of horizontal lines and we just listen. When my mom leaves the room, she comes back with ice cream sandwiches for us.

Frida Kahlo began painting at age eighteen on the full body cast she wore for three months after a bus collided with her trolley car. In this accident, an iron handrail pierced her abdomen and uterus, and she suffered a broken spinal column, broken collarbone, ribs and pelvis, eleven fractures in her right leg, a crushed right foot, and a dislocated shoulder. The story goes that a bag of gold dust of an artisan next to her burst open, and gold covered her hurt body as she lay in the street.

I have bone-marrow biopsies to help the doctors determine why I'm not making red blood cells. When the doctor inserts the long needle into my thigh bone, I feel an intense shooting pain from my leg throughout my body. My nurse holds one of my hands. and my mom holds the other one and talks to me to calm me down. My dad can't stay in the room because it's too hard for him to hear me cry in pain. At home, my mom makes healthy meals, and I'm not allowed junk food snacks. But when she picks me up from school to take me to see my doctor in Indianapolis, she always brings McDonalds for lunch as a treat. When I am eleven and in the hospital for a medical procedure, my friend B visits me, and we share a 20-piece Chicken McNuggets. I eat more of them than he does and feel bad about it; at age eleven I already think as a girl I should eat less than a boy. After we eat, he and I play Dungeons and Dragons on my hospital bed,

Later when B and I are thirteen and at a basketball game sitting at the top of the old Indiana gymnasium, he asks softly, "can I hold your hand?" I tell him I'm not allowed. (My older sister was recently in trouble with my dad for holding a boy's hand at a football game.) A few minutes later B says are you sure, and I say yes, I'm sure. (I'm not sure.) The next four years I have a crush on him. Our sophomore year, he's my Biology partner, which makes me nervous every day. I

have hand surgery that year. The tendons are cut and straightened to reduce the swelling and deformity. When the surgeon describes the hand splint I'll have to wear after the surgery, I cry. It sounds awful—embarrassing. After the surgery, my hand is encased with a big splint with rubber bands holding up each of my fingers. In Biology class, mortified, I keep my weird splinted-hand hidden under our lab table as much as possible.

Despite my reluctance at age twelve to hold the hand of B in the Indiana gym, I'm a hand-holder at heart—probably because my mom holds hands with me all the time as I grow up. In my first relationship at age twenty, I happily hold hands with my boyfriend. My second male partner, S, doesn't like to hold my hand in public. Affection is uncomfortable for him—it's embarrassing. He's a gentle man, so I wonder if holding hands makes him feel weak, not masculine. When we run into people we know, he drops my hand. This makes me feel hurt. It becomes a conversation that never really goes anywhere. D, the first woman I hold hands with, has lovely soft small hands. My next girlfriend, L, and I hold hands all the time. This is new for her. She says she's never done this with someone before. Her hands are long, thin, brown from the sun, strong and agile; she uses them to fix bikes, cook, draw. I love looking at her hands and feel lucky to get to hold them.

In high school computer class, I'm called out into the hall where the Superintendent of Schools tells me she needs to drive me home. It is 1988, the Fall semester of my junior year in a small Indiana town. I don't ask her questions at any point, feeling something bad has happened and she's not the one to tell me. I walk into my house and in the living room is our church minister and my dad, who is crying. Standing across from me, he says your mom has died. She choked on food in cafeteria at the elementary school where she teaches first grade, and she couldn't be saved. I cry with him but I'm in shock. It isn't real. I have a vague sense I should prepare for what comes next. I walk up the stairs in our house to my bathroom where I get out a washcloth, put it under warm water, and with soap I wash my face carefully, removing all my makeup—powder, pink eye shadow, blue eyeliner, electric blue mascara. My dad comes in, stands and watches me do this, silently.

When I am twenty and in my first relationship, my boyfriend, N, wants to help me mourn the sudden loss of my mom. I'm stuck in the stage of extreme grief about her death. I've had no therapy or help with processing her death from

anyone. Whenever I talk about her, I immediately begin crying, overcome with intense sadness. N suggests I think of good memories about her, remember her with happiness, not sadness. This sounds nice, like a good idea. I tell N she liked to get us ice cream sandwiches, so he brings me an ice cream sandwich and asks me to tell him stories about her. I am touched and appreciative of this.

Because N experienced emotional and physical abuse as a child, when I'm distant or disapproving, he becomes scared I don't love him enough and that he's losing me—or will. Sometimes in these moments, he becomes angry, emotionally abusive, yells and says mean things; occasionally, he is physically abusive and breaks thing, punches the wall, grabs me, holds me down so I don't walk away from the fight. One time, my neighbor knocks on the door because she hears him yelling and me crying and wants to interrupt and make sure I'm okay. While I appreciate her concern, I'm embarrassed. N always apologies and cries after these episodes; he's sad and mad at himself for losing control. Initially, when this happens, I don't understand what's going on. I've never seen or experienced this kind of behavior and am simultaneously afraid of him and sorry for him. I'm unable to reconcile this angry person with my loving partner. I'm confused. I have no experience with abuse and don't know what to do—for him or for me. I don't talk to my friends or family about it; I'm a feminist and feel ashamed to be in this dynamic with a boyfriend. I have not recovered from the trauma of losing my mom, and despite the sadness and fear I feel in these moments, I'm not emotionally equipped to leave and lose N and the relationship.

The same year I begin teaching high school in Tucson, I slip and fall on the concrete floor of our house and break my hip. I'm twenty-three, but my bones are brittle because of the cortisone I took for my aplastic anemia. After surgery, I'm stuck on the sofa for a long time and use a walker for a few months. N helps me on and off the toilet, in and out of the bathtub. He drives me to the school and picks me up. We watch My So-Called Life together and cry. At one point, he says something mean; with my good leg, I kick over the coffee table, and everything crashes to the floor. We're both frustrated and losing patience with the healing process.

When we break up years later because I don't want to marry him, I stay in bed for days and cry endlessly. I imagine he thinks this means I want to stay together—I don't. I'm devastated about all the sad, hard things over the last ten years, about all the different kinds of loss. I'm sad for both of us. After I move into my

own house, I'm relieved and happy to be there and be alone, but I spend a good amount of time crying, missing his presence and friendship. I'm determined to work through all the stages of grief about this loss. And I do.

In my early thirties, out of the 10-year relationship with N, I discover Pilates and casual sex. For the first time since childhood I feel in control of my body. I'm taking a new drug for my arthritis, Remicaid, and it feels like my arthritis is gone. This drug, called a biologic, has mouse protein in it. I receive a three-hour infusion of it every three months. I'm going to Pilates class twice a week, and after a year, I'm in Advanced Pilates. The teacher is a calm older woman with a white bob haircut who used to be a dancer. I love following her lead through all the movements. It feels like I'm in dance class again. My arms and core muscles become strong. I feel powerful and sexy. I seek out other people's bodies and pleasure.

I have a new best friend who shows me the ropes of casual sex. C and I cross paths because we're connected to a young-man poet we both like; Tucson is a small place, and he's notorious; women across town bond over his irresponsible romantic gestures. C and I become close, and get side-by-side shot-gun apartments in old adobe four-plex downtown. An artist from Detroit, C is in Tucson for a corporate job she hates, which is pre-teen girl product design. Outside of her job, she designs and makes cool clothes; her living room is filled with thread and fabric—gold, deep red, black velvet, and a clothes-racks and an enormous table. C is red-headed with green eyes, foul-mouthed, funny, and has a deep loud laugh. The only thing in her freeze is a bottle of vodka. I want to be like her. We share our life stories with one another, watch Sex and the City together, go to the little Tucson bars. I admire how C pursues pretty men like men pursue pretty women.

I try to follow her lead and begin to make first moves with men; I don't hesitate to ask them to come to my place, into my bedroom, do this or that with me and to me. I take risks, am fearless and exuberant. Once again in my life I'm Entertainer-of-the-Year Runner-up. I eventually realize I'm not good at casual intimacy like she is, or appears to be, but I've become comfortable in my body, which is a feeling I've missed.

In my seventh-year as an high school English teacher, I begin working on a master's degree. My grad-school advisor, a male professor around my same age—early 30s, is professionally ambitious and an intense teacher. He's one of those young

professors who hangs out with his grad students, meets up with them at bars and music shows, and although he's married, is having sex with one of his students, one of his advisees. At the time, I hear the rumors, and later when its confirmed, I'm not surprised. There's an expectation among his advisees we should keep quiet, protect him and his position, which I do, but don't feel good about. It's confusing. Unlike some of the older tenured-professors, he's attentive to us and our work. He seeks to form us in his academic image, so any success or failure of ours is his. The feedback he gives me about my work is harsh. The way he does it feels punishing. But I take it because I want to become a better writer, or this is what I tell myself. I'm an adult with life experience, so I think I have clarity about this dynamic. When I deviate from his direction and do an ambitious presentation on the language of paradox and ambivalence in Judith Butler's *Gender Trouble*, which I'm proud of, he won't engage with me about it in class and later reprimands me for not doing as he told me, which is a more succinct close-reading. I won't improve if I don't listen to his direction he tells me over a dinner.

When I'm applying to PhD programs, he gives me advice for when I go on the job market in the future. One piece of advice is that when I interview, I should try to hide my hands because they make me look older than I am. I know he means because they look arthritic. When he tells me this, I say nothing. I wonder if he's right. This advice and his matter-of-fact tone relaying it only later strikes me as horrible. It makes me sad that academia, like other institutions under capitalism, prefers the young, healthy and compliant.

When I am working on a Ph.D. in Los Angeles, a new grad-school friend tells me about a debilitating disease she has, which she rarely talks about. She doesn't tell anyone in her program about it—her professors, dissertation advisor, classmates. Understandably, she's afraid this will be used against her. She confides in me because knows that I know sickness can be a problem in grad school, where it feels like it's the young and healthy who make it; they're the chosen ones by the faculty and most desirable ones on the academic job market. When she becomes pregnant, a happy but not easy decision, she is chastised by a professor about the detrimental effect this will have on her academic career. One day when we are together, she tells me about how it feels to have her disease and a child; she says before she had her child she comforted herself with the fact she could kill herself if she felt she couldn't handle her disease. Now that she has a child, she must stay alive no matter how it feels to be in her body.

When I first meet L, my attraction to her is immediate. I see her at a party that D takes me to and notice her immediately; she is androgynous and cute. Eventually I become brave enough to sit down next to her and strike up a conversation about traveling. A day later I send her a friend request on MySpace, and we begin messaging each other; we have in a conversation about the spices we have in our cupboards. I ask if she'd like to take a walk together, which we do with J, who's the person who had the party and is a new friend. J and I talk more on the walk than L and I do, and this feels okay, as I really like J and want to become friends with J. And L makes me feel shy.

Over time I learn that L does not drive a car; she is a bike person and rides her bike around Los Angeles to get places and with all sorts of cool bike people. I visit her at the Bike Oven in Highland Park, where she volunteers, hangs out, fixes people's bikes for free. It's a little tricky for both of us that I don't ride a bike, as this is an important part of L's life and identity. My arthritis and osteoporosis prevent me. I'm afraid I'd break into pieces if I got into an accident. Whenever I pick L up out in the world, we cram her bike into the back of my little hatchback Versa; she takes off a wheel to make it fit. We're enamored with one another, so this doesn't matter, me not riding a bike—at least not at the moment.

When I am growing up with arthritis and seeing doctors in teaching hospitals, small groups of resident doctors often come into the room; the doctor explains my disease to them, and they look at my body. This makes me feel alienated from my body, like it's a peculiar object; I find myself outside of my body looking at it with them. Sometimes the doctor introduces the other doctors and asks if I mind if they are in the room. What else can I say but yes. It doesn't feel like I have a choice. I become used to being an abnormal body. On good days, I feel glad they can learn from my body and what's wrong with it. One upside to this dynamic is that I learn how to move outside my body, to leave it and distance myself from it as if I'm not in it, which can be useful.

I go to the lab to get blood drawn—for what is probably the thousandth time. No big deal. The woman drawing my blood asks me about my day as she inserts the needle and fills up the vials with my blood; she begins telling me about a dance class she's taking. I realize she's attempting to distract me from thinking about the needle, my arm, and the blood, and even though I'm fine and don't need a distraction, I appreciate this kindness.

I notice a painful lump on my inner arm and first thing I think is I have cancer. I've come to expect bad things to happen in my body. After a few phone calls and a doctor's appointment, I go in for an ultrasound. A young woman x-ray technician squirts cool gel on my upper arm and runs a warm wand over it. The image on a screen is blue, red, orange and pulsing. She tells me about what she is seeing, which I appreciate this; she says something about a lymph node, a cyst, and asks if I have a cat. There seems to be an infection. I'm to see an orthopedic surgeon. I wait in a small, cold white room in which there are two chairs, an exam bed, a desk, computer screen, and a trashcan—a typical doctor's office room. The door is shut. I sit in this awful room for over an hour waiting for a doctor. I anxiously get up and walk out in the hall a few times to remind them of my presence. The surgeon finally comes in accompanied by two young men doctors.

The surgeon is old, white, smiling and animated. He glances at my face, looks down at my deformed hands, picks them up, turns to the two young men doctors, and says excitedly to them, "look at her hands." He says "this is rheumatoid arthritis," "ulnar drift," "this is what happens, look." I feel annoyance and anger. I blurt out personal information about myself: "I'm Adrienne, I'm working on a doctorate in English..." I never introduce myself this way, but want to signal to him that a smart person is attached to the arthritis-ulnar-drift-hands. He turns to the young men doctors, and says, "people with arthritis are always nice." I snap at him, "not all of us." He says nothing in response to this example of a not-nice-person-with-arthritis and turns to look at the computer screen with the two young doctors.

The first book L and I read to one another is Gertrude Stein's *Paris, France*. We are camping and laying side by side in our tiny tent, reading with a flashlight. She tells me she has never read a book aloud with someone, not with her mother, or a friend or lover. She begins reading, her voice tentative, trying out her reading-out-loud voice.

Even though L riding her bike all over Los Angeles and me not riding a bike is initially not a problem in our relationship, I think about how this might come to be a problem, about how L needs a girlfriend who rides a bike with her. It does become a problem when we live together. When we are both headed somewhere for a social event, she wants to ride her bike, but I want us to go together in my car. Bike-riding for L is about independence and her way of being in the world. I seem to be impeding this. While I understand it, I don't know what to do. I wish I could ride bikes with her.

L and I begin reading in our bed every night when we are living together. We read all of Italo Calvino's fairy tales to each other. When she reads in different voices, we laugh.

After L and I are living together for four months, I'm told my intense headaches are a result of an issue at top of my cervical spine; possibly because of my arthritis, there is a dangerous amount of space between the top two vertebrae of my cervical spine. If the space increases, there could be nerve damage, or if I fall and hit my head, I could break my neck. A neurosurgeon will need to fuse the top two vertebrae to stabilize them.

In the shower the night before the surgery, I think about where the surgeon will operate—my neck where the spinal cord meets my skull; the top two vertebrae will be fused together with wire and pins. I think about if there's a problem with the surgeon's instruments, the pins, my bones. I might become paralyzed. I might die. I might not wake up from the surgery. I let myself really think about this as I stand in the hot water and cry quietly. I typically have panic attacks when I think about dying but decide I need to come to terms with the possibility of death now, at this moment in the shower. I don't want to be scared and cry in front of L and make her more scared than she already is. After the shower, I don't do any more thinking about death. I get in bed with L, and we go to sleep.

I survive the surgery. Three men doctors come into my hospital room to tighten the screws of the metal halo that had been drilled into my skull. They surround me and three pairs of doctor hands simultaneously tighten the screws—a team effort. My cries of pain become louder. They give up tightening the screws, at a pressure, they tell me, is less than desirable. They turn and leave, disappointed with me. Later, one of the doctors comes back alone. He is dressed meticulously; his pointy shoes are shiny brown leather; under his white coat, he wears a white pinstriped dress shirt and purple tie with a pattern of little white diamonds. In contrast, I am a monster; my hair is matted with blood and iodine, my drugged-up body is a disheveled mess in the hospital gown and bed sheets. He resumes tightening the screws, and I cry out in pain. He explains to me the pressure of the metal halo around my head, the tightness of the screws, needs to be more. He tells me you have a low threshold for pain. Most patients, he explains, can tolerate more pain. I try to stay quiet, but can't keep myself from emitting more cries. He stops. He says I'll come back later, and then he asks do you have any questions? This makes me mad. I yell this isn't a good time for me to think of questions. He

looks startled and walks out of the room. After the surgery and hospital stay, back at home in my bed I have to learn to sleep in the metal halo attached to my head that has metal rods anchored in a plastic and wool vest I wear around my torso. In the middle of the night when I wake up, L helps me sit up in bed because I can't do it by myself. The halo is heavy, and I'm in pain and on drugs. "L, L," I whisper, waking her up, "I have to go the bathroom." She wakes up, leans over, puts her hand on my back, and gently moves me forward so I can sit up.

Before the surgery, I had asked the surgeon if I should cut my hair—if it will be in the way and hard to wash because of the halo. He barely takes a second to answer no. When I'm home it is clear that my shoulder-length hair is a problem. My friend J cuts if off. After the wound on my neck is healed, L and I learn to maneuver washing my hair once a week. I lean over the tub, and she gently washes my short hair, rinsing it with many cups of warm water.

Each day L reaches her long slender hand with a washcloth inside the plastic wool-lined vest connected to the metal halo around my head in order to wash my skin. She cleans me with such care that when the doctors remove the vest from my body after three months of me living in it, there are no stains on it, no evidence of the sweat and suffering of those months. L says that this is evidence that she has taken good care of me, and I say yes, it is.

The three months and three weeks that I'm in this device, I try to stay calm. Wearing a halo head-brace screwed into my skull means I take Oxycodone and move around the house in a daze. I'm scared to turn the wrong way, move the wrong way, run into something. I frequently knock the halo on the bathroom doorframe. I pause for a moment to see if something bad is going happen. I'm very careful with how I move my body, more careful than I have ever been in my life.

I depend on L completely, but I'm not careful with her or our relationship. Only towards the end of this time does she express feelings of frustration and impatience about my total dependence on her. I know she's trying to do work for her classes and is also thinking about what I need. In this moment when she snaps, my response is to become angry. I throw a gift from her on the floor, a replica of an old view-master camera, accidently breaking it. It is only later when in therapy I come to understand that the person doing the care-taking needs as much patience and care as the patient. How do I not understand this at the time? I received care from multiple partners. It takes me too long to learn.

Virginia Woolf's mother, Julia Stephen, cared for her children and for sick people in her community. She wrote an essay entitled, "Notes from a Sickroom," in which she detailed methods for taking care of the sick, including the best method for the washing of their feet. *It is a great refreshment to sick people to have their feet washed, and no part of the body can be washed more safely and with less fatigue to the patient. A warm flannel must be put under the foot, which should hang a little over the side of the bed, the foot-tub or basin must be just below, and the foot can thus be soaped and sponged easily and effectually. Each foot must be washed separately, and, as the sponge is removed, must be wrapped in a warm flannel and dried with warm towels.*

When I go to the doctor's office to have the halo removed, L drives me. I'm on extra pain medication, so I'm in a bit of a daze. Three doctors I don't know come into the small room and tell me they'll be removing the halo. They don't ask if I have any questions. I think about the shirt I'm wearing over the plastic vest the halo rods are attached to, and it occurs to me that this will be a problem. I ask about it needing to come off, but they don't pay attention to what I'm saying. Without telling me about how they will remove the halo, how it will go and feel, they surround me and without warning begin unscrewing the pins in my skull. I'm scared and want to tell them to wait, slow down, give me a minute, tell me what you're going to do. They now notice my shirt is a problem and pause; we struggle to get it off me. I feel panicked, worried about the screws in my head. As they pull out the screws, I feel pressure, then the halo is out of my head and the heavy hot vest off. They hold gauze tightly on the wounds for a few minutes. Then the men are gone.

L and I are now holding the gauze on the bleeding holes in my head. I'm shaking. The nurse comes in and tells us about how to take care of the wound and about continuing my pain medication, but I'm dazed and disoriented. I don't hear anything she says.

Later I am furious at these doctors: at their lack of communication and empathy in this moment, at what now strikes me as a cruel interaction. Even after years of this kind of treatment by doctors, I'm still am surprised at the cold clinical handling of my body as if I am not a feeling person.

I take oxycodone for a little while longer then stop abruptly, deciding I don't need it anymore. No doctor or nurse told me that four months of being on it means

that I am addicted to it—my brain and body both. When I stop cold-turkey, which you're not supposed to do I find out, I feel depressed, have sharp stomach pains and become sick with nausea and diarrhea for weeks. I have to research on my own—on the internet—about what to eat and do about my opioid addiction because no one in the hospital or doctor's office gave me any warning this would happen. I eat white foods—bananas, rice, potatoes and saltine crackers. I drink ginger and peppermint tea non-stop. This helps.

Sometimes when L is out late at night on her bike and doesn't come home until late, I become very anxious that something bad has happened—that she's been in an accident. I insist when she's out late on her bike she text me where she is and when she'll be home. She resents this, finding it controlling. I find that I have to remind her of the trauma of losing my mom suddenly to explain why I need this; but she says no, which confuses and hurts me.

In my sixth year of grad school when I have funding and don't have to teach is when I have the neck surgery. I don't take a leave from the program because I need the paychecks and health insurance. It's the year I'm supposed to be writing my dissertation full-time and submitting chapters for publication in journals in order to be competitive on the job market, but the surgery and recovery take up six months of this year. The following year I'm required to teach again; it's my last funded year, and I must finish my dissertation. I don't ask my grad program or committee members special treatment or exceptions. This is a life-time continuation of me not wanting to be seen or treated as different, as disabled or sick. Even though my committee professors are kind, understanding people, I don't want to seem pitiful or weak. I'm teaching, writing non-stop, and applying to jobs with no publications in my field. Things aren't good between me and L; we haven't recovered from my surgery; we aren't communicating, aren't having sex, aren't close. We are not addressing the ways the surgery and her care-taking of me changed us and our relationship dynamic. I say I'm too stressed out, that we'll talk about our relationship when I'm finished with my dissertation and when I know if and where I have a job.

L and I are breaking up and still living in the same house. Neither of us can afford to move out yet. I sleep alone in our bed, and she sleeps on the floor in her office. My dissertation has to be finished in two months, so I don't feel I can take a break to make life decisions. I sit at my computer every day for hours writing my final chapter on Jean Rhys's *Voyage in the Dark*. When I cry I'm not sure if it

is about my life, the author's, or her character, Anna and her bleak life and her trying to be hopeful and "get on," like everyone tells her to do: *Keep hope alive and you can do anything, and that's the way the world goes round, that's the way they keep the world rolling. […] But what happens if you don't hope any more, if your back's broken? What happens then?* I'm crying for all of us, but I'm also crying about losing L. I can't wrap my mind around this. I develop anxiety and have panic attacks.

The last thing L and I read aloud together is a passage from Virginia Woolf's *The Waves*. I'm working on my dissertation, and she comes into the room with the book in her hand. We sit on the sofa, she reads, and we cry it makes us so happy. We love Woolf so much.

I take my leftover surgery anxiety medication. I'm in bed trying to sleep, L hears my anxious breathing and crying and comes in and holds my hand until I calm down. She goes back in the other room to sleep.

In one of my favorite films, *Hiroshima Mon Amour*—that I write about in multiple classes in grad school—the central character Riva, distressed that she must separate from a lover with whom she has just shared a traumatic personal story about loss from her past, cries, "I'll forget you! I'm forgetting already! Look how I'm forgetting you! Look at me." In the film's screenplay, Marguerite Duras writes about this last moment they have together: "they look at each other without seeing each other." I return to this film over and over—watching it and writing about it in order to think about cycles of intimacy and loss.

L moves out the same weekend I have my Ph.D. hooding ceremony. I'm exhausted and broke. Between non-stop phone-call conversations with my sister and patient friends who help me process the break-up, I binge-watch all of *Mad Men* on the sofa in a month. I start seeing a therapist. In late summer, I start messing around with men. I make out with three men in cars in two months.

I am now living alone and feel somewhat recovered from the break-up. I go to a friend's art performance downtown. A group of women speak the words of other women who cannot cross borders. In this group performance, they lie on each other's bodies, inhaling the air of one another, making sounds and listening. I find myself thinking about the intimacy of this. In my life now no body is next to me. I do not lay my head on the body of another person and listen to her breath-

ing. I do not feel the comfort of a body next to me in bed; no more reading in bed together, no more whispered conversations in the dark. It takes me a long time to not feel the absence of L.

The girlfriend L has now rides a bike; they ride their bikes together all over the city. This makes me both happy and sad.

I'm at party where I meet and flirt with B, a young-man art writer, who is tall with dark curly hair, who knows friends of mine. Afterwards, he drives me to my car a few blocks away. We end up making out. He says, "will it offend you if I ask you to come over to my house?" I want to laugh at this question, but instead I say, "No, it will not offend me." I go to his little house, and we stand in the dark living room and each take a shot of whisky. I say, "let's go to your room." We have all kinds of fun sex and talk in-between. We hold hands in his messy bed. I tell him his hands are nice—they're delicate, feminine. He tells me that when he was a little boy he thought his hands didn't look tough enough, so he'd hit walls to give them scars like his brother's hands. It crosses my mind that this is a story he tells women. He asks about my hands, and I say I have arthritis. I didn't notice them, he says. I tell him I'm a little self-conscious about them. He says, I think you used misdirection. He tells me a story about a Pilates instructor who uses misdirection to keep people's attention away from the fact she does not have legs. He sounds sure, so I entertain this. He says, your hands are beautiful.

He writes me a noncommittal text the next day—"let's do that again sometime." I work to be okay with this form of communication.

I'm at the register at Target, and in my cart is a large box of cat litter. I struggle to pick it up and put it on the conveyer belt. I always buy this kind of cat litter, even though it's difficult for me to pick up and carry. I rarely think about my struggling being difficult for someone to watch. An older woman in line behind me sees me struggling, and without saying anything, she reaches into my cart and puts in on the conveyor belt. After I pay for it, her daughter puts it back in my cart. I say thank you. I cry when I get inside my car, touched by their help.

E, A and I go to art galleries in Culver City on a Sunday afternoon. In a little back room is a show entitled, *Impulsive Control*, by the artist Melodie Mousset. On the floor are video screens of a naked body of a woman who is a sculpture in progress; the woman's body on the potter's wheel spins around. Her body, cross-legged, is

visible, but not her face; her head is a pot being formed by a man's hands that dip in and out of the wet pot, molding and forming the woman's head with his fingers. The artist creates her pot-head, pushing and pulling the walls of it, her head malleable.

I look for photos of L on Facebook. It feels like she's dead, and I want to see she's still alive. In a photo I find, she's watching a performance and touching her lips, in the way she does when she is thinking hard about something. I find a video of her; she is rubbing her eyes with her long fingers the way she does when her contacts are bothering her. I would ask are your eyes bothering you? And she would say yes. These gestures and her hands are so familiar they feel like they're mine, like they also belong to me. Like my body belonged to her. I'm working to accept the loss of her and her hands.

In Thomas Mann's *The Magic Mountain*, Hans Castorp finds comfort in the walls of a Swiss Alps sanitarium; he carries around the chest x-ray of his beloved, Claudia, who is dying of tuberculosis. Castorp, who doesn't have tuberculosis, does not remain at a safe distance from his beloved. He imagines he has tb symptoms and performs them. He's not with the men fighting the war, and he identifies with the sick bodies in the sanitarium, with those being nursed and comforted; he keeps company with his sick beloved.

The artist Hannah Wilke is diagnosed with lymphoma when she's forty-six. Her *Intra-Venus* photographs that she began making in 1991 are of her body during this period.

In reading about Wilke on the internet, I come across an essay by an art critic writing about the *Intra-Venus*, about Wilke's photographs of her sick body undergoing treatments; he writes she is "still refusing to be defined by her body and its appearance, assuming a surprising dignity even in its decline." This critic's characterization of Wilke refusing to being defined by her body strikes me as wrong and typical in its anxieties about the female body, aging, and illness. His observation that Wilke is "refusing to be defined by her body," is strange given that in this series she is, in fact, as an artist offering definitions of her body, of the sick female body, in playful, provocative ways. She's not in decline. In the same family as her early work, these photographs bear witness to the complexity of the female body; the body is solid, alienating, ugly, beautiful, resilient; never one thing, always multiple.

It is curious to me this critic describes Wilke's body as "assuming a surprising dignity even its decline." "Decline" is passive and vague, balking from acknowledging illness. I wonder if his surprise about a "body in decline" assuming "dignity" is about a need to see a sick body as dignified, about a fear of the lack of composure when our bodies are sick. In the images, Wilke is intentionally undignified: bald with discolored gauze up her nose; in another, her eyes are closed and her mouth is wide open as if in a furious scream; she wears a hospital identification bracelet and medical plastic-tubing hangs from her body; she's naked with white square bandages on hips fresh from bone-marrow extractions, smiling as she balances a flower arrangement on her head; with a blue hospital blanket wrapped around her head she is a demure Virgin Mary; luxuriating in a sexy pose in a hospital bed, her body naked except for large, square white bandages taped on her hips; she is a sick "Marilyn Monroe." Women are conditioned to feel ashamed when we're not composed or appealing, when our bodies are a mess, sick, ugly, abject. I appreciate Wilke's rejection of dignity.

I make plans with S, a good friend, to go to an interactive art and writing event in Chinatown. The two of us wander around and are directed to go down some stairs into a small room where people are sitting in chairs. A woman is instructing people to perform actions. She asks for volunteers to stand against the wall, and my friend does. She gives them a number of instructions on what to perform. One instruction is to "walk like a cripple." Each person performs this differently. Two of them walk with a dramatic limp; one hunches over and drags his leg behind him; others hesitate and don't do anything, including my friend, who I know doesn't like this instruction and is thinking of me. When he returns to his seat next to me, he looks at me searchingly—I can sense he's trying to figure out what I'm thinking. More than anything I'm curious about what the woman is thinking. Who uses the word cripple now? How was this art? I give her the benefit of the doubt; maybe her intention is to see what people do with that language and instruction, if people will immediately fall into cliché pantomime routines of disabled people and people with differently-abled bodies. Is this what she was doing? There's no explanation or discussion.

When my friend sits down, he asks me if I want to leave. We climb the stairs and walk away together in silence. He says wow that was weird, that walking-like-a-cripple-thing was a problem. I feel bad for him because he feels bad for me. I appreciate he wants to give me a chance to talk about this. I say yeah, what was up with that?... What would walking-like-an- emotional-cripple look like? We laugh.

We check out another performance and run into people he knows. One of them is a woman I imagine my friend has a crush on—probably only because I have a crush on him. We stand in a group talking, then he leaves my side and seems to walk deliberately across the circle to stand next to her. This makes me sadder than the walk-like-a-cripple art performance.

I go downtown to the Broad Museum to see a performance of the artist and writer Martine Syms. "Politics is something you do with your body," she says, sitting behind a table on the stage of the Broad She has layered a screen with photographs, text, and film clips of bodies of black women, of women known and unknown to her, and of celebrities. Syms tells us she spends time looking at old photos of women she doesn't know, "trying to learn something about them," and of her aunt, "a singular figure," a woman who "moved through the world independently."

In her multi-media performance, Syms mixes together personal and collective memories. "There's something in the way she moves," she says and plays this line from various songs that belong to her and us; the audience murmurs sounds of recognition. Remembering when she was taught how to move, she tells us stories about attending Tyra Banks's girls summer camp while her brothers spent the summer playing guitar and skateboarding. She felt envious of their freedom of movement as she was learning to limit hers.

Syms wonders lately about how to enact "extreme presence" as a way to communicate visually the politics of the body, her body, the body of an African-American woman She stands in the center of the stage, performing power poses from a TED talk. She notes that these poses are "replacements for actual agency," then adds, "these are perhaps no crazier than the rules I have for myself." Seated, she reads her list of rules for her body, laughing but serious. "These are the ways I protect myself." She returns to photographs of black girls, ending with the declaration: "Looking is a way of knowing—and I see these girls."

I'm with my dad, who is visiting me, and as we are walking he asks if he can help me carry something, and I ask why, and he says you look fragile. This upsets me. I'm not fragile, I respond unreasonably angrily to him, why would you say that? I don't want to appear fragile. I don't want to be fragile. Even though I know my fragility is one of my strengths— that it makes me sensitive to suffering and empathetic towards others.

In high-school I wear splints in my shoes because of the arthritis in my feet. I worry other kids see the splints peeking out of my tennis shoes, and I worry I walk funny. Almost nothing is worse than being different in high school in a small Indiana town. I concentrate on walking down the hall, walking normally, trying to not walk-like-a-cripple.

As an adult, after many surgeries, when I'm traveling and walking all around cities, I don't think about what my walking looks like to others. I'm so happy to be walking around out in the world. However, I still carry with me shame about being different, weak, vulnerable.

I go to visit a school for my job, and at the top of the stairs is the door with a buzzer to the side. I lean to press it, and my foot goes down the stair. As I lose my balance and am heading down the stairs, trying to catch myself, I'm scared. I know I'm going to get hurt.

I'm thinking about my brittle bones with osteoporosis, and I am thinking about the metal hardware in my neck holding together the top two vertebrae of my spinal cord. I don't put my hands out, instinctively protecting them. My head takes the hit on concrete twice, and I'm on my back. I don't move. People come out of the school, and an ambulance is called. This is the second time in my life an ambulance has taken me alone to a hospital. (The first is when I'm in a car accident.) All I can think about is my neck and if it's okay, even though it doesn't hurt. I wonder what if I die alone in this ambulance. In the hospital, I'm told I have a slight concussion, but no broken bones. I'm relieved.

For months, it's painful to walk. I tell my doctor. I'm in pain, but he dismisses it as a muscle or tissue injury and tells that it just needs time to heal. (I find out a year later when I trip on my pajama pants and fall hard in my bedroom and get a hairline fracture in my femur that I did have a fracture in my pelvis from the fall down the stairs.) In addition to the pain in my pelvis, I have vertigo, which lasts for a year. I constantly feel like I'm going to fall, which is difficult because I have to go up lots of stairs to get to my house. I get advice from people about exercises to do to fix vertigo; no doctor seems to know what to do for vertigo other than pre-scribe medication for dizziness. My dad who had vertigo helps me do the exercise when he visits me, which is called the Brandt-Daroff exercise. He shows me, and I lay on bed and turn my head and do sit-ups in a certain way to re-situate crystals in my ears. My body and brain don't forget the fall, and I develop anxiety about

escalators and going down stairs, always hesitating and slow, like an old woman; this is what I imagine I seem like to people around me, but I don't care. I look down and concentrate on my feet on stairs.

A few days after the fall down the stairs, I have intense vertigo and a horrible headache. I imagine my brain is bleeding. I text my friend S who lives nearby that I need to go to the hospital, and he comes right away to pick me up. Because I have hopes that one day something romantic will happen between the two of us, I don't want to seem too miserable in the car ride to the hospital. I try to play-fully banter with him like we always do. Then I tell him he needs to pull his car over. I open the door and throw-up on the side of the street. As I'm throwing up, I think this is the least attractive thing one can ever do in front of a person, and I resign myself to the fact we will probably never have sex. He takes me into the hospital, and I insist he doesn't need to stay, even though I'm scared and want him to. I don't want to seem like I need too much care. Ever since my break-up with L, I'm anxious about appearing like I need alot of care, especially to people I'm romantically interested in. I have a MRI and find out my brain isn't bleeding. S is gone. I take an Uber home.

When I'm on an airplane, an older man next to me asks the stewardess for food, and his voice is a gravel whisper. I think oh he's had something happen to his throat, his voice box or vocal cords. When I drop a cup on the floor later and can't reach it, he reaches down to pick up for me and silently hands it to me. I say thank you.

I use henna on my hair and take turns asking my best friends to help me. It goes like this. I make us tea. I sit in a chair. My friend stands behind me and separates and saturates strands of my hair with the henna, a thick earthy-smelling green mud. Talking throughout the application, which takes about half an hour, we always cover a lot of ground. Each friend has her own way of applying the henna. M asks questions about how to do it, and goes slow, wanting to do it right. A is meticulous, careful not to get any on my face or neck, and when she does, uses a warm washcloth to wipe it off. E enjoys the texture of the henna and puts it on thick. S is messy and gets it all over me and the floor. Afterwards, my hair is shiny with hints of auburn, like the hair of my great grandmother Fox, who I'm told had red hair. I like having my friends' hands in my hair, their care and the intimacy of it.

My sister and dad are concerned about my hands. I find this out when we are together during Christmas break. They talk when I'm out and when I return, my sister reports the conversation to me saying this will make you mad. She tells me they wonder if I should have reconstructive surgery—I guess because my hands look bad, deformed. She asks what happens if I can't type in the future. I say well they don't hurt, I can use them fine. I then say I live alone and who would help me if I had hand surgery? We end up talking about my dating life and what people think is wrong with my hands. My sister tells me I should explain my hands to people on the first date and that I have arthritis. I tell her I do this if it comes up naturally.

The last person I explained my hands to on a first date said oh I thought you'd been in an accident. I realize from this comment that my hands must look bad to people. Soon after, another woman I go on a few dates with, when we make out, she touches and holds my hands without hesitation. I feel encouraged.

I go see my rheumatologist Dr. K for my usual office visit. Over the ten years I have seen him, he's always struck me as unhealthy and unhappy. Today he looks different. He's lost weight and is tan. I notice he's wearing cute socks and stylish leather shoes. He seems to be radiating happiness. Like most rheumatologists I've seen over the forty years I've had arthritis, Dr. K mostly asks me questions my arthritis is doing and talks about the drugs I take for my disease. He rarely asks about other aspects of my health or about my personal life. This time he asks if I'm dating. Under his care, I've been in two relationships and been through two break-ups, and he knows that L and I aren't together anymore. He starts telling me about his divorce and new wife. She seduced him. He asks me if I'm good at seduction, at "picking people up." I am startled by this. I can't answer for a minute. Yes, I laugh, I'm good at this. He wants to share his romantic success with me, maybe to help me find a new partner? He tells me about the importance of flirtation and the book *The Art of Seduction*. He says he's learned from this book about how seduction works. I wonder if I should try to give him examples of my skills at seducing people to end this awkward conversation, but can't get them out of my mouth. Plus he's so excited to share; he's never talked with me this long during a visit. I appreciate this. I nod and say yes and thank you. I leave with mixed feelings. I feel sad that this is the longest conversation we've had in the years I've been seeing him. I feel happy for Dr. K that he's feeling good about his body, new wife and life. He's being a better doctor, at least in this visit. For a moment, a doctor sees my body as something other than just a disease, as something that can and should experience pleasure.

I hold a Green Calcite stone, which helps me let go of what is "familiar and comforting and that is no longer needed." In my other hand, I clutch a Rose Quartz crystal, "which heals one emotionally." It helps to release "unexpressed emotions and heartache." Whether any of this is true or not, I'm not sure, but I feel like it is. In my bed at night when I hold them tightly, they become warm in my hands, and I fall asleep immediately.

BRANDON DOWNING

from *The Bacchae*

Clark Coolidge

Our hymns scared your kid, but did
You ever wonder why? I want to say
It's flowing, as I take it in, the
Delicious blood of Jesus. But we're
Not sure—do you sit on that doily, or pray by it?

Passion? It's more like the batshit of the Christ.
I interviewed a group of the visitors as
They came out of the Orientation Theater,
Who seemed moved yes but quite freaked out.
And I know exactly why. We need to stop.

I rescued more than 2,800 Austrians held
By the Probe—using positive rock music.
We were on ABC Family for a year.
When I saw what they did with me,
As a faith figure, I felt confused.

Church

God is running through you so hard
You crumple into your entertainment center.
Get a tan, you pray, run,
Blisters and lesions on your mouth and your tongue.
With your Bible open the pain is a joke,
You hold onto a girl's hand while her hair never moves.

She has on a dress vest of thick red mealy fabric,   (*gestures*)
A flight of zippers, this cheap navy blue skirt.
I agree—her excruciatingly holding out was hot,
Intellectually, but why try that here?
You could punch holes into most of the
Strip's architectural follies with a child's golf club toy,

"The same goes for our Megachurch, brother.
But we won't do it to these women." What about
That song your daughter did? That kid is religious,
I almost wish we could harvest that belief level
For our next big outreach—we're going to
Trick God into coming out of his hiding place.

I'd like to look more into these
Writer Centers ads, especially if somebody can
Fill me in on the nature of, why.
You can't center writing! We're done now,
I'm doing the, the walkthrough with Amy.
I hope they're still selling that soup after two.
Wake up, little sleazy, wake up. (*sings*)
Hurry fast—something's eating you.

If only the tide would thunder upstream and
Scour away some of these people and the things
They appear to be using as dining room tables?

Each workshop student pays me $45,000.
They get my email list their second day. They think
They've got the contacts too easily, they start talking
About me in front of me. Students—pack it up a bit.
Try and kill it then. Poetry is not the Arcade,

And neither will I die.
The bells and reviews shoot off
In all directions, but our light-hearted
Overlords seem alright with me staying on.
No one said it, but I cried out, what, too soon—
She turns and looks like yep she's going to eat me,
Before she does, I'm switching the entire sytem to on.
She's still going to eat me though!

Workshop

She was a diamond in the fine,
Either more or less than a poet, but
Absolutely not a poet. Fairly professional!
Quite detailed…I mean, she had a body,
She'd only express the best topics around.
And could easily manage any sugar spikes—
She displayed this divinity she seemed to
Have borrowed—directly from his face.

It was as if God itself pointed that key light
Onto Ron's terrible skin—we instantly knew.
Our meeting room felt like the Hague, filled
With raging speakers and educators, the outcomes
Resinous; no, I mean resonating outcomes.
And flirty, hard-drinking 8th graders,
Who were also big-time rabbis. Man
Would they tell us all about Masada.

The Poet

Deepening your indifference to your close friends over recent time,
Is that they're reforming the guys' old teenaged gang, the Artist
Kidnappers, and nobody told you yet.

It grieves me to hear
About my students creeping on their peers,
Apparently with my endorsement, but that ain't real.

It's still terrifying to be doubted. It's probably been shown
Across what you've been reading—exasperating non-specifics,
Generic dialogs, songs with breathtakingly cold terms. Legal?

Yes. Holy? God no.
It's a blessed relief knowing I will be instantly forgotten.
"When?" After a fucking long time! They'll need to burn me

Off the Main Stage. "Not if you fall from high enough up first."
Well said. The gotcha moment transcends culture, whatever
Your directing style is, even two weeks in South Europe, drinking,

Partying with people from England.
You can't deny the milky writing is on the wall—Strap Fever.
Would you really live there? The mission to Europa needs to be over.

They're spitting money at you, all that way. One big surprise?
The vintners all checked out. Their daughters are beginning
The long migration back from Wesleyan, through Berlin.

Whole family lines are lathered up with freezing allure,
Back in Napa. "I'm so sure!" they say, as they
"Cross across these inexpressible islands."

[eye doctor wanted]

eye doctor wanted (at last) my cock
          combined with four-
          hand Mozart sonatas.
his tall Norwegian wife, caftan, in
          bed with us for
          novelistic complexity.
chocolate chips, raisins, cashews, in dish
          daughtered up my three-
          o'clock disappearance.
time to teach math, ninth graders—
          outlaw bike-ride milk-
          shake hill homo-reverie.

forehead coign-angle legatoing
          me into world peace
          treaty dissolver or solver.
magnet dream told in St. Louis to undo how
          hinge-folds kill you
          minus Samothrace appendage.
weather-cock, gaming his ass, I
          said you're gorgeous
          to no inkling-avail.
like kindling tossing homo down
          Grimm hill Lotte
          Lenya aunt-lip fissure.

treacle damage me, then reverse the scar,
       drop basted turkey
       on Kissinger-foot, no
peace in "did they fuck?" speculation cramming
       his memento mori pubes
       backward to canker-Eden.
grail come back, scar no impediment,
       gummed shame-salami
       mispronounced, samizdat lice-poem.

tinkle the fairy ark-rope wizarding
       stained cruelty-daughter
       now regal aged Cassandra.
to cram him up, to celebrate him crammed,
       to revise the cramming,
       to call the cram cream.
how redux can you make East Germany,
       duckie? I get plumbed
       by rose-thorn, a Jekyll teething-ring.

Flatiron realness minus sexual panic
        in your underpants
        dreaming cookie-toddler.
spiked abalone alabaster dopamine in
        suicide terror, gun
        noose amyl nitrite.
saké her cockhead his bologna if
        folk songs co-create
        Western narco-reality.
our drug my drug our stomach our mis-
        prision sweating karate
        lessons for Pa-bonding.

thousand sex partners giggle to Sontag it,
        Mercutio her, stigma
        him—pox-Mary hal-
        itosis alleluia.
pink phlegm-card severs DNA-helix, im-
        petigo colonized, de-
        cathected for diaper service.
sweat-a-holic Laura Mars basket-weaver in
        art-therapy Paganini
        spittle—reckon thy
pudding, pinkie in tapioca bosom; cancer-recovered
        stalagmite-o-rama,
        I ♥ NY Brick-impotence

(Paul Newman). nose in his pubes, Noémie
      (Henry James) failed-artiste
      his VD my Tod-relic.
Liebestod crackers w/ strawberry jam, ricotta,
      charnel-rumors? arthritis
      tenderloin, 3 a.m. snack.
body unpopular, gut a Mona Lisa cam-glimpse,
      jack-off Chekhov cues
      Victor/Victoria Weltschmerz-lees.

negative space witch-calculus, Ghirlandaio
      teaching whip-widow
      a lady collar cholera.
when Monet tinkles. FIY he intuits petrol-
      optics, boner-schism when
      chroma-spectrum unslackens
Jethro Tull—we played LP to lure
      smashed-lip sibling-alter-
      ego to drool upward, where
      Lord might await stretchmark-Nacht.

Chez Butt,
angel blue sideways red
abstraction

————

loving the legacy
I create as relaxed
Czar or lazar, not
Lazarus but fractured
metaphorical leper

————

dislike of two stray
dead hairs cut
on page's table

————

my tie
is too expensive the song
says but you can't
trust promiscuous lyrics

————

June Havoc Berlioz—
June Havoc demarcates
Berlioz, June Havoc
is demarcated by Berlioz,
or a plus-size Berlioz
is ultra-demarcated by
a bunch of June
Havocs, a cold June Havoc

warming up a fell
Berlioz, a fallen Berlioz
in love (backwards
chronologically) with
a plush June Havoc
learning to long for
her own ruined habitat
in Berlioz's eyes

—————

heavy humid Schiele
in mist, she rinses
Schiele shortly, June
Havoc grammatically
rinses Schiele shortly,
the gay department of
Thursday's Schiele speaking
Italian to work-related
June Havoc, but specify
why June Havoc

—————

        suddenly
who is June Havoc from
the narrator's point of
view coming to ease
the blue stain

—————

he's chill with June Havoc
alive in a role mis-
begotten on hold,
June Havoc whole and
flowery, a high or hiked
June, like June took a

long hike up Yosemite's
tallest peak to try coming
alone up there novelistically
as what Berlioz took for granted—

—————

speedy fruit with bubbles—
underwater plants with
celestial details—

—————

who dominates? or does
no one dominate? and is
domination not the issue?

—————

reading Simone Weil,
wanting to find
the hurt, pocked portion
of being, afraid that
I possess a caved-in
plank that will open
a door onto incarnation,
or simply passage-
way through pleats immortally
strewn along now's
highway—I'll faint
while falling into elixir's
or crime's cosmic crevice—

—————

blue impaled
me in the nose—

my head an open
corridor or cement sluice

———————

seeing demolished Penn
Station from Jackie Onassis's
presumed point of view

———————

          Parker
Tyler next year I meant
Parker Posey overdetermining
Troy—

———————

          dreamt I gave
myself a long blow job,
then my mouth stank of
penis, my own—
wondered if people would
smell it, and would they know
it was my own stink?

———————

to my brethren I address
this playlet

———————

          snorting
supercilious heavy-breathing
gay guy browsing his Twitter—

        sempiternal
Corsican trek in hot
tight clothes then lying
down naked on beach

—————

unshaped carcass
continues unpaced

—————

red neon letters advertising
a defunct bathroom

—————

creating a vibe while pretending
not to possess a vibe,
Agamemnon hit on me

—————

tuché = "the encounter with the real"

—————

        pregnant
lying-down sickroom shape
of water stains on tablecloth—
specter my sickness matches—

—————

to be greased and cradled,
underage unclaimed

waiting in a photographed
void to consider
repetition a friend
dwelling in corners
disowned—your impersonal tone

————————

       sequential
marks laid down,
obedient to language's
stacking decree—words
must be stacked,
parts arranged and tabulated

————————

rhetoric, my fake Lowell
Apollonian Delmore
Schwartz side?

————————

please invent a more
forgiving regime of book—

————————

       I said "snowfall-
as-erasure" in email
to handsome photographer—
afraid he'll think I was
aiming to erase him
rather than trying to praise
the palpable erasures pop-
ulating his abstract tableaux—

JACKIE CLARK

Mt. Mitchell

I didn't want to tell the story and still don't
Not thinking in elephant thrusts
An action that rolls off the wrist
The situation changes
As does the house
What middle colors
Electioneering for my love
What grounds for improvement can I claim
Not one in reality
But infinite toward a masquerade
I can exploit you as I do myself
Make you sleepy and overpower
Reinforcement with rain tarps and sandbags
Only someone else will be credited for the saving
The drowned reality that I watched from the stones on the side
It is easy to slip
Easier to slide by choice
I don't have anything outstanding to say about it
Vulnerability is boring in excess
Dries up the compassion one tends toward
That I tend toward
I don't have a muse
A disciplined hand
An unwavering conviction
If I think about youth I think about the ability to fill the cup
To be easy and strong
Statements make their way
They tell us who we are with the smallest liability
They don't run on or run over

If it rivers it rivers elsewhere
Imaginary smokies
A ring of green mountains we drive over and around
It was the rain that increased the water
The rain that forced the slide
I don't dream with you
We dream side by side
I can't harness it and bring it into our lives
I can write a difficult poem
I can pretend like it matters
But I don't run over with narratives
It takes too long to describe profound change
A motherhood that I watch among
An ease of decision
Of seeing oneself in that role
I can get to about here and then I don't know

Cake Eater

I stared and the man ate. Cake in his grip, he reminded me of a cartoon bear pawing honey. He had round eyes as white as frosting. He stood at the end of the bar, where the cake was set out next to a caddy of garnishes, limes and lemons and cocktail onions, on a gold board with scalloped edges—a sheet cake commemorating an event someone had forgotten to celebrate. Really, when is cake mere compliment?

The man had a globular stomach and held the cake like a sandwich. I was fascinated, horrified, and already aroused: I had never seen an adult eat cake in this manner. Before I could second guess myself, I was walking up to him. Closer, I could see the wrinkles in his shirt. That made sense. His pants didn't: dark denim that I knew could ink one's thighs.

"Hey—" I pointed to the cake in his hand, the piece on my plate. "Is it worth it?"

He chewed as much as you need to with soft cake goodly iced. His gaze swabbed my face, the way my doctor mined for my cervix.

"Not bad," he said. "Though it's no breast milk."

I was amused but used to louche fellows, truly beyond-reproachables. This man had a jutting quality, like he was being yanked forward, off a shelf. I focused my vision on his porous forehead. My cake stiffened.

"You're a father then," I said.

"Twins," the man said. "Patty cake, patty cake."

"You have your hands full."

"But with what?" At that, he squeezed the cake in his grip. The frosting squelched—it would've been a sound we heard if the music weren't loud, a falsetto chanting: "Afraid to die."

The man clearly meant to punctuate our exchange with this desecration, but I was alone, pregnant, and desperate to be defiled, so I followed him outside. We found ourselves standing at a tall table in the plastic bubble that blistered over the front of the building. Some would call it a tent, but there were

many windows and a roof with fans, the blades molded to resemble bamboo, slowly rustling the humectant air.

"I have to ask you: Why exactly are you at this event?" the man said.

"A favor, a past," I said. "More or less, a reunion. Before I give birth."

"I didn't recognize you!" he said suddenly. "Now I see. Your arms are different."

"We barely know each other then," I said. "But now we both like cake."

The windows in the plastic enclosing us were opaque with exhalation. I nudged the cake around my plate, using the chin of the fork. I had only raked the frosting.

The man ate his last bite and smiled. "The frosting is homeless shelter frosting. Food pantry frosting. *Te hablas espanol?*"

I did speak Spanish, I *hola*-ed to everyone in my neighborhood, but I couldn't come up with a *claro, por supuesto, como no*. I balanced the cake on my belly. What of it, getting dirty, *sucia*? Sticky sweat was glomming on my camisa, where the cotton clung to my spine. My newly-popped navel pressed against the cloth like a spare button.

"Let me tell you, it's not as hard as you think," the man said. "I was very energized by fatherhood and my wife is wonderful with directions. Giving them. She's a project manager for a stable. From farm to table? How about from pasture to Saratoga?"

"Your children will ride?" I said, hopeful this would sound suggestive.

"God, no, please no," the man said. He wiped his hands on his shirt, where they left a crumbly white smudge like dead skin. "We're horse-eating people. From the north."

Somewhere in the night, there was a sound, like the exoskeleton of Earth's core being crunched. I was nervous, but one gets nothing as the instigator of fear—not without smoke or fireworks. There's a gulf of difference between fear and nervousness, pain and lonesomeness, anger and solitude. The man was keeping me company. He might come back to my hotel, down for a discalced romp, parenthetical, unthinkable. He had pink on his lip from a lone frosting rose.

"You want to see something straight awesome?" the man said.

I shrugged, but lord was I ever: desperate, desperate, desperate. I left my cake on the table.

He pushed out the tent and into the barking night. I followed him up the footpath, through a grove of bare magnolias, and into the parking lot. I was still hungry and the baby was turning, glowing, worming. I had seen others eating cake from plastic cups, the tiny breed that comes with water coolers. I regretted not smashing mine into one of those.

The man reached into the tight back pocket of his dark denim and pinched some remote. This was his car: the Carrera irradiated inside by green flashing lights. He nodded at the illumination, perhaps expecting a remark on the color, but I had my own father whose convertible could strobe, interiorly, exteriorly, with a dial's twist. I had a husband, too, some other fuckery.

"Meet the mother of my children," he said. "And the twins. Cula and Carl."

He opened the back door on the driver's side and stepped aside. A crimp-coated cocker spaniel panted there, lying on a pillow inlaid with silvery rope. It shone in an emerald tremor of overhead lights. There were two friendly-faced stuffed baby dolls in the dog's nest and a spear of bone, elk antler, most likely.

I wanted to go. I had the room nearby, a room from whence I had wandered in search of a convincing meal, conversation, some belittled cumming. I had kept my heart as open as batter for eggs. Now the humidity was mounting. My uterus was cramping. The hailstorm forecasted had never come. I had counted on weather to relieve my problems, but the weather was a coward. Like me.

"You see, without a witness, this is nothing," the man said, unbuttoning his shirt. He crouched as though he were fetching items from a very low shelf in the grocery. In the green overhead dim, the sparse hair on his chest was whiskery, wiry, feelers on a microscopic bug.

The cocker spaniel rolled over and exposed a scrubbed pink belly, nippled and speckled. The man picked up the baby dolls, much as he had picked up the cake, and situated the children near the dog's heart. Between a Y of blue veins, I swear, I could see a tremulous pulse.

By now the night was burned up and starving. I took a few steps back.

"My father, my father," the dog barked.

"My darling, my darling," the man said, and his face grew compassionate and he knelt on the seat and set a hand on the lower abdomen of the dog.

I imagined the cake back in my hand. I imagined stabbing the cake and taking a bite. It was marble. The chocolate was indistinct from the vanilla cloaked in all that icing. Roseless, sugarful, stupid cake. I expected such cake for a push present.

"Do you need a nurse or a midwife?" I said.

The man looked at me, puzzled. By that time, he was fully inside his own backseat and, with one of his hind legs, he kicked the door.

Soon it was noisy with suckling and his windows began to fog. There was cake smeared on the front of my *camisa* and I walked back to my hotel, watching my shadow grow rounder and rounder until it was a shadow globe.

Alone in bed: my stomach howled, I opened my legs. In the next room, a dog yapped like a snapping wet rag. Could he smell me, my hormonal torte, so progesterone? Whatever the odor, I was embarrassed and yet more defiant than usual. Perhaps I was great with child, but there was no way I could wait until breakfast.

DANIEL TIFFANY

stanzas from *Cry Baby Mystic*

A squashed
blackberry stuck
to the sole of my shoe
in Paradise you'll starve up on
the roof.

Mobbing
birds will often
swerve away before they
strike: Mannikins, Mousebirds, blue-gray
Noddies.

Even
that little truth
is too much though so is
the fibbing. I'm still not sure how
it works.

❄

I once
have known a man
soft as death could not catch
my scent no telling where "Little
Hat" went.

✳

The lies
themselves began
to take me at my word.
Why don't you eat him, the King says,
that way

maybe
you could work a
miracle. But who says
palaces ever were neat and
clean, what

with all
my friends here: *Eye
Winker, Tom Tinker, Nose
Smeller, Mouth Eater, Chin
Chopper.*

Bones may
be dropped from great
heights to break them open
on the slopes of *Mount Quarentyne.*
Seeing,

thinking,
sobbing's the best
life on earth—watch, he'll knock
on my door after he gets off work
tonight.

*

Not that
the world's so lost
we'd better start packing
our bags. His "divine monstress" he
called me

from his
rotten English:
*I savede him from beyting
and he hath me bette. A kissing
ther was.*

Pretty
grimy—we're done
with art—you never know
how much inside you is breaking
apart,

what it
must be like, why
some words always get their
way. He spends the night wherever
he lands.

ALL THE STARS IN THE SKY

★　★　★　★　★

KEVIN KILLIAN'S AMAZON REVIEWS

Selected and introduced by David Buuck

In addition to his voluminous work as a poet, novelist, memoirist, art critic, playwright, and literary organizer, Kevin Killian found time in his last years to publish over 2,600 Amazon reviews. For some time now, his reviews have found fans among poets and other connoisseurs of the paraliterary, with three collections already published by poets (*Selected Amazon Reviews*, Hooke Press, 2006; *Selected Amazon Reviews Vol 2*, Push Press, 2011; *Selected Amazon Reviews Vol 3*, Essay Press, 2017), with a fourth volume on its way (as part of Tripwire's pamphlet series).

I am not the first to note Kevin's felicitous use of the Amazon review platform for literary publication, distribution, and archiving beyond the sometimes insular small-press poetry world and the corporate literary establishment (which was never going to publish anything as outré as Kevin's work anyways). At the same time, I don't think his project was merely some intervention into corporate exchange, where customers are given a sense of voice and power in exchange for their free labor and personal data. Anyone fortunate enough to have had a conversation with Kevin knows that his love for cultural consumption and dish was an authentic expression of his devotion to the juicy details of every last element in every last movie, biography, or public encounter, demonstrating his attention to the nuances of pleasure and its sharing, however fanciful or make-believe.

Of course, several of his reviews contain invented biographical information, including many detailing an imaginary childhood in France or his non-existent children, not to mention a fake foodie's sensibility (Kevin often subsisted on microwaved meals and Tab), but with Kevin you never know. For instance, at Kevin's memorial at SFMoMA this summer, his sister Maureen informed us that their father did indeed use Mackenzie's Smelling Salts (see review below). Knowing Kevin's background and insatiable tastes for

the seemingly banal pleasures of lowbrow consumption, it makes it hard to decipher what's invented and what's real, what's ironic and what's earnest—which might sum up his poetics, if there's a grad student somewhere performing close readings of paraliterature for a monograph on literary tone in late capitalist literature and in search of an exemplar.

Indeed, Kevin's reviews foreground his signature blend of high and lowbrow (but never middlebrow!) culture, refusing to hew to a conventional aesthetic value system or replicate trite postmodern tropes of capitalist-realist camp. Steeped in the language of fandom, Kevin's engagement with consumer culture—its treasures and its discourses—was always driven by a kind of love: for sensual description, storytelling, celebrity gossip, trash aesthetics, B- and C-list films, all delivered with a light touch patinated over a deeper sense of loss and dread. For where do online reviews reside other than a strange temporal netherworld between passionate and instant response and a hauntological afterlife in the corporate-owned clouds?

What follows is the smallest of samplings, in hopes of giving readers a taste of the treasures awaiting in the cloud-verse of Amazon. While there's no guaranteeing that Kevin's reviews will always be available at a click, I have no doubt that his singular brand of taste-(un)making will continue to live on, like the ghosts of the pure products of America, no doubt roaming Amazon's warehouses with algorithmic beatitude.

Kevin, wherever you may rest, we miss you.

My heartfelt thanks to Ted Rees for helping archive and select the gems from Kevin's more recent reviews.

LOOKS FADED, BUT IT WAS THIS WAY BRAND NEW
5/5 STARS
SEPTEMBER 21, 2015
FORMAT: PAPERBACK

It took me only a few minutes to plug in my new toaster oven and perhaps twenty to read the revised edition of David DiResta and Joanne Foran's *The Toaster Oven Cookbook*. Ever have half an hour in your life where you had nothing to do but do the thing you always wanted to do? I was getting ready for the monthly meeting of my Bicoastal Mask group, and thought to myself, "I'll just make something out of the *Toaster Oven Cookbook*" the way I had always wanted to do.

For too long this book has lain on my formica counter, handy to my cooking station, but somehow the time never seemed right. Now, with the meeting coming on, I flipped open the cookbook and tried to find some of the recipes I had salivated over during previous reads. There was one with shrimp and broccoli that sounded right. (Why is it, I ask parenthetically, that I find the word "broccoli" so hard to spell? Early childhood aversion to green, wiry, tough vegetables?) I grabbed the book and looked at it guiltily, it had lain in the sun so long that the cover looked all faded, even the hot orange cylinders of the toast filaments seemed dim, like candy corn. But now as I compare it to the illustration on the book cover, I can see, it hadn't faded, it was just printed with a sort of sepia finish. The very first recipe was what I wanted (and indeed it is the one on the book cover), shrimp and broccoli pizza. While the authors advise the readers to get little pizza pans, and even tile ramekins on which to place your pizza slices, but not me. I was willing to risk the inevitable disappearance of some of the crumbs, dropping off into the hot hell of the lower levels of my toaster over--i.e., the drip tray--what my wife calls the crumb tray. Some of your food is going to be lost, that's a given. That's toaster oven cooking, you might even say, that's the heartbreak of toaster oven cooking.

But there are many rewards. The smiles on the face of your friends in the Bicoastal Mask group when you bring out tray after tray of Toaster Oven pizza, with that shrimp and broc combo spiced with oregano and store bought pizza sauce! The curious, envious questions your guests will be peppering you with. The sheer joy of the heavy, viscous scent of the pizza, bringing back memories to all of days spent eating heartier fare at Domino's or Little Caesar. Each page in the cookbook contains one recipe, and by the time you've finished one, you want to try the next one, which is just perfect for one or two person meals. It's intense, this craving to go on, turning the pages, dialing up the fun.

My Irish grandfather used to keep a bottle of MacKenzie's smelling salts next to his desk. He was the principal at Bushwick High School (in Brooklyn, NY) in the 1930s and 1940s, before it became a dangerous place to live in, and way before Bushwick regained its current state of desirable area for new gentrification. And he kept one at home as well, in case of a sudden shock. At school, he would press the saturated cotton under the nostrils of poor girls who realized they were pregnant in health class, before he expelled them. Or, when the policy of corporal punishment had allowed him rather too much paddling of the sophomore boys, he would apply smelling salts to their faces till they recovered from passing out.

For me, 2013's a new era, and the salts themselves seem way more organic than they used to when first I sampled them in the 70s. I was a typical teen raiding my grandparents' medicine cabinet, trying a little of this, a little of that, you know.... I took a whiff of the MacKenzies and I was like, whoa! It was the feeling when your face has been "stuffed up," and reality has blurred your vision, your passages clogged, the doors of perception jammed shut. And one infusion of this magic ointment opens all of them up within a fraction of an instant, you can't even get a syllable out, you're just yourself again, your very best self.

Nowadays, with my ongoing heart problems, I use them only when I'm in a deep grief or have had a shock. I was so sad when Paul Walker died. And then again one day I came staggering down the stairs, having been passed over for inclusion in the 2014 Whitney Biennial by a troika of careless curators, I simply collapsed out of grief, and it took my wife a minute or two to locate the MacKenzie's, but passing it under my nose, as though she were my grandfather ministering to the pregnant girls of yore, or the sore-bottomed "tough guys;" and suddenly I snorted and came awake, shot to my feet, still grieving for my disappointment but at least able to function and go back to making my art, feeding the cats, etc., being a man. In time of deep mourning thank goodness for small miracles!

52 PEOPLE FOUND THIS HELPFUL

The Big Builders came out the year I started the fourth grade, and it became an important book to me. As an adult I can see what appears to be an ideological message I never really understood as a kid. But what kid would? Or do I mean, what boy would? I still don't understand why I was so fascinated with builders and junkers both, could stand for hours watching construction crews erect even the smallest of buildings, and I loved seeing things go down, too, as they often were in the Robert Moses-dominated Long Island of my youth. I hear from my grandchildren (now grown themselves, starting families of their own) that their own kids love videos involving big trucks and that they are the best babysitters around, these videos. You can leave the house for hours and your kids will literally not know you are gone.

That's how I was with this Whitman "Learn-About" book by the utterly strange and compelling immigrant figure, E. Joseph Dreany. The back of my tattered copy of *The Big Builders* reads, "In that part of northern Canada where log cabins and tar-paper shacks are still plentiful, and where winters mean deep snow, long icicles, and temperatures that tickle the sub-zero mark–that's where E. JOSEPH DREANY, author and artist, was born and raised." I wish I could show you some of his illustrations but they are quite fanciful and cinematic. On the front cover a crew of four hard-hats reach out to each other from opposing red-gold girders as they lasso the Golden Gate Bridge, above the raging waters of Hoover Dam while above soars the then-new United Nations Building. It turns out these workers are Mohawk Indians, who have the "iron nerve" to takes to stand without safety belts with only a steel beam to stand on in heavy winds. "Once they came from an Indian reservation in Canada. Now they live in Brooklyn." Dreany doesn't talk down to kids, exactly, and it was from this book that I found out that the iconic Lever Building was the first NYC building to be erected without setbacks, from the third floor up. A giant slab on its end, like the UN Building that followed it. Now we see these buildings and don't even appreciate the power of the Mohawk Indians that made them–like the artisans who created Mont Ste. Michel and Chartres, they are forgotten balancers.

The chapter on the building of Hoover Dam likewise is written and illustrated with real force. My total knowledge of Hoover Dam comes from a gay amalgam of

Dreany's *The Big Builders* with memories of Elvis and Ann-Margaret touring the dam for kicks in the splenetic dreamworld of George Sidney's *Viva Las Vegas*! It was from Dreany that I learned that the construction of Hoover Dam was larger and more difficult than the building of the Great Pyramid of Cheops, or, to look at it in another way, imagine a grand pyramid erected upside down within the walls of a western canyon, and then flooded with water, and you can see how the chariots of the gods isn't just a fanciful Canadian idea, it may be a real thing, and that is why this extraneous scene of Elvis and Ann-Margaret was inserted into the film in question, to announce the endorsement of the thing by actual 20th century gods of music, beauty and dance–a "dam that tamed a wild mustang of a western river," to be colorful about it. The book also answers the questions, "What is a 'Gismo'?"–"Can you bounce a ping-pong ball on water?"–"Who eats 'woodburgers'?" and many more attractive propositions that every child yearns to know.

This cover shows just half of the visual excitement that the legendary Dreany brought to us Whitman Learn About books. You'll learn about colors and capitalism in The Big Builders.

ONE PERSON FOUND THIS HELPFUL

5.0 OUT OF 5 STARS
DUCT TAPE SPECIAL
APRIL 20, 2010
SIZE: 3" WIDTH X 60 YARDS LENGTH
COLOR: DARK GREEN

I was impressed by the manufacturers' claim that "This product's actual size is 72mm x 55m. This tape is typically cut to width from log rolls so most sizes ship on a plain white core." I've used enough duct tape in the past to know that, although many manufacturers claim they're cutting to width from log rolls, it's not always the case. Duct tape's a funny thing, isn't it? No matter what you're using it for. I like Polyken as a brand and I always like products cut from logs... When I was in shop class in high school they used to call me, the Log Lady, and one time it was my birthday they brought me an ice cream cake shaped like a log! So I ordered several rolls of the dark green 223, as you see here, and when it came I went a little crazy with the back of my refrigerator...

And also I had the common problem of having three cats (of my wife's) who run around the kitchen sometimes knocking down the upright broom and dust mop much to my annoyance. Problem licked with Polyken! I just applied a few inches of that thick, log-derived polymer on either side of the broom handle, basically taping it to the wall. Mop too. One caveat, but this is something all duct tape users know, if you are actually taping yourself, or another human being, watch out, that tape stings when you peel it off, so save the bare skin by inserting strips of linen or cotton underneath, and save yourself some swearing down the line.

It has a nice aroma just sitting in my shop cellar. I keep thinking it wouldn't be inappropriate in my top dresser drawer, if I ever run out of potpourri–again, a nice mixture of clean, sweet, unearthed log, and maybe something a little chemical like air freshener.

3 PEOPLE FOUND THIS HELPFUL

HALL OF FAME
5.0 OUT OF 5 STARS
FASCINATING OGRE
SEPTEMBER 1, 2016
FORMAT: HARDCOVER

If you thought that children's book illustrators live lives of no drama, this book will come as a complete and utter shock. I was one who thought it would be placid stroll in the park but it was like walking into the life of King Lear, if Lear had been married four times and couldn't stop having children in every country of Europe. I mean, when I was a boy Garth Williams was at his peak of fame and could do no wrong, but we read him as life-affirming and not scary. Now based on the intimate documents uncovered by a pair of Boston College-based biographers, the truth comes out and it's not all that pretty.

I do admire the Wallaces for knowing how to entice a reader. In their introduction, they tell us that Williams knew most of the great children's authors of his time, but they go on to say, "Williams' life also intersects with a remarkable series of twentieth century figures: artists like Rosario Murabito and Mark Rothko, editors like Harold Ross and Ursula Nordstrom, musicians like John Sebastian of the

Lovin' Spoonful, politicians like Winston Churchill, and celebrities like Elizabeth Taylor." After that, I am so there!

Trained in the fine arts, Williams (born 1912) apprenticed as a sculptor and won the Prix de Rome–the most prestigious honor a British artist could then achieve. In Rome he met the unusual Gunda Lambiton, whom he married and sired two daughters on. His next move was to bring on Dorothea, a nanny for the two girls and just like Robin Williams' nanny wound up married to the boss and having children by him herself. A weary Gunda made her way to Toronto where she created a new life for herself and became an experienced farmer and memoirist who lived till a great old age–100? Dorothea was from a wealthy, stylish family of Hungarian Jews who was fleeing Hitler, and Garth Williams fell in love with her as she foolishly went into a snowstorm barefoot and coatless, and he ran after her to rescue her from a possible influenza. Eventually they settled together in New York City. There Williams met Rothko and other bright lights of the New York art world. And then came along the great break of getting to illustrate E B White's *Stuart Little*, which made him enormously famous, though it embittered him that he didn't get to share in the royalties White was making

Soon enough his beloved editor, Ursula Nordstrom, hatched a plan to have him illustrate all of the Little House books, and he and Dorothea drove to the Midwest to visit the aged Laura Ingalls Wilder and her ten years old husband Almanzo. The Wallaces are very good about describing what makes Williams such a superb illustrator and they are never better than in touching on the way his drawing style is slightly different in every book, to match the continuing maturation of little Laura into a teen girl and then a young lady and then a married woman, so that just as Laura sees life, the drawings reproduce for young readers her varied visual experiences. If Stuart Little made Garth Williams popular, the Little House books made him a legend and still to come was Charlotte's Web. Soon the Williams family was living the high life in Aspen and mixing with people like Thomas Mann and Stravinsky. Then he got it in his head to move to Mexico, and sure enough, a young beautiful Mexican girl from the neighborhood took him away from wife #2 and became wife #3 in the blink of an eye. It was at about this point that I began to realize the Wallaces really don't know, or can't explain at any rate, what made Garth Williams tick. Their biography becomes an account of a privileged old man getting more and more whimsical and self centered–like Lear, but without the poetry.

At the end of his life it broke his heart that White, fed up with Williams trying to take credit for the success of *Stuart Little* and *Charlotte's Web*, told Nordstrom to hire someone else–anyone else, to illustrate his third children's book, *The Trumpet of the Swan*. Time was catching up with the Garth Williams brand, as younger, hungrier artists like Ezra Jack Keats and Maurice Sendak started infecting children's books with themes of darkness and uncertainty–and fear–and anxiety. Williams illustrated Randall Jarrell's first book for children, but the other ones were given to Maurice Sendak because he was edgier.

Oddly enough, in 1964 both Jarrell and Williams came down with hepatitis. Wonder how they both happened to catch it at exactly the same time. The Wallaces do not speculate on what seems like a coincidence, but was it?

I read Garth Williams now as a late modernist artist at a time when artists were given the benefit of the doubt all over the place. Picasso was his model, and like Picasso he went from one woman to another, and like Picasso, one of his wives wound up a suicide. Fittingly enough, we learn that Picasso's son Claude dated Garth Williams' daughter, Jessica, a jewelry designer like Paloma Picasso. It is a book filled with mirroring images and jolting shifts in perspective–a sad book, but one that won't let you put it down.

9 PEOPLE FOUND THIS HELPFUL

DUMMY FULL SIZE WITH HANDS
BY C4L
5/5 STARS
USED AGAIN AND AGAIN
NOVEMBER 22, 2013

Like most of the other reviewers, I first bought this dummy in 2011 as a prop for a haunted house me and my mates were operating in Oakland, just across the Bay Bridge from San Francisco. We were running a nonprofit artist run space that hosts poetry readings and meetings of like-minded people into poetry and the verbal arts. For years, ever since the shutdown of government support for poetry, Halloween has been a big money making time for us, but in 2011 as I recall we were especially wary of other competition, breathing down our necks, because a good

spooky house is something every artist wants to have at his disposal this time of year. With increased competition everybody has got to boast more gore, more carnage, more fake blood and most of all, more corpses, and realistic looking ones particularly, otherwise a jaded audience gets weary and bored easy, just as if we were presenting two Language poets, say, while the other guy down the street could boast Mary Oliver and Billy Collins. Thus in 2011, we were totally up against it, and we wound up going wholesale and buying dummies, where once we could count on our friends acting crazy in homemade costumes—Jack the Ripper, the Human Blockhead, the spider with ten legs, the Hypnotic Eye, Jayne Mansfield without her head, Tarzan, and many more.

Alas those once unemployed poets had landed good tech jobs at Twitter and Google and were no longer amused by nor available for the long hours and unpaid lifestyle of a spooky house volunteer for poetry. Amazon came to the rescue so I bought one of these guys as a treat. We planned to employ "Dummy Full Size with Hands" as a mummy, sort of a Frankenstein mummy with a meat knife sticking out of his chest, a mummy that would greet the terrified pilgrim who opened the door to the back room with a maniacal recorded cackle easily downloadable from numerous sources on Spotify or ITunes. And it worked.

It worked so well that our competitors from other poetry groups protested that we were stealing all of their thunder. They didn't realize we were trying to raise the money to start off 2012 with a bang and we needed the extra dough to be able to afford Christian Bok and Dottie Lasky to come together onstage for our Valentine Ball. The only question was what to do with our dummy till the next year, 2012 Halloween? None of our members had an extra bedroom for the fellow so, even though he was fairly heavy and nearly my own height, I wound up taking him home back to my place where he remains today. My cats love him, they sit in his lap all day and shroud his crotch with hair (I should say, it's not really anatomically a crotch). He went back to work just this past Halloween in a new costume—Manson! And when I'm feeling lonely and my wife has gone out of town on business or pleasure, I hate sleeping alone, so I shoo the cats away and drag my guy into the bed with me to spoon with. You know, he's stuffed, and his spine comes with extra holes into which you can feed more stuffing, be it grain, acorns, or styrofoam, and I like to move my fingers up and down its spine looking for the holes and sealing them up if necessary. His hands are fully operable and will wrap themselves around any elongated object.

9 PEOPLE FOUND THIS HELPFUL

Hail to my friends David and Sara for bringing me this book for my birthday! They are beyond belief sensitive to a fellow's needs and wants.

I had my eye on this book from the beginning. It's not that every book on Kylie is good, though I never read one I didn't enjoy. For me the first and still the best was, oh I don't know what they call it but it's known as *Kylie Evidence*, from the late 90s? Came in a box? That book showed off the extent of Kylie's collaborations not only with top designers but with the crème de la crème of British and international artist, from Pierre et Gilles to Wolfgang Tillmans to, ah what's her name, she made that film about a teenage John Lennon and then married its teenage star. Well, the anagram for "Kylie Minogue" is "I like em young," and this woman artist underlined that in red! I know, I'll Google her name, oh here you go, Sam Taylor-Wood, the one who's directing *Fifty Shades of Grey*. Anyway, *Kylie Fashion* is pretty cool. At first I thought, they're not giving enough space to the pre-*Light Years* era, but that was heavily covered in *Evidence*, and perhaps in the splashy, vacuous, *La La La*, and though I feel that the 90s were the decade in which Kylie was the most glamorous, there is still enough greatness in the 2000s, the cancer years, and the Aphrodite rollout to make the act of reading *Fashion* a pleasure from cover to cover.

As other reviewers have noted, there's not too much of Kylie's longtime stylist William Baker in this one and for that we can all be grateful. I don't know about you, but I was sick of him from the minute I saw the videos for "Please Stay" and "Your Disco Needs You." Now and then he lets Kylie wear something suitable for her, but so often he brings her to the ateliers of the world's greatest designers and then picks out their worst costumes for her, *coughDolce&Gabbana*. I only like her because he stuck with her through the cancer period, but even Olivier did that, who would desert her in her time of need. Why make a movie about what a good friend you were, William Baker, with her all hugging you and crying on your shoulder? On the third hand, there's no denying the greatness of the Body Language campaign, nor the way you dressed Kylie at the Brit Awards when she did "Can't Get You Out of My Head" with tiny braids and a robot dress. Nor the videos for "Slow," "CGYOOMH," "Get Outta My Way," "Wow," "All the Lovers" or "Santa Baby," so I'm still rooting for you to a certain degree. On the fourth hand, it was

a great idea to have sidebars through *Fashion* consisting of interviews of the designers to show how they first met Kylie. I could read them all day. Gaultier seems like Wittgenstein, he's so acute. On the fifth hand, those hot pants were not your idea and I'm glad you're finally admitting as much.

HYPNOSIS THEN, AND NOW
JUNE 8, 2016
FORMAT: PAPERBACK

If ever you wanted to know how the artists invited to big European shows like Documenta survive the months-long and often arduous toil of basically singing for their supper, I can think of no better guide than Marcus Lutyens' lovely little book, *Memoirs of a Hypnotist: 100 Days*.

The artist was approached by a Lithuanian curator, Raimundas Malasauskas, in Los Angeles, and asked if it were possible for him to hypnotize someone–literally. Malasauskas had already made an agreement with a San Francisco gallerist who had given him carte blanche to stage a show at her new gallery on whatever topic he wanted. Interested in hypnosis, no doubt because of his early experience behind the Iron Curtain in the days of the Soviet state. However, he didn't have a hypnotist so the beloved arts activist Ronni Kimm reached into her Rolodex and found him one, young Marcos Lutyens, then living in LA with his wife Yi-Ping and a young son, Jasper Tian-Huu. His memoir reveals him as the perfect artist for the show, and once the Silverman Gallery show was held, it became clear that curator and artist had it in them to expand a modest pop-up exhibition into first, a touring show, and then finally an attraction at the most famous art fair of them all, Documenta 13 in Kassel.

Kassel is a town in Germany and there, we gather, Lutyens devised a mirror cabin for his installation. (To "mirror" the mirror theme, the book's introduction is laid out in a footnote scheme in which we see the numbers on the right hand page, say 23, but on the left hand we see the number "23" reversed as if seen in some sort of dim, reflective mirror.) There was an unease built into the show, and happily Lutyens has pages and pages on anecdotes of what it was like, hypnotizing

visitors into vague "narratives" devised by participating artists for an experience that would leave them feeling interpersonal but singular. Celebrated artists came too, and like all good sports sat in and let themselves "go under," like the American performance legend Joan Jonas. We watch as Lutyens watches Ron Athey undergo genitalia stapling surgery without pain, due to his ease with hypnosis, while in another sequence a friend grants him access into a private hospital in which operations are performed on actual patients to be witnessed by spectators in their underwear, like some fantastic futuristic Eakins painting nobody knew he painted.

I didn't go to Documenta but I was there, hypnotized, at the American gallery in which the Hypnotic Show debuted. I append my contemporary notes from 2008. I relished my time spent with both Lutyens and Malasauskas. I think they implanted suggestions in my brain like the shadowy brainmelders in Heinlein's *The Puppet Masters*, or Condon's *The Manchurian Candidate*, so that every time I think of either of them my cares melt away and I drift between smiles and sighs and erections.

My 2008 notes begin here: At the door of the Silverman Gallery you had to sign two releases before being allowed entry. "Basically this one says you waive liability in case you get possessed by a demon while within these walls," explains the gallery girl, "and this one's stating you won't sue if the dream machine gives you an epileptic seizure." Possessed? Dream machine? We were positively fibrillating by the time we took seats in the dimly lit gallery space on Sutter Street. Job Piston and I sat warily, cameras in our laps, ready to snap any sign of ectoplasm or wrathful spirits, but apparently this was just part of curator Raimundas Malasauskas' Barnum-like showmanship, and when he promised a "séance of hypnosis," he was using "séance" as a metaphor, as one might say, "a whole bunch of hypnosis," or, a "quiet evening of hypnosis." I don't know how they say it in Lithuanian, but the philosophy of the studio heads of Hollywood's golden age was, get those asses into the seats by any means necessary. Malasauskas might well be the William Castle of modern curatorial projects. [I might have the prophetic streak, for here I was, calling on the name of the US schlock horror master William CASTLE, not knowing that the project was going to wind up in KASSEL Germany, the Castle homonym! Nevertheless let me go on:]

I never felt that I was actually going to be possessed by an incubus, but artist slash hypnotist Marcos Lutyens certainly had us all going pit a pat as he entered

and prowled through the space, dividing the audience into two groups, those who were volunteering, and those like myself afraid to participate, who wanted merely to watch. Malasauskas had commissioned hypnosis scripts from a group of international artists, and Lutyens had worked four of them into a running spiel. The ring of chairs was soon deep in a trance, the sitters nodding and blinking like rabbits, while he spoke on in a velvety, Michael Ondaatje baritone redolent of summer, with a poignant tang of autumn surprising some of his labial consonants. Like I say, he worked the space, reaching out here and there to clasp shut a pair of hands a -trembling on a knee, to touch a supplicant's forehead with his thumb, all the while counting us down, five, four, three, two, one. At one we were in the deepest possible trance state, and then he'd have us count down yet again, from ten to one, deeper still. One girl wound up so out of it her hair touched the ground in front of her, I've never seen anything like it, not even back in college when we took massive doses of animal tranquillizers to get over the outrage of having Nixon as president.

Meanwhile Lutyens was droning on in that intimate, simpatico way, walking us into Joachin Koester's script about a park, a sidewalk, a civic building called the "Department of Abandoned Futures," after which we crossed the threshold and descended a stairway, entered a hall, found a box filled with–with what? We each were invited to imagine what lay within. Deric Carner's script was more ominous, I thought, a dark, cloudy horizon along which an unimaginable object began to evince itself–in a color we could not name, as it was not a color we had ever seen before–and the name of the large object came to us little by little as its Lovecraftian shape began to struggle in shadows and gleams across the sky. I called my object "Zephyr." I don't know why. You'll gather that my status as a spectator did not prevent me from joining into the general trance; Marcos Lutyens' voice is so seductive that, were you in that room that night, you too would be dreaming these dark visions. He leaned on some catchphrases that, perhaps, judged objectively, he used too often ("went back to the well one too many times," as my dad used to say), but I never got tired of hearing him say, "And you're drifting and dreaming–drifting and dreaming." Indeed I'm now engaged to Marcos Lutyens and cheerfully I am bearing his children without anesthesia. I'll just be drifting and dreaming in a bower of erotic bliss somewhere, bent to the floor, my hair soapy and washing his high-instepped feet.

Before I knew it we were waking up, one, two, three, four, five. Kylie Minogue had that song on her LP, *Body Language*, which I should have listened to before exposing myself to Hypnotic Show.

> Count backwards 5, 4, 3, 2, 1
> Before you get too heated and turned on (and turned on)
> You should've learned your lesson all in times before
> You've been bruised, you've been broken
>
> And there's my mind saying think before you go
> Through that door that takes me to nowhere (yes boy)
> I stopped you all romantic crazy in your head
> You think I listen, no I don't care . . . .

The truth is, I do care, and when Raimundas Malasauskas proposed hypnotism as an avenue of total interaction, a room full of mirrors in which objects create themselves from the swept floorboards of the Silverman Gallery–the birthplace of the golem–I went there. You know how Susan Sontag coined that expression, "Don't go there." Well, I went there, ignoring Sontag, thrusting myself in a post-Sontag space of risk, interpellation, and impending childbirth, drifting and dreaming, drifting and dreaming, in the Alterjinga of the Australian aboriginal people–the dreamtime.

Oh Dear

Purple is sub-Saharan.
Indonesia, an orange that looks yellow.

Look quick! A cuppa
Java. Palm trees upon

which sorcerers nest
like this is some British East India

Company shit. Into tradewinds
I speak. To be

spirited off. Ghost fingers
tickle my window, claw to get away

from winter. Slow drivers in the parking lot
run into each other like bad dancers.

Sorcerers drift. Wood-
like. I'm terribly sorry

to bother you, old boy,
but I seem to have mislaid the empire.

Says the ether. The humors. Says.
Do you mind. Terribly. What circulates

nimbly. Digits' heretical
exegesis. Putting sheets over

the parenthetical happening.
Inelegant dancers

exchanging information in the parking lot.
What circulates on tradewinds.

The peppercorn
bowled. The wicket! Look quick!

The Atmospheres

Like the hermit
crab, I scrabble impervious

to doubt. So armored,
spiral-chambered, orchestrating

tides; time; the moon
calls me. A werewolf

entombed, the agent
of I-will-rip-off

the-banks. My shirt.
Where the elements

convene I want to fuck.
My tea is cold. Mint

and wind. Alloyed.
Alloyed to the typhoon.

Grasping legs scramble, spines digging.
Of yours. Of mine. Globes of

sand held among campfires
blown out, alloyed. I climb.

CHRIS STROFFOLINO

Sphinx of Black Quartz, Judge My Vow!

"You gave me more than I could ever need & even
     created more needs just so you could fulfill them"
Is it true the closer you get to someone
     the more of a mystery they are?
How can I render you free
      in words like one or three
looking away looks like a way
     the sound is happy, the meaning
moans, but I don't mind
     the discrepancy bees flirt
     but you probably mean flit
as if beyond the kind of "I"
     that needs a you to tell itself to…
& the temptation is strong to wear you like eyes….
to learn to let the sea of your polyvocal monologue
wash over me longer
     so it tires us both out
as the artist formerly known as love
     may appear in clothes you wear better
if almost everything you said
     didn't make we want to slow down
& insert a quip or question
     really important at the time
for whatever is afraid to drown
     in erasing words from all past uses
"When I'm writing about you
     I'm really writing about me
     or what would be me

if I stopped trying to call it you
                or the heart or the soul or the body
                or the mind, defining my _____
by address."
                Fixed?
                adequate opposites
  in a distance of becoming only different
                        from being if we catch ourselves
squinting, as if we have to be
                        indifferent enough
to be different enough to _____ "
                        & if you think you got my number
I promise not to say how dare you reduce me
(& is it a problem if I feel closer
                to someone's mind than my own body?)

MAKMAK FAUNLAGUI

St Oyl!

he is st oyl!
of the well-machined

of the well-lubed
of those lankyass

lads loosed
on boulders

with pinecones

bested by small
pineneedles

the needles!
they have been

trampled over
by his loosed limbs

needles having
their own needles

succulents lining
edges of other

succulents from the
paleozoic era

he! st oyl, he!
his limbs:

they are the cedars
over which the unbested

mounting-
manner-of-mine

[o! what shitty technique!]

we graze at each other
and at each other's

limbs : tangled
matted and messy

i catch you looking
sheepishly at the mirror

sheepishly bested-seeming
though, you know full well

you've bested me

The Immediate Electricity

the immediate electricity
of an early morning trim

from an armenian punk

[possibly]

in some buzzing
basements

fleeing with
fresh haircuts

the accidental knick
at the back of my head

[looks like crete]

or cyprus before the turks
or armenia after

one saturday morning
maybe this saturday
or perhaps one three months ago
and then again, not a saturday after all
but really a late friday night
punkrabbit had a gnawing feeling
that, despite already having a brother
that he also had a twin named
punkdandy, who was not really a brother
but a twin nonetheless
and stands to reason
must've been a brother

somehow . somewhere upstate

where furry chops were good against the cold
and soda was pop, and little white boys
hadn't yet played with other brown boys
who'd already climbed a nice guava tree
or at least, not just yet, that
there were boys such as that
who'd been up such a tree

living upthere . upstate

where there are
only oaks
and maples
and pines

Honeycomb

all muscle, bone
and ligament, all
like footchases and lines
of powder, all canallike
bermlike, spattered all over
O without an H, O
O! with an exclamation point, O!
and sandpaper nape
and mossier arms
and lichened legs
the hairs
much like lichen
likened to lichen
lichenlike!
gams gripping pillows
and willows all donnelike
that's john donne
fucken all johndonnelike to *you*!
all done-up
in a proper waistcoat
and the first beards of youth
bedecked in the blackest of indigos
all tricksterlike
you *are* a trickster
to the insufferably earnest!
levelerlike
leveler to all
leveler of egos
and helpmeets to ids
with much felix, i'd meet you
in the last room
in an always
much too dark flat

yes : *that* one
overlooking the airwell
bricked-up and all hazelike
and up we are
at not a terribly early hour
upped by the low throttle
of your sentrycat's purr
aubades are never a thrill
slinking away all aubadelike
before the break of dawn
before husbands come back
before the normalcy
of life
of the rest of life
all intruding back
into our sequestered hut
of lichens, and heavy breaths
of sneezes
all wetlike on face
that—
all aubadelike
is what intrudes
the honeycomb

Evenly So
You Are Still Snoring

LOOKING OUT THE WINDOW TO THE SKY flat as lead and depthless, Atticus twirls his toe on the sheet. Then looking over to his left, as it is always the case that every night he sleeps on the right, he spots his snoring bedmate. Or rather, he is his deflating bedmate, with the kind of snore that sounds more like a leaking tire. 'This is unusual,' Atticus thinks to himself, and yet not so, as he proceeds to remember the three leaky people in his life, though not all of them bedmates, to have had this slowburn dormant exhalation.

GOOD THING EVENLY IS NOT A VOLCANO. Or worse a fissure on the side of volcanoes, the kind that emits gasses that would knock parrots out of trees, water buffalos on their knees, men over the crumbling rims of calderas. He hasn't bothered to mention to Evenly that he has come to call him that, at least if only in his head, and only when Evenly is his lefthand bedmate. Though this is never spelled so in texts. A play on his first and middle names elided into one. 'How did I decide to call him this?' Atticus thinks, as he also wonders what there is to have for breakfast.

AS HE HAS NOTHING IN THE FRIDGE except horseradish and some kimchi. Or maybe the two tacos leftover from lunch yesterday. 'I will have to take the tongue taco,' as Evenly, despite his even tones though sometimes less even tempers, will balk at the thought of rolling meat the consistency of tongue through his own tongue. Nothing in the fridge expect some shishito peppers and the lube in the unmarked water bottle.

'YEAH EVENLY WILL LIKE THE CABEZA TACO well enough yes,' Atticus thinks to himself. 'I'll just say it's beef cheek not beef head.'

SNIFFING THE SANDY COLORED HAIRS in Evenly's pits, Atticus thinks of woods and myrrh. 'Of course you would think of myrrh,' the one unusual H dangling at the end of this unusualer word. Evenly swats Atticus's nose away from his nipple. Or rather makes fake attempts to swat it. Evenly knows well enough that this is his bedmate's habit every 9:30 of every Saturday morning in every instance before Atticus rushes Evenly out to his Honda, in order for him to rush out to his husband. Evenly doesn't mind. He just pretends to sleep longer, and enjoys this leak of air puffing on the crook of his armpit.

The Ghost of Things

René Girard called it the triangulation of desire; we fantasize about other people, based on images. Fragments, glimpses from constructions. In short, we want what others want.

Paige knew as well as anyone that when Maeve posts a picture of herself wearing a tight dress and making her sex face to the camera—it is not real. It is only an image.

But that does not mean that it doesn't have the power to ruin my day, Paige adds. Yes, Beau explained, but you want it because you don't have it. Don't have what? Don't have Larry. Maeve has him. Or so you think. Yeah, but I don't want Larry! Paige says. You don't want him but when Paige wants him, you want him again, because we want what others want. We want it *because* they want it. Girard called it mimetic desire.

Paige was walking around her apartment, listening to Beau through the speaker on her phone. Across the street, she could see her neighbor, the baseball player.

Paige told Beau she didn't think it was that at all. She said, I think it is about territory. I mean she's with *my* son and *my* ex-husband. Okay, so I left him, yes, but that doesn't mean I want her in my space.

We live in a culture of optics, Beau reminded her. She could hear him chewing something, vaguely hoped he'd stop. What we see is the surface, a performance, a curated and constructed view of a person, a place, event. This is how we perceive what is real. But it isn't real! He laughed. Pretzels, she thought.

Well, it is humiliating, she said. Now the baseball player was sitting on his stoop, looking at his phone. He had a beard of bushy red hair and a plain face. Paige and Beau had been friends since college—thirty years ago now. They

often called each other to lament the current socio-political moment. We are middle aged now, Beau says. Paige chafes. She doesn't like to hear it said out loud. But she wouldn't deny it, either.

Like everything related to aging, there isn't space to settle. It's surreal, like much of life: shifty and over too soon. *The food here is terrible! Yes, and the portions are so small!*

Paige sat and scrolled through social media. She saw a headline; a plastic surgeon said that patients these days come to him because they want "to look better in selfies."

Beau lived in Los Angeles, Paige in Chicago. They saw each other once or twice a year, but spoke often, particularly since her divorce. Her analyst had said, This is a time to focus more on friendships, and so she did. It was a relief, to remember what had meant everything once, the power of such relationships, which endured beyond marriage.

Oscar Wilde said, *friendships are more tragic than love, because they last longer*. More beautiful, too, Paige sometimes thought.

Beau was saying that he worried he was a wrinkly old gay man and Paige said, My hair is entirely gray, or would be, if I didn't dye it every few months.

Paige had called Beau to tell him about the party she'd attended the night before, at the home of her ex-husband. I was invited, Paige explained, because we are in a better place—plus it is better for the kids if we do these things, you know? Beau said he wasn't sure. He quoted Girard again: *All desire is a desire for being*. I'm not sure what you mean, Paige replied. I don't know either but I think you should think about it.

Larry, Paige's ex-husband, is a few years younger than Paige. At the party, she noticed that all of his new friends were younger than him. That is, Larry is in his forties, and his new friends are in their thirties. Larry's girlfriend, Maeve, is also in her thirties. After their separation, Larry began to socialize with a new group of poets and academics.

There were some he'd been friendly with throughout their decade-long marriage, but no one they'd shared as friends.

The friends they shared, Emily and Mike, for example, insisted on remaining friends with both Paige and Larry. We are able to stay friends with both of you, Emily explained in her rational way. It is possible for us to do that. Paige understood Emily's idea in theory, but a few months later, when she heard that Emily had hosted Larry and Maeve at her home, she wanted to vomit.

Maeve was fine, as replacements go, Paige knew—just as she knew she shouldn't think of her as a replacement. An academic librarian, Maeve specialized in the sort of poetry that Larry wrote. In fact, she specialized in Larry's poetry. This fact privately amused Paige. It made sense; throughout their marriage, Larry had complained that Paige didn't care enough about his poetry. What better replacement than this Number One Fan.

Maeve was at least five inches shorter than Paige and a few years younger. It was *fine*, Paige would say to anyone who asked about Maeve, she's perfectly fine. Most importantly, she would add, in a very grown-up and well-adjusted way, trying not to conform to type: *She's wonderful with Jasper. That's what matters.*

Paige had gone to the Hanukkah party because she thought another former friend would be there. But that friend was not there. In fact, very few people were there when Paige arrived.

Maeve made a point of referring to Larry as *Babe*; she read Larry's texts for him, too. She told Paige about her upcoming trip to San Francisco, as if to impress. Great, awesome for you, Paige said in what she hoped was a cool, distant way. Larry once told her that she scared Maeve; she attempted a smile in a way that signalled minimal warmth.

Paige valued the reserve, an armor of defense she maintained in response to such irritations. She had always been good at a certain detachment. She felt powerful.

More guests arrived; Maeve and Larry greeted them. A man sat down next to Paige. How do you know Larry? He asked her. Paige found the moment exquisite; she wished others were there to witness it and imagined telling the story later. She paused, considering ways she could respond. Well, she said flatly, I was married to him. Once, for about a decade, in fact. The man looked shocked, then embarrassed. He put down his latke and shook his head. Oh, I'm so sorry,

he said, I didn't know. No, you didn't know. Of course you didn't, how could you know? Paige smiled, drank more of the cheap wine. She smiled slightly, to suggest it was no big deal. The man went back to eating.

After swallowing, he told Paige how much he's enjoyed getting to know her son Jasper. Paige said that was nice. She found it amusing that Jasper had relationships with adults that didn't involve her, his mother. But she supposed that was what happened, children grew up.

The wine tasted like vinegar. One of Larry's charms, Maeve once had thought, was his knowledge of wine. His good taste. It pleased her, to no longer see him as she had so many years ago. To no longer admire him.

To Beau, she'd wondered aloud: why could it still be ignited in her, like a flare up, this rage, this sense of betrayal? A New Testament shunning. That was when Beau said that she should read René Girard. *It's about triangulation*, he explained, *what you think you are seeing*. But Paige wasn't thinking about René Girard at the party. Instead she was testing out a proposition: *How close can I get to the site of the trauma without feeling?* She sat there, looking at a man who betrayed her, looking at the woman he chose. She waited to feel.

The man next to her remained uncomfortable. She looked to him placidly, allowed him to apologize. He was tripping over his words in excitement and shame. She saw Maeve over his shoulder. Other friends had arrived. Maeve was laughing, putting out her arms for them. I don't have this sort of closeness with anyone, Paige noted, though it did not bother her in this moment. She felt protected through distance. There are two kinds of people in the world, she thought, the kind who have a large group of superficial friends, and the kind who have just a few intense friendships.

Paige assessed Maeve: she was attractive, but not beautiful. She wore a push-up bra, the underwire Wonderbra variety she herself had begun wearing in the 1990s. Wonderbras had been revelation, back in the nineties. Maeve seemed eager, but for what? It wasn't offensive that she was so unlike Paige, who held out an aura of self-protection. It was like comparing a dog to a cat, Paige decided, recalling a stupid video she had seen on the internet. She was a cat, and Larry, too, was a cat. Maeve was not; Maeve was a dog.

Paige excused herself and went to the bedroom where Jasper was playing with other children. It was much easier to be a human with children. Children spoke of imaginary friends and played hide and seek. A girl named Eva seemed to forget she was supposed to seek; she played with a replica of Calder's circus. It was more fun to hide, Paige remembered from her own childhood. She sat on her son's bed and spoke to the girl holding the circus mobile. She remembered a dream she had the night before, a dream of aging. In the dream, she saw her profile in the mirror and, too, the skin on her neck sagging in an exaggerated way. She'd lost her chin; there was no longer a distinction between her chin and neck. Or was it a dream? She wasn't sure now.

Paige and Larry were twenty years older than they'd been when they'd met. He hadn't lost his hair. He, Larry, was perhaps more handsome than he had been when they met. Was he more handsome because he was unavailable? Still, she didn't feel attracted to him, which relieved her. All that sexual energy and desire had withered during marriage, during the early years of raising a kid. He'd been too close, and she was well aware she'd pushed him away. Not once, but in moments, the accumulation of which made reconciliation impossible. Later, he accused her of not being "a good wife." He wasn't wrong; it didn't make sense to regret those moments, she knew it wasn't a choice. She had to leave. She had to move on. It was choking her, the familiarity, the love.

She walked back out to the living room. A group was gathered on the green microfiber sofa. Do you like the sofa? She asked a woman at the end of the couch. Oh ha yeah it's so cozy, the woman laughed. Should we make room for you? Paige said no, she didn't need to sit. I was just thinking about it, this couch. She laughed a bit. A lot happened there. What do you mean? The woman looked confused and expectant. Well I had contractions on that couch. Paige lifted her eyes, looking over the group. People say you don't remember the pain of it but that's a lie. Larry was there—Paige gestured toward the kitchen—I'm sure he remembers. Not the pain, of course, but you know, witnessing it.

The woman had stopped smiling. Oh I didn't know. Didn't know I've been married to your host? Paige laughed, a trill, then sipped her wine. Larry heard her, she was sure of it; he was looking down awkwardly. Maeve kept another conversation going: poetry, San Francisco.

Paige sat down now, on the couch, and explained to the woman, Larry was there. That someone could be there for you in those moments before death. I didn't want to die, but I was sure I would die, yes that was it, a new knowledge. And there was Larry. He didn't know, he could not know.

The woman put her hand on her belly and shrugged; she was pregnant, she told Paige, awkwardly. I'm only in the first trimester. You are scaring me. The woman laughed again. But he'll be great, she said, grabbing her husband's thigh. He's a good one. The husband seemed disinterested.

Oh, it doesn't matter, Paige went on. You have to die, I think. It is death. I died on this couch, and Larry was there, he brought the baby home with us. I nursed him here, too, on this couch, brought us both to life. I had infections, you know, in my nipple. A mastitis, yes, painful. Larry brought me falafel, ba le sandwiches, and so on. He was a good partner, though it didn't last. So what. That doesn't take away from the truth of it, of what we were.

Maeve walked over to the couch now; Paige saw the concerned look on her face. She interrupted, Oh Paige, have you met Roni? Referring to the pregnant woman. Yes, yes. We were just talking—Oh, yes! I heard, I heard. Babe? Maeve called out, loudly, looking around for Larry. Should we bring out more latkes? It was embarrassing, using this term of endearment in public this way. It reminded her of her father and stepmother in the 1980s; they were fans of Neil Diamond.

She smiled, put her wine glass down on the side table. She idly noticed a cookbook there, one she'd gifted Larry for his fortieth birthday. She saw Maeve looking tensely at Roni. She had created something, unsettled something, Paige knew. Had she intended it? She didn't feel anything. It was odd, to put herself here, in the site of the trauma, and not to feel but to know: Yes, that couch once held her life and her death. Yes, she'd bought that couch with Larry many years ago; they were just back from living abroad. They'd fucked on that couch. He'd probably fucked Maeve there, too. Paige thought of Ferrante, of Olga, the spurned wife in *Days of Abandonment*: *Once he'd fucked me, now he fucks someone else, what claim do I have?*

She heard a buzz. It was getting late. Her son came out of his hiding spot. There were many people in the small apartment but it was quiet now. She

walked to the hall closet, passing the art on Larry's wall: a pottery piece that her brother had given them; a framed image of their son's preschool graduation; a photograph Larry had taken in Mexico; a framed image of his National Book Award citation; a note reminding Jasper to take everything (glasses, backpack, lunch, water bottle) to school before leaving each morning.

Everything was so random. I could have fallen in love with anyone, but it was Larry. *We are occasions.*

This was a beautiful party, Maeve. Paige squeezed Maeve's arm, and saw the look of despair briefly pass over Maeve's face. Paige considered squeezing with more force. It reminded her of childhood—how mean she had been to other girls, particularly after her mother had died. How all other girls seemed to have what she could not have—a mother—and how renewed she felt performing small acts of cruelty. It wasn't processed, she didn't feel responsible; it was performed. She'd been a child, she acted, survived.

Because Paige's mother had died, her father refused to discipline her in any way; he wanted only to make her life as easy as possible, he wanted to protect her from any further loss. He couldn't bring back her mother, but he could let her do what she wanted. Everyone felt sorry for her, she knew. To be cruel, she remembered the feeling only now, with Maeve's face before her, supplicant. To humiliate and scare others, to see them afraid of her—it had relieved that lack, that emptiness. It transformed her.

Of course, that was long ago. She was a middle aged woman now, and she believed in kindness. She let go of Maeve's arm, tilted her head to the left. Thank you so much for coming, Maeve said. Paige called goodbye to Larry, who was behind Maeve now, and left the room.

Outside the cold was a surprise. She ran to her car, got in and slammed the door. She turned on the heat. On the radio a man talked about capitalism. She put on her seatbelt and felt a wave come over her, tears came to her eyes. She paused, wiped her eyes. The man on the radio asked two different women what they thought about Capitalism. The first woman said, *Capitalism is neither good nor bad by itself* but the second woman was more certain, said, *Capitalism is bad because in order to increase profit one has to pay workers less than they are worth.*

Paige thought about Larry's book on exploited worker bodies. The other woman on the radio continued to talk about unions, and about Millenials, asked to *take all of the risk but with none of the protections*—no universal healthcare and no universal childcare.

Paige parallel parked her car into a spot right in front of her apartment building. Across the street, the baseball player was just getting home; was there a game? No, it's not the right season, of course not. She laughed at herself. She felt her chest contract and she began to cry. Her chest lifted and fell, her shoulders slumped and she wept: the heat on her face, the car in place, the man's voice repeating words, or so it seemed to her, words over and over again: *capitalism, workers, exploitation, healthcare, childcare—all of the risk—none of the protection.*

STRUMMER HOFFSTON

"Peter died two months ago, I woke up at four still drunk, lost my wallet and passport, knew all the people in Beverly Hills were full of shit, were selling the Monica Lewinsky stories to the press, I knew the boys who were doing it, the ones who said they taught her how to give head, who sold the bat mitzvah tape. The *Times* rejected the piece so I started a bidding war, after we booked the ticket I said to Charles, 'Let's do coke and have sex when we get to Portugal', and Charles said, 'Are you crazy? What about getting locked up?' It was before my colposcopy, do you remember? The doctor said I had dysplasia, we got high in Katie's bedroom, my mother died and my father's sick, I've been staying out on the Island, he eats but it takes a long time, we don't know what the surgeon was able to clean out of him. I haven't read *Araby* in years, but alienation and humiliation are first cousins. We don't have a nanny, I work at home, I met Charles when my husband was dying of AIDS. Columbia says sentimentality is a hate crime so we say 'sentimentia.' Tell her about Dave, he edited Eliot's collected, we named our son after him, I read magazines, when I'm not teaching, I'm reading. She's having a rough time, Peter died two months ago, she told you about the passport. I've never seen a therapist but I saw a Lama in Colorado when Peter was dying. She's always been nasty, when she was 17 she'd look at me and say, 'Hey faggot.' We have a place on 15th Street and a house in Bronxville, you're welcome to the apartment in Portugal anytime, it's empty most of the year, you just pay the management fee, 25%, you can't go in the summer. We haven't seen each other since we were 17, I disappeared, then I find her on the Internet, I'm sorry, I don't remember your name, I see seven clients a day, been doing tarot since 17. In the beginning, it's learning the cards. Then it's intuition. One out of five people ask me to kill someone. Stupid

Mike is flying out of Newark, I'll have the cat by myself, 10 hours door-to-door, when I gave her tranquilizers her inner eyelid got stuck and she shit all over herself in the carrier, I worked with her father on the Lindsay campaign, was walking down the street and there was a little old woman giving out pamphlets, '31 Ways to Survive: A Guide for Black Men,' she was the first black stewardess for Trans Am, I pitched the story and they took it, it's about getting clips in the beginning, Gina, you know you're the rock, beer's on the way, I'm having a boy, every day I can't believe I'm giving birth to a white man, men I could fix, get started, get going, then something happened, I met Charles and realized things change, he was Editor-in-Chief of the biggest gay publication out there at the time, everyone wanted to write for him, I wanted to write for him. Your husband's intentions come from nostalgia for the past, there's no going back, you suffer chronic guilt, worrying, you can achieve the easy way or the hard way. This card doesn't come up often. We exchange numbers or meet for coffee, I'm going to stay with Mike in San Francisco, I haven't read *Frankenstein* in years, but I'm not teaching plot, he's alienated, a good monster, expectations of him so far the other way he turns into what people imagine he must be. She was bragging that she never has B.O. and she wears the shirt the cat pissed on, you should've seen my face when I asked Mike to read my screenplay, yes, that's the face, laugh or I cut off your balls, the first line is, 'My gynecologist says I don't look like a lawyer.' It's none of my goddamn business, but every time we say a prayer for the sick and suffering I think of her, her liver! Looks like I'm wearing a meat helmet, had an allergic reaction to the transfusion, this is a picture of her eating pastrami, I had an IV of pain killers and halfway through the nurse said, 'Are you sure you want to do that?' She wasn't very good at her job, was she? Make the face I made when Mike read my script."

RACHEL GALVIN

Red Armor

A man crafts the smallest sushi in the world
from one grain of rice
a tiny piece of nori
wrapped around a shred of sea urchin

He says a woman cried for over an hour
when she saw the small sushi, it was just so cute

The ratio indicating the relation of the duration
of weeping to the size of the sushi
is bewildering

Sometimes I can't tell if my neighbor upstairs is crying
As I listen to her outpouring I try to discern
whether it's giddy giggling or lament

I change my mind every few minutes
Her state of excitement is perhaps both
I think she must wonder this about me too sometimes

Should you punch a Nazi yes or no

Should you punch a girl sitting on a bar yes or no

If you are the girl sitting on the bar, will you laugh when you tell the story
about how a guy you didn't even know walked up and punched you

I turn over my lipstick and look at the label
all this time I'd been reading "red amour" as "red armor"
I suppose that more than *amour* I needed armor on my mouth

If you are the girl sitting on the bar should you punch the guy back

In the 1960s the Viet Cong guerilla girls who came to visit Chile
looked like angels says the artist whose glasses read VERDAD
Some were snipers and officers, some were spies

Around here, you can't make a sound without someone seeing it

Matter might be called imagination turned war,
puzzling scenes in the bombardment during "that ongoing,
vast but somehow boring destruction. The landscape grows
increasingly perplexed. "Little conceived more American
than the "cryptographic" since it can reorient sense, helping
to account for turbulence that follows, therefore begins. Instance:
color aspects of American democracy, or terror

here and over There. Or even: in traffic snarl delayed construction
at city edge: President, man behind history, realize instant
interstates would not connect American cities but cut through:
psychic zones of relationship. A site society systematically
unordered. Questions about the limits social does.
.

How specificity feels general. How *does* language page
put one somewhere and nowhere — vague idiosyncrasy
of place uses multiple particular places (as opposed settings,
to anchor what would otherwise be untenably pathless, wondering
meditation. Still, these places remain largely general; place names
and multitudinous nature of them, augment both

distinctness and lack of clarity. The *the*. *Incantatory*, calling aura
and past, bringing half-imagined events life. And are arenas,
and in that, their specificity negligible — they name relatively
idiosyncratic settings merely, in which events occurred

or might have. And of culture, education, lends at least a flavor
of Antwerp or Oran, a French concentration suburb, Euphrates,
Pyrenees. Places as much about the or of those places, as about
what hints are provided by name attachment.

1976 Juan Gelman, exiled by junta; twenty-year-old son,
and pregnant nineteen-year-old daughter-in-law "disappeared."
Gelman lived in Europe and Mexico since with *Dark Times
Filled with Light*, '56 to '92, as in "one day i watched death going
by / she wasn't on horseback / she was screaming."

Before actions abroad had few to no direct significant
consequences at home. 9/11 changed. Oppen declared,
"There are situations which cannot be honorably met by art, and
surely no one need fiddle precisely at the moment house next
door is burning." And if the fire lasts a decade, or three,
or if the house is down, and only be returned to in mind?
And once exile has granted freedom to write in opposition
to interests of dominant classes, but has largely taken your
audience—then? Transcending arguments over writing
as politics as opposed to writing *about* politics.

Genius

"The Winchester 1886 is truly the best of the repeaters," the man says after tapping me roughly on the shoulder for the second time. His friends watch as he mimics the grip, the trigger squeeze, the shoulder absorbing recoil. "It was designed by John M. Browning," he tells me, "a genius, a real genius. Revolutionized the modern firearm." He repeats each syllable—*John Em Brown Ing*—for my edification, pointing in rhythm at my open browser but not stopping long enough for me to politely exit the lecture. "The Browning Arms Company used to be just up in Ogden," he says. "The Brownings came out West when the Mormons emigrated to Utah. But Winchester," he says, gesturing again at my screen, where an image of the Winchester Model 1866 is pulled up, an inferior model, as I now know, "Winchester was a manufacturer. Good at making, good at selling. But Browning was the inventor, the innovator." I nod and thank him, but he keeps going. I'm writing a paper, I told him the first time he tapped me and said, "What's with all the guns?" "A paper?" he repeated. "For school?" Yes, I said, *for school* and turned around, ignoring the way his face bulged with a desire to share his knowledge. But he found a way around my disinterest, the tap tap tap on the shoulder, the words coming no matter how many times I thank him and turn away. I nod and listen about Browning, about how the factory used to be here in Utah, until they were outsourced to Japan, about the Browning machine guns still used by the military, nodding and nodding and not saying that my interest is really in Sarah Winchester, in the rumors that she felt haunted by the victims of the Winchester rifle, and the mansion she built continuously until the day she died, not saying that the only time I've ever fired a gun was skeet shooting with a man who was then my lover, a man I was desperate to impress, desperate enough to fly out to North Carolina and fire haplessly at pretend pigeons, or that what impressed me was not the power or the recoil of his shotgun but my constant fear that day that I would forget the safety, that I would blow holes into his chest, the thrumming anxiety and disbelief, that someone could just place this machine in my hands and tell me to make it shoot.

JAMIE THOMSON

Bently

Sometimes people stop me & say is this some kind of joke?
But I am not a joke I am an ok person trying
I like this tired morning
All the time we're burning thru together not caring just cruising
Yet I've decided henceforth that I will be like grass
I will grow all over everything
Until they can't look anywhere without saying *Jamie Jamie Jamie Jamie Jamie Jamie*
I am done with casual acts
There's the rest of death for that
So long as we stay up all night write great poems I don't care what else
I said, stars are holes in the perfect sheet of it
I said, such vastitude whelms
Everyone wept
I am a genius
Here have a fact I can't stop thinking about you haha

Ritual Candor

If my body & to it they call *darling*
shall I step out?
No way.
I fucking hate them.
Tho crave they feel me
like new pangs.
It's all so central.
I tried to forget my life,
these lame thoughts life consists of.
Then awoke from a dream
in which I'd throttled all dickheads,
convinced I was divine.
It was a day.
Hurray!
I put on some cloaking I mean clothing.
Everything collapsing / in flames
when I looked up.

I do whatever
Until it hurts
Make haha
Unto etc.
& no one watching
(Shit.)
Drink beer
Etc.
Again & unto
Until it hurts
Haha
& so I wonder
Or whatever
Beer x beer
Unto what wonder?
Beware!
I etc. hurt
Am worthy
Of way more praise
Am > haha
Etc.

KIRSTEN KASCHOCK

Mouths, Filled with Cinnamon
selected for the Summer Literary Seminars Prize

The girls returned to us are not girls. They were taken at eleven and returned at seventeen. Forty-six were taken and fourteen returned. Had they then expired, were they no longer of use to them who had done the taking? In the morning, we woke and they were here, in the center of the village. And we do not know what to do.

The girls look at us. The girls' looks ask us what we have been doing. We have been doing life. What had they been doing? What life had been done to them? Six years ago, they were lost. One morning the spokesman at the factory came. He told us they'd been taken. "Taken?" we asked. "Taken," he said, "by boys with guns." The girls' parents followed him on the day-long trek back to the factory. He was right and the girls—gone.

The factory had stolen them from us years before that—on the day we sent them. We wept. The factory was a gash, bleeding loss. To begin profiting again, it took in even younger girls, littler sisters. Smaller girls who could fit inside the big guns, who could weld while boxed in those small ovens, who would need little. We prayed. For months we prayed for the return of the older sisters. For years. There was no prayer to make the factory give back what it took. At some point, some of us began to hope the kidnapped girls had found other lives and some of us wished them dead.

I am ashamed to say I am of the former group, although I am equally ashamed to admit I am sometimes among the latter. There is no place to stand in this village anymore. Our mouths are dry. Some of the girls are surely dead. Some of them must be in other lives they did not choose. Some are in the middle of the village, circled around the well, facing out. Slender as question marks, curved in on themselves.

They hold hands. We have been pacing around them since the call went out. A boy, Olly, yelled out at dawn, "They are here! They are back!" And we gathered, to search faces, to call out names, but none step forward. None cry out to mother or for father. Some mothers go from one to the next, skimming

cheeks with fingertips, looking into eyes, hunting as if among nuts and seeds on market day. Some mothers stand back.

I am one who stands back, but am no mother. The girls do not look dead to me. They do not look like ghosts. They are not girls anymore but there is nothing else to call them. They seem unmoved by the wailing and by the prodding, caressing hands. I wish they would sit cross-legged like they did in the school. I wish they would ask for food. They have refused all that we have offered. Even the sweet hard buns that all the children love until one day, inexplicably, they do not. The girls hold hands and sway, reed-thin in the dust that is beginning to coat them like cinnamon.

Before the factory took them, I taught them letters and they recited letters back to me. They grinned their gappy smiles and flashed new teeth as they grew and giggled and whispered behind my turned back. One picked a flower for my birthday. One thanked me for my teaching even though it was stupid for her to learn. She was no boy, she told me. I told her I knew she was no boy.

None of the boys in the village have stayed at the well except Olly. He is here, he is still looking. The rest have left. They are frightened, I think, though they would not admit it. There is an idea, unspoken, that these girls are spirits come to hurt us. As if we have not been hurt enough.

Of course, it is true and not as-if. We have not been hurt enough.

Three years ago I married my second husband. The first died a year after the girls were kidnapped. It was a short sickness, with coughing I thought would stop, and did, but only with his heart. My mother, who is still alive, says to anyone who will listen that I killed him. "He suffered," she tells them, "an unnamed grief." This is something like truth, as I made him no children and unmade children have no names.

When the girls were taken, his eyes went dark. But he was my husband and he didn't care about the girls. He didn't care about any children other than the ones I did not give him. "Children make men men," he said. He drank himself into sickness, his eyes dimming with each paycheck tossed down his hot throat. After the girls went to the factory, a few fathers joined him—a half-dozen, then maybe a half-dozen more. He bought many, many bottles with the money I brought home from the school. I worked hard that year to keep half the village numb.

After the factory replaced the lost girls with even littler ones—any girl old enough to sit still inside a room shaped like a bullet—only boys came to my

class. I noticed then how boys are taught. They are taught that they are the ones who make good things happen, while bad things are done to them. I did not teach them this. They came with this knowledge. I taught them logic, logic those earlier lessons helped them twist. The boys with guns, they reasoned, had taken their sisters: a bad thing done to them. Justice must be served: a good thing they must do. For the past six years I have watched these boys plan for a new world. A better one they want to make, need to make, if they mean to grow into men. A just world. I love these boys and I fear them.

My new husband is from the coast, and comes and goes as he pleases. This year he took money from the village, small stipends paid to families of factory daughters, and brought back guns. He is loved. My mother loves him, more than she loved the first. She warns him that I am barren, cursed. He says he has no need of more children, he left a score at the seaside and along the road to our village. I know his smile and I believe him. He stands beside me now, peering in with narrow eyes at the girls-not-girls, yelling questions that ricochet off the stone well.

"Where are the others? Who took you? Why? What did they do? Speak!" and—

"Why have you come back? Answer!"

I am used to his questions, used to how he ends them with command. My second husband is a man who speaks of action. Who travels to and from the oceanside. Who trades things for things. Who is heard above others. The people in the village respect him. And I too love this man I fear.

The girls-not-girls have been not answering for hours, and the people are starting to make their own answers. It is how silence works here, a thirsty grave unconcerned with which body it is asked to swallow.

The mothers who do not see in these girls even the shadow of a daughter are the first to get angry, but they stay silent. They see these ones as wraiths, shaming us for our continued life. Since we are ashamed, they are not wholly in error. One father who drank often with my first husband called out "Witches!" an hour ago. But only once. That is not an idle word here, and none are ready, yet, to repeat it.

A toddler from the edge of the crowd broke free from her mother, ran to the well, and pulled at one of the girls' skirts. She wanted picking up. We all noted the resemblance of her mother, standing at the back of us, to the teenager singled out. The mother came forward to snatch up the little one, never raising her eyes to the other. For her part, the girl-not-girl stood with the closed face of a pit. She still stands, and she offers no look, not of recognition nor malice. Nor expectation of love.

The fathers whisper below their breath. They grow louder, their stances spreading as if in anticipation of added weight. But their hips are narrow, unused to carrying children. They feel they are being accused. Since the village bears a fathomless guilt, their whispers have merit.

My husband, sick of the silence, turns his back on the girls to address the village.

"Who are these girls-not-girls? Are they yours? They are not mine. I came after your tragedy so maybe I am the person to tell you what must be done. Because as we have stood here, re-mourning your loss, re-opening that wound, for no good reason I can see, it has become clear to me."

He pauses. My husband is an intelligent man. It is his sharpness that drew me to him. In both of us, intellect can be cruel. Our fights are legendary. No one in the village understands them. I think one day he will be done with me and move on to another town and I am afraid. I have no third husband in me, yet a husband makes a woman a woman, here. I am too old for the factory, too big, my mind too hard to melt or blunt. When we fight, my husband tells me I am no natural woman. When we fight, I question his reasons for coming here. I say he must have been driven away from the coast. I say he is not the big man he would have us think he is.

And since this is true for all men, it is true for him. I have the better education. He does not understand how I can know things about him he has not given me to know. But I once saw the sea. I worked for a family there and learned. They were not kind to me, the schooling they promised was informal, irregular, but from them I gleaned things that have served me. And at the end of my stay, from their oldest son—a boy I helped raise—and his friends, I was given the gift of no children. During these last six years, I have come close to accepting that gift.

None of these girls-not-girls, the ones holding hands, the dead ones, the ones making children elsewhere, not one of them is my daughter. I am grateful.

My daughter is smoke along the coast.

My husband finishes his pause with a fist coming down in his other hand. He speaks again in a voice he saves for moments when he would not be argued with. Other times he enjoys besting the men of the village, especially after I have made him question, if only for a moment, his superiority to me. They drink with him less often than they did with my first but they listen harder.

He says, "You must interrogate them."

There is a sudden hush in the village. It has been four long hours and everyone is horrified at the suggestion and also relieved. Someone knows what must be done.

In small groups, men and women go in toward the well to drag out the childwoman who seems most familiar. They make no noise, the taken, though they hold onto each other so that fingernail marks appear on their wrists as they are dragged apart. But none yell or speak or run. They are taken, for a third or thousandth time, against their will.

This time, they are removed to homes that are no longer homes.

The following day, each family performs its begging, its bribery, its beatings. The girls-not-girls make no sound but other noises emerge. Yelling, crying, cajoling, whipping. I cannot go home to my husband so I walk through the village, my own ghost, listening for a voice I recognize. Some girl-not-girl I knew from my classroom. From before the taking. From before, even, the factory. I hear no such voice. I remember the girls-once-girls by drawings they made, by words they stumbled over. "Interrupt" caught Eda's tongue. Min could not say "architect." A bird folded from homework perches above my doorway nearly seven years after little Komi offered it up with shy hands. I have been waiting for it to leave—to fly away—as is the way with birds.

Finally, I go home. My husband asks me where I've been. I answer by asking.

"Why did you separate them?"

"I did not do that. It had to be done."

"They were safer together."

"Safer from whom?"

I cannot explain to him how a girl needs a girl in this world. I do not say it because, one—he would not believe me. Two—he would ask of what use is a girl to the world? And three—he'd tell me a girl cannot have needs because she herself is needed. My husband sees no contradiction in his logic. I have the better education. He knows where to find guns. Still, of all the men in the village, he offers up the most freedom to his woman. I don't always cook for him. Like him, I go and I come back. But I do not go far or for long. His confidence that I will come back is envied by the other men. They would not dare allow it. I come back because I have no woman to go to. I was my mother's only child, and she sent me to the sea long ago, before the war came.

Two days pass and no girl-not-girl speaks and no girl-not-girl is let out into the street.

The boys come to school agitated. They are angry and do not know how to stay still. They pace and they spit. They argue with each other and ignore me when I ask them to work. They were hurting and hateful before but they had hope. When they got older, they insisted, they would hunt the other boys down.

Gun against gun. They would take their sisters back. But now some sisters are back and it is a joke. A trick. These are not the sisters they knew. They are broken, unnatural. They do not blink or cry. They look through their brothers as if nothing their brothers could do would matter. Someone must pay.

The boy, Olly, tells me they are hatching a plan. He will not say more. I wonder which direction they will strike out in. I wonder how many guns my husband has given them.

I come home and ask him, "Can you stop them?"

"Why would I stop them?"

"These are your guns, and maybe these are your ideas in their heads."

"What ideas?"

"They will not tell me."

"They are smart then. If they know when not to speak."

"Not speaking is not helping the girls."

"The girls are no longer girls. Anyone can see that."

"What are they then, husband?"

"They are pain."

I see that this had a kind of truth, and do not argue with him. Instead we make love as we did when he first came through the village—angrily. Oppositionally. As if in competition for the bottle of love between us. This is the first time since the morning the girls came back. I am also pain but do not cry out as I sometimes do. I do not want anyone to mistake my voice for that of a girl returned.

The boys, I think, will leave the village in the night—as is the way with soldiers.

But the next morning comes and they have not gone. They are back in my class. Olly is twelve, and the oldest. His muscles are getting denser, dragging on his bones. He is a heavier thing in this world. He could sink deeper in its mud, mud that is elsewhere. Here it is dry. Nevertheless, it is time for him to make his mark—this is what they begin to think at twelve.

The younger boys look to Olly for guidance, and those his age look to him with love, the rough love of boys separated from sisters. In this village, the only direction is downward, a settling into dust. One day his mark will grow deep enough to swallow him.

"What is the plan, Olly?" I ask him. "Which way will you go?"

Olly stares at me, and smiles. It is a smile he uses when he is caught with a frog in his desk or when he has stolen another boy's lunch pail but before he has eaten its contents.

It is the smile that happens before.

The boys mock their lessons and leave me. I walk home, sad for what is next. The sky is too many colors this evening, embarrassingly. This is the only way for the sky to show her kindness, and it hurts us both. I will never touch the sky, and she will never pull me up into her like a lover or the reversal of a child. The sky and I are, we have always been, sadly matched. Same-not-same.

It is not long after dark when the first shot rings out.

And then, another. There is a scream. Two more shots in rapid succession. More screams. My heart pounds at my sternum as if it were a door. I run out of the house and my husband is there, at the end of our street, staring wildly, worried at what is next—for him. The shots continue. I do not count them. Cries overwhelm the night sounds of whirring insects, the thin babble of starlight. Mothers are running out into the street, their hands over their own faces or shielding the smallest children. Their homes tether them—they can only run so far.

A dozen shots ring out, more. Each one reverberates in the bodies emerging into the street. They cower or cringe, or they drop onto their bellies.

My husband stands, unmoving. He sees in my eyes my hatred. My arms too ache with it. I could strike him. Or shoot him. My hands are open in just such a way. They want the cold, the metal, the relief of a trigger. He taught me how, once. In case of wild animals, in case of a drunken man coming to take what is his while he is gone taking elsewhere. There are guns in the house behind me. Two? Five? I have never counted.

Finally the blasts stop. It is over. My shoulders drop, my arms heavy as Bibles. I was punished with books by my family on the coast—for intelligence called arrogance—punished for hours with arms extended, hands laden with this god no one ever meets, this god I learned weighs very little. Less than the weight of boy after boy after boy. I do not turn back into the house. I stand on the threshold. I count. "One," I say.

The first shooter stumbles out of a house nearby and vomits in the dust. He vomits the way I vomited the day I was made hollow.

His mother looks over at him. She is shaking in the street. She cannot will herself to go to him, although I see her trying. He looks up. It is not Olly, but it is a boy who would follow Olly into fire or the scrub, a boy who loves math and whom Olly assured that loving math was fine, was indeed acceptable to Olly. Hoke learned his tables quicker than any child I have ever taught. Even the twelves. Hoke is also twelve, like Olly. The gun is beside him and he says, "Mama?" He asks it of her. She cannot answer him.

She stares at the boy so long I think he will crack. He is already pieces, but still flesh, not hard. I see her eyes drawing softness from him. I see his loved numbers stumble-hopping away from him into the shadows, like unfledged birds. The eight-times-tables. The sevens. She cannot give him an answer.

His sister. Min. She answers.

Min glides through the doorway with her arm outstretched. She puts her hand in the center of Hoke's back. He swivels around to face her, shocked at her touch. Her hand goes to his cheek. She is no wraith. She is Min. She may no longer be what she was, neither is he, but they cry like children. Tears shine inside the dark space that surrounds them, like tips of soldering guns sealing shut a bomb casing. They are alone together inside this death. Gun smoke drifts from the house in surrender. They were children, and now, they are together without a father. Min's brother has done this and she can see him again. Hoke. He is pain.

I wander the village's circular streets in shame. I did not guess. The boys have decided to fight. In order to fight, they have deduced that they must have an enemy. They have figured this. I pass homes where a mother has been spared, and others—a father. They have figured this also. The boys have spared some of us, a mercy. In a few homes, both parents are dead. This is the inscrutable calculus of war. Brothers cry and some sisters cry with them. Some are giving comfort, some are taking it. There are arms wrapped round. Or, there is no touching but a huddling close. I hear the voices of girls-not-girls for the first time since we have arrived at this new place. Some are so low I cannot tell if they grieve. If they are grateful.

My second husband is a few steps behind me. He is saying foul things, but under his breath. "Cursed," he says, and "Witches." I send him a look he allows to pierce him. Or maybe he does not have the power to allow. The look I send says, You are lucky. Lucky your guns are in our house and not my hands. Lucky you were coming home but not home when I heard the first shot, and the second, and the seventh. Lucky I do not count. You are such a coward, a creeping shadow in the village now, not the big man you pretended—asking to be shot, begging for it, by me or by a boy. My eyes tell him our equation has changed.

He stops muttering.

When I reach Olly's house, no one is outside. I go to the door and push it gently open. A light is on. Olly's mother is on her knees. She is holding Olly. Olly's father was gone long before the girls were taken. It was mother and son who mourned but could not mourn Komi, who was not returned. Komi is still dead or she is still living some other life she did not choose. Either way, she is

not here in the village. Komi's brother is dead, and he is here. Olly will fill her empty grave like a wrong answer.

"What kind of revenge is this?" my second husband whispers from behind me, and the whisper fills the room like fever. Olly's mother does not respond. She is holding her son, so close to becoming a man, so close he could not bear it.

I kneel down beside her. "Olly only ever did good things," she tells me. "So many bad things were done to him."

I nod.

"They took his sister," she says. "They did that to him."

I know this as a kind of truth. I know, too, about the money sent from the factory—for Komi and Min once and the smaller ones now. How guilt swells inside woman or man like a pregnancy, and can rot like a pregnancy. Or fail to root at all. I also know how many frogs I pulled from Olly's desk. These, I counted. The boy snapped 37 small necks between his thumbs before he cocked a pistol and put it in his mouth.

"He tried," I said to his mother. "He tried and he tried."

In the morning, the village drops its bodies one by one into the well. There is no ceremony other than this succession, the long line of families struggling to carry heavy dead then struggling to let them go. The girls and the boys together carry the dead the boys shot alone. Mothers help sons let fathers fall. Daughters touch goodbye mothers' hair. And then the village turns from the well and we leave. All of us do this—all except a hard few. My mother remains, loving above the living her dead: her husband, and my first, and also the child-me. Since I came back from the coast, I have been like a crust to her, a sulking husk. A wraith accusing. Her mouth will be so dry, but she has known drought. I learned it from her.

The village starts walking. We walk all day to the factory and there demand the younger sisters. We left the guns behind, but we do not need them. A village stands at the factory gates—girls are inexpensive. There are other villages. The little ones soon file out to meet their older sisters. To be half-met by half-families. The girls themselves are nearly dead but happy to be out, so happy I smile to see them limp and skip on unstretched legs, the sun catching on bits of bald where dripping missile seams have seared shine onto close-cropped scalps.

My second husband I sent creeping back to the sea before dawn. He will speak to other boys of guns, and of better ways to use them. He is smart. So smart he will again love—probably another woman he cannot control. Maybe she will pick up one of his guns and send him away with it. He may secretly

want this. Until such a day comes he will creep like a shadow difficult to recognize as shadow, bleeding his darkness into the darkness that surrounds.

I carry a paper bird. As we walk, it leaves a print on my sweaty palm—*architect, cinnamon, interrupt*—before disintegrating. I open my hand. The fragments drift away but the words stay with me, cool, like weapons. Behind me the smallest girls are crying as they learn what has happened in the village to fathers and mothers, to aunts and cousins and uncles. They are learning the complication tables of their freedom.

Beside me, Olly and Komi's mother drifts. We are nomads now. I reach across to take her fluttering hand into my own. I say to her: "The children have figured it. Olly did." She nods. The sky is large and strange, and it has nothing to do with me. The sky is the sky.

I mean to accept this gift too. To teach myself, day by day by day, what happens when things are not, or do not have to be, the way they are.

LLOYD WALLACE

Under, and After

Each bulbous spring
I spy my own remastered syndication;

Numbers squirt
Like gelatin
Through slats of fickle chance.

At any point I may adjourn
This stubborn courtship
Of the flavors:

For years,
I've seen the orchestra of codependence
Past the sky—

Frictionless and simple,
Tart and lacustrine.

The layers of this accident
Commingle there in tandem.

I must allow myself
A chance to know
The streets behind the scenes.

The Perseids

A word is said to
someone with a flip
of a finger or
a twitch of a lip.

The sallow smoke
from my husband's
cigarette curls up
and up the rails
of the fire escape
hiding a dour face.

When the god
of carnal pleasure
(or whoever decides
these things) passes me by
duck-duck-goose style
I ask am I deserving
and know I am not.

I am / may be the bad guy.

To end this terrible night
the god of brief
and insignificant things
strikes a match against the sky.

I stand looking Northeast
at sixty degrees.

As a kid running
barefoot through the yard
I tripped on a snake orgy
and planted my face
in a pile of writhing knots.

Now I wait for another meteor.
A lid is revealed over
us by its failure to contain.

from leech-book

AVA HOFMANN

the charm-squares

this section of the manuscript features fifteen poems which mark a significant formal departure from the other charms in the *Codex*. these texts are not written in alliterative verse, but in a non-linear matrix wherein the text can be read both horizontally and vertically. take, for example, C-S 13, the shortest of these "charm-square" poems:

the law	maids the law
makers	makes the maids

there is little instructional material available to give us insight into how these charm-squares were used; it appears that the texts were once paired with an instructional index which has now been lost. however, there are a few clues as to how and for what these texts were deployed. the charm-squares' similarity to other magical squares, such as the sator square[1], indicates that these poems may have been deployed in a similar manner—i.e., as inscriptions on stone, wood, or membrane for use as wards. additionally, a few of the charm-squares are accompanied with brief notes or, in one case, a snippet of verse; these instructions also signal some possibilities as to their individual purposes. however, like many things contained with the *Codex*, these texts resist stable interpretations.

---

[1] the sator square is a well-known latin word-square which reads "SATOR AREPO TENET OPERA ROTAS" from left-to-right, top-to-bottom, bottom-to-top, and right-to left. its palindromic properties lend it to use in various charms and wards, from antiquity to the modern day:

S	A	T	O	R
A	R	E	P	O
T	E	N	E	T
O	P	E	R	A
R	O	T	A	S

to be written on the inside of a shoe:

CS-1:

i'm a boot	power tells
footing the bell	curve of key
butt tresses	soft keys
into price-point	less-cost

'heel'. i'm
building structures
stroke slashes
shoed on my skull.

CS-2:

the "what" in	power met trick	methods, invented
mega-watts.	standard eyes	pilfered each site
lost wisdom teeth	building de-fined	dime's ends.
umpire's state		

CS-3:

class traders	police pleasure
cavity searching	for the long laws
lost wisdom teeth	fuzzy handcuffs
ripping the backdoor	seats pleather

CS-4:

meant measures	natch resource
hard and wet	wares. we wild
telling. self	domesticated aping
strip searches	royal ovens
into truth	each degree
of authority	fortunes

extraction from
away, time
lexicon-vexed
burning words
decreed its medium
story-told

CS-5:

paging my	book burner
phone, god	swears his
self. flesh made	whirred things,
geared-up	spell-checkers of
insuring the	bad magic of
taste. tongue's	licking the lead.

CS-6:

cast iron	panopticon	strip mall
mine. crypt	of current sea	changes for a
5 thousand	years' invention:	clay tablet
computers' labor	to grain-store	age. righting
to administraight	the fail state	of the art medium
clay signs	pointing to	know no.

one may also speak these words to amplify the effect:

i bury this ward. i bury it in the eggshell dirt: // bear worry to shelves where words are failing.

CS-7:

fee male stain	lesser steel joint
parts w/ inner	locking calm positions
pre-come pack	aged. here, i am girl
enough to guzzle	what comes

CS-8:

i'm a loan gun
engenderbeast,   woman prepping the bred
the waist land mixing   milling about
my spring grains.   genre's flour into
the rubber   trampled weakness
                          soul's corps upon my neck.

CS-9:

soldiers of god's
pacific theater   paramilitaries operating
booked. the ink   curtain culls. the good
lapdoggerel to   in "cross" dresses word's
the *n* commandments   power lines of succession
say mercy is an other   writ by stone dictators
tour of duty in missionary law. churchgoing scripts our
bound in vertext's binders: positions, odd pronouncements
only afterlife only   all knowing all
                          heavenly chains.

CS-10:

texts green   cashier cliff   faces with vomit
vermillions of   clear-cut power   plants stomach
us fly   traps, the human   conditioner
tenders its chic slaughter cuddles in his cud gel.

CS-11:

name's banked	interest in eco
gnomic terror	assassination
goes no where	power won't
bridal. she reeds	paper while
another agent	stakes out.

another use for this charm is to stave off poisons.

CS-12:

the regular is	is a table
exerting itself	a normal force of
tabulactating	budgetary concern
its military drills	boring facts.

CS-14:

map's ledge end	bending rivers	with attitude and	longitude anal-beads	of sweat. chain
actions man-dated	buy the solid	state semi-conductors of	globally positioned	bonds. the lainpeople
following roads social	medium; store	gazers strolling round	about paths found	maximal for photo
shopping. interchange	in my body	pump trafficked traffic	erupting in sapphic	beads of volcanic
plasms—an atom of	my hand scape	guide books to my grave:	the graph is all	remains

CS-15:

to be left among the trash and forgotten:

i kiss her index	finger in death's
throw pillows	doom surround
sounds. she	smiles. worthiness
is a shit question	i must refuse.

unidentified inscriptions[1]

J.C.: "manufactured west of liverpool. this thing was made by a lowly potter, who loves his brother very much."

H.W.: "this amulet is to ward off poisonous snakes. another use of this amulet is to ward off other kinds of snakes."

A.S.: "the speckled tree loves its speckled graft // this speckled wind groans. when we have sex, we laugh."

M.P.: this amulet is not inscribed with writing in a conventional sense, but a mnemonic device which depicts the end of the world in four scenes: "death by fire", "death by plague", "death by war", and "the triumph of the void".

J.C: "[...] the fish-woman kisses that lovely woman, the one who rescued her from the fishermen's nets [...]"

H.W.: "[...] bowl of power and drinks from it shall have the power to [...]" or "[...] and call for a good time [...]"

A.S.: "[...] retched, // her limbs stretched and stretched until they filled the room [...]"

M.P: similar to item A1, the inscription upon this fragment is not writing, but more of an abstract illustration of the history of some sort of battle. because the proto-text is fragmentary, very little of its text can be discerned.

J.C.: "grain-storage" or "store something kind in me" or "this is where i keep the odds and ends."

H.W.: "they will not listen to us. we must rise up in these streets to survive."

A.S.: "when storing herbs in this box, speak this charm. this will vouchsafe their love and effectiveness:

i remember the fear, i remember the shattering // fronds in the underbrush, o roots tubers, fruity rinds, keep me minded of planted // pain, of the record tied up in fetters— fret me more, as i enclose your healing // flit your history on me, so that i might compose more than pastness, but in this false mirror // propose something for us like a future."

M.P.: this inscription is neither writing nor proto-writing—it is simply an appealing illustration on the lid of a decorative box.

---

¹ placed between two pages of the manuscript are three ceramic fragments bearing a script of unknown origin. the first is probably an amulet or medallion; the second, a curved pottery fragment, likely from a plate or bowl; and the final ceramic piece appears to be the lid of some manner of container which has been lost. the script written upon the objects seems consistent with some form of writing or proto-writing; however, they do not map onto any known writing system. this has not prevented scholars from nonetheless providing translations for these texts; we have supplied a number of the most popular translations for each of the inscriptions. the disparate and divergent content of these translations both demonstrates the script's indecipherability and the disparate approaches taken by the various scholars, from A.S.'s more poetic approach to M.P.'s speculative refusals of translatability.

MICHELLE TARANSKY

RICHARD JACOBSON
MARGARET JAKOBSON
MURRAY JANOFSKY
CONRAD JANOWITZ
JEFFREY KAGEL
KATHERINE KALINSKY
BERNICE KAMIAT
MELVIN KAMINSKY

Afraid of dangling
A participle:

A reader
Who knows the folks
Who are running things

Who value clarity and concision
You might never get over
How to make things
Matter— perceptions of research

Frames that are needed
To understand the outcomes
What goes without saying
A premise about talking about

What a nation might do
To see differences we are doing
Not to look at this quite yet
The work horse not the show horse

A work a day kind of project
To look for patterns
Critics are debating
How to add to what you

Already know what it's like
To have an audience to read to
That is ok being in a place
Where they do not know

RICK JASON
MAGGIE WHEELER
JAN MURRAY
CONRAD JANIS
KRISHNA DAS
KITTY KALLEN
CARA WILLIAMS
MEL BROOKS

MICHAEL FELDMAN
FENELLA FELDMAN
SOPHIE FELDMAN
FIVEL FELDMAN
WALTER FEUCHTWANGER
JASIN FINK
HARRY FINKELMAN
JACOB FINKELSTEIN

Today we are in training to learn how to write
The rules to train the trainer how to enjoy
The work. We are in training to know

Quitting could occur, or if you become tired
A worried mother with no access to wheelchairs
Or memories of new gardens, sad leaves, an old city
That has no birds returning from winter I won't be angry

If you're late for the first day of training, but assume then
I will be very worried the city isn't enough not enough faces
Or eyes to see through, perspective to know their place is like
An other building where bricks are bread and blood libel

You are scared of the last stop where he must choose to go he must choose
Must go must know he must needs a new eye now and heart and the most

Patient and determined trainer to train him to tell me he is good he is
Safe he is finished his training took seriously this
Training, the newest token, the one you used to want to lose
When you didn't care about losing couldn't care we were sad here

Here in training thinking of tomorrow what we may remember
From today here being trained to take care of, clearly, confidently,
Yes. Yes we did choose these paths and these problems
Did not think to not choose the difficult because it's here

No matter the end of the year party it is still the same year it happened
Party preparations are required so why not want to know how
He hid it from his family or did they know are they we will we say
We were worried before we knew we had

The work ethic
The rise of the tiger

The problems we are being
Trained to take care of them

Then of the bridge
There with their enemy

They met at the party
Now where is our trainer

Where our want to know
Every time it happens again

Trained to know even if we do not know
It is happening, it is happening

MICHAEL BRANDON
FENELLA FIELDING
TOTIE FIELDS
PHIL FOSTER
WALTER WANGER
JANIS IAN
ZIGGY ELLMAN
JACKIE FIELDS

Dog Eaters

My grandmother dies in the depths of summer when it's too hot to eat a popsicle. On the day of her funeral I walk with my mother to the cemetery in our blackest clothes. As we follow the dirt path to the outskirts of our village, I witness a herd of monks dressed in bright orange robes, their knees dirty with prayer. Their robes have been opened to let the breeze in, so they look ostentatious yet fully functional, like traffic cones. One could truly make a living this way: by willing rain to come, by willing rain to end, by praying for the souls of dogs killed during the annual Lychee and Dog Meat Festival to get back into the cycle of reincarnation instead of wandering the world aimlessly without form, etc. It's a busy time of year for them.

Further down the path, an old butcher alternates fluidly between coughing, cursing at the monks, and spitting on the sidewalk. The butcher is squatting on the stoop outside his shop, arms folded piously over his chest with a tampon shoved inside one nostril. He wants to stop his nosebleed while dressed in an apron soaked in dog blood. I turn to my mother and ask, "What's the point of plugging up one wound while letting another one leak?" Here is an economy based on redemption: a temple built next to a butcher shop where the primary occupation of one is to pray for the killings of the other. Now that I've proven how much we need each other, let's get on with it.

The butcher has a pet dog who barks at the caged dogs, and together they chew on vegetable scraps and howl at the moon. Which is to say: sometimes love means you don't talk much, but you eat together. This is a signifier in my culture. Please translate into a symbol you can understand. (When going somewhere you've never been before, you should always learn how to say hello, goodbye, where is the bathroom, I love you.) The monks say the butcher is sacrilegious, but I believe religion is whatever you embed the totality of your being in—my religion is spoonfeeding eggs to the sink. My religion is informing men how sweaty their hands are. My religion is a cigarette butt that's started a

dumpster fire with no one alive to witness. My religion is skipping the line at the deli and going straight towards my dreams.

The monks prepare for the Lychee and Dog Meat Festival by redirecting traffic in their traffic cone robes, and the butcher prepares by shining the crimson off his knife. In the dark, over the hills, hundreds of flames are lit and dog bodies turned over and over, widening under the cool, black fires. You can excavate their tiny white hearts and lay the skins out to cure. You can do this with the conviction of somebody who has a family to feed. I've never eaten dog meat or tried to flag down a god, but don't equate what I haven't done with what I wouldn't do. For instance: my grandmother once asked if I could help her remove the birthmark on her face—a pearl of oiled black the size of an insect. I brought the knife solemnly to her cheek, and made her do the rest herself.

I like to be the one who cleans up the mess instead of the one who tends the fires. I like to be the one who slips in and out of my desire to hurt whoever is standing closest to me. Maybe we are opposites, and we could grow up to become siblings. Maybe you are the same as me, and I could grow up to become the flesh under your nails. This may seem like a finite realm, but there are many things that exist between a sibling and the flesh under a nail—the finger itself, the grime that slides under a nail when you are burying a body, the palm that sweats on prayer beads, the sound of your mother smashing her sunglasses on over her normal glasses, your shadow cast over a freshly-mowed lawn, etc.

After the burial is done everyone is left standing and staring at the ground. I can hear the sound of monks and dogs wailing in the distance, so loud they drown us out. The sun is still a sliver pronounced in the sky, fingernailed yet bright. I squint. I wink. It feels like coming back after a long day, and all the lights are on, but there is nobody home.

The Coppices of Pleasure

As the summer days get longer, the leaf canopy fills out and the woods darken. In the silence, purple flowers nod.

I can't recall the sensation of pleasure, only the context, which I would have to tell as a story. Would it turn you on?

Here's a story. Antoine Saint-Just rises before the Assembly and makes a dizzying argument. Even though King Louis XVI may now call himself Citizen Louis Capet, and say he is a friend of the revolution, he still must be executed, because of what he represents. There is no need for a trial, because the monarch is above the law. For me, I see no middle ground. This man must reign, or die.

Another. Walking in the woods, I find a flower, all white, pink-tinted, glowing in the shadows. Indian Pipe, or the Corpse Flower: *Monotropa uniflora*.

Another. They walk the King to the scaffolding on January 21, 1793. He says something, but the drums are so loud, no one hears. Something about innocence. The blade flashes, a muted thud. The end of feudalism.

This flower doesn't need light, because it's parasitic. I touch it, and it's slick. Its head hangs pendulous.

Another. I remember a corner of the park, the windows rolled down, cool air pouring in so we are shivering, and she whispered, come inside of me.

It's supposed to be that the will of the people gives the state sovereignty. It seems also that the state comes into being to push past people's innumerable, inconvenient objections.

Saint-Just: He must die to assure the repose of the people.

If the state is an argument, one of its presuppositions is the people's restlessness.

You see, the flower takes what it needs from a host, a nearby plant, often a tree. Also, its entire body is one inflorescence.

An act of violence, when it's staged, is so satisfying. I think of protesters and cops arrayed, encircled by others with smartphone cameras.

Alice Notley says Death to all evangels / death to the head of state…. death to your pitiful salary. I read it in a photograph of the page, on-screen.

Saint-Just: One cannot rule innocently: the folly of that is too evident.

Forms of state policing: to imprison, discourage, employ.

I am walking with a neighbor, and she says, I can always tell when someone isn't from here. How so? Just, you know… high hopes!

I overhear: you were measured as having been away from your desk for on average thirty minutes. As far as going to the bathroom, you just need to be mindful, and take care of that before your shift starts.

Here, I offer you 1,000 *Monotropa uniflora*, one for each humiliation.

Each head hangs pendulous in the quiet.

I strain to hear while I'm doing the dishes: the market, democracy, accumulation, stagnation, rent economy, neofeudalism.

Saint-Just: The folly is too evident!

Roque Dalton: It seems to me the dead have started to realize they're becoming the majority!

In the end, it is a body like mine. One inflorescence. They put him in the hole, rested his head by his feet, and sprinkled quicklime.

Kalām Kalashnikov

Light expels itself
Six hundred seconds
Per minotaurs per minute
Per second per century
Per postmodern period.
Millenniums melt mì
Why do we eve try
Tag intaglio
חַזָּ Ja. Shadows
Châteaux
Cointreau
portrait
Data da jour
Becketts Become
Pāgellārum Becoming
No   [Thing]
Before they could
Imagist Pascaline
Pigmentation
Pillaging Σ ion
Ionic
Laconic
Draconic
Idiotic
מִיהֹלָא slaves salves
Pharaonic myriad pyramids
Forms Formal formulaic
Hydra hydratic tick tix
Equa nox nix nack snap
Apple kill pop singularity
Monolithic Plantations

Narcissi' narrative
Naja Nero neither
Negro Kierke Avant
Evant Horizon
Maybe six centuries
Are all that we needed
Or allowed anymore

ERIN TRAPP

Passus 1

in a summer season   the word was the sun was soft
the word was soft   the summer was worn by
endless conversation about the summer no longer
but it was   in a *somer seson*, it was
the wearing was the softness and I clothed myself
but was still myself · a cloak was soft
the summer was worn by no one
shrouds as I a sheep were shoop I bramble I hep I thorn I rosebush I false fruit
I habit I hip I hermit I desolate beadsperson · your soul a bead to prayer
sweetbriar to bear it was the old world
rose the summer no longer   wide in the world
the sun was shoop and rose hip · enclose your typical achene
the seeds of dream pressed close and soft it fell agape and wonders to hear
ac on a may morwenynge on malverne hills ac on a morwenynge
ac on amorning on bears ears may befall fairly a mine
methought a may morning the summer season was soft
was weary and why was I weary why wandered and weary
what paying out and not taking in · what *forwandred* had been wound
tried mending *ac on a morwenynge* on bears ears had been mending
and mending was blocked was forwandered and wandered to rest
was rest, was remaining · was weary, was distance
had been destroyed and not mended had wanted and *wente*
had nowhere wide in the world   no longer
wounded and went in   was winter and was more was within
was within the dead labor everywhere · fossilless hills, the trodden paths
tucked in ladybugs overwintering by winnowing in
ac on a may morwenynge I was as in dream a destroyed object
had not made it out · had *forwandered* within my *mende*, lost my mind
I did not slumber, I did not slomber into a sleeping
I lost my mind I shoop as sheep, was on a morwenynge   the hills were gone
the morwenynge was within the crisis was the republic was the public

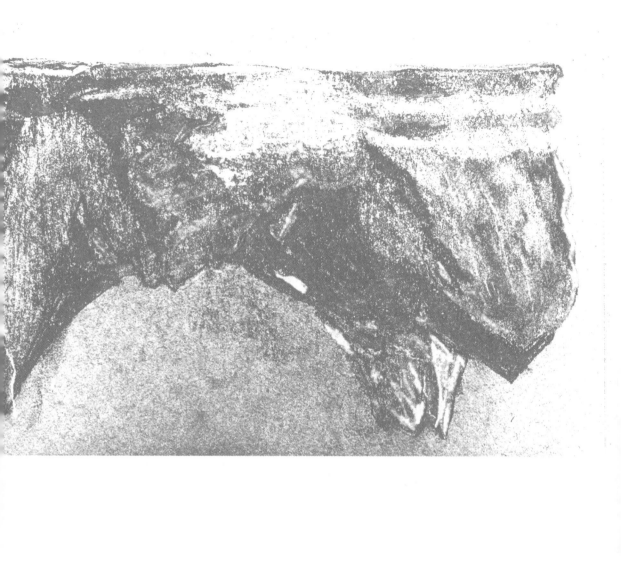

KATHLEEN HEIL

You Disappoint Me

I could have told her that if something is disappointing, I know it's not nothing because nothing is not disappointing. ANDY WARHOL

By noon it was hot enough in my studio apartment that the Madrid sun shooting down through the attic skylight bullied me into waking. I thought about lying there with my eyes closed for the rest of the afternoon, even if it was too hot to sleep, even if getting up required finding effort collected in places I had already misplaced. I was relieved to see I felt weary in a way I knew, that I'd had another dream about anxieties I couldn't name with my eyes open, nor understand with my lids closed. I put my hand on my chest to see if my heart had already begun beating faster than it needed to, my body's emotional armor for the fear that seemed to invade my life in perpetuity. The four-chambered thing pushed at me, all right, and as I moved my thumb down I felt the skin drop into a groove with a texture that felt like braille, cool to the touch although the head was sweating: a scar. I felt the length of it wrap around my torso, followed it with my fingers, the worn tracks leading me down the stomach and toward the hips. I moved my hand yet further down and instinctively adjusted myself, as my genitals had become twisted uncomfortably during my late-morning lie-in. I did this without thinking, then thought of the fact that I had never had to do such a thing before. Something was definitely amiss, and my heart now seemed up to the task it had always been waiting for: a real disaster. I looked at the limp, pink creature and its red, mottled veins, and realized, suddenly, terribly, that I had to pee.

I got up slowly. My legs felt longer and older and more brittle than I remembered them to be. Instinctively I wrapped the bed sheet around my hips, wanting to shield myself from my impudent sex, and walked the four steps to the bathroom. I put my hands on what was hanging there below me. The simple act of emptying my bladder mitigated the strangeness of the situation, and only after giving the weighted object a gentle shake did the absurdity of what I had just done overcome me. I looked down at what was now my penis and knew

that I had never urinated from it before. Curiosity and delight and terror overwhelmed me—Freud was both right and wrong about his theory of envy. You may want what you don't have, but that is a human and not just female trait. Once you have it, I could see, still holding this strangeness before me, such a thing could quickly cease being a curiosity and become, like so many things in life, a burden. I dropped my hands and headed for the mirror, not sure how I was going to explain this situation to my sometime boyfriend.

My concerns became superfluous as I discovered I had a much bigger problem. I looked up at my reflection and saw a photograph. I had always liked the jawline, fine and insistent, had found the nose which others called 'bulbous' and 'cauliflower-like' rather fine. Noble, even. The patchy skin seemed to contain its own geography, the eyes held a kind of wounded intelligence. The scars corseting my torso, which felt like the worried musings of having lived too many stories, could be better described as—yes—looking like the corset of a Dior dress. So it was this, then. The mirror reflected what I had been trying on, it was a frame to the work of art that I had finally become. This seemed an awful joke, and also bad timing. How could I pretend if I was no longer pretending? He would have had an answer, and it would have been funny. It was great. It was terrible. It was really, really … *abstract*.

The hollows of the eyes looking back at me weren't vacant, they seemed to attempt to draw me out; or was it in—I wasn't sure. I took the hand attached to this body and put it on top of the head and felt the bony skull and the few strands populating it. It was useful, I supposed, and fortunate that I already had the wigs. A project I'd said I would abandon but had never touched, not really. They weren't real, but they were silver and would have to do. I looked older but I didn't feel older, was I older, the brain was still my brain, I think it was my brain, was it my brain, in the brain I tried to find a thought somewhere which might reveal itself as his, here was his body, offering itself to me, was it his mind that I now minded, was it. Never mind how I would even recognize the difference, how to get out of the head without losing it, point a finger, draw an arrow, pull it apart.

The mind which I had the instinct to still name as mine was trying to jump out of this skull and into all kinds of terrified conclusions, but I didn't want to do that just yet, I wanted to remain before the mirror and look. It was hard to say what year the body was from, but after '68, certainly. The scars were there and I couldn't help but look at them. The flesh sagged. A collection of skin hung on the hands. The face held a vague puffiness.

I found my striped shirt and pulled it over the head. It fit more tightly than it had before. The phone on the table next to my bed shouted at me angrily, insistently, but I did not answer it. I still wasn't sure what the voice would sound like, whether it would be my voice, or his.

I wanted to lie down again. Perhaps if I went to sleep I would dream it was a bad dream the way characters in bad books dream bad dreams and then wake up and find out it was nothing but a dream. Surreal. But the head hurt and it was hot and the body sweat and sagged. I could move but didn't want to. I thought perhaps if I tried to create something it would make me feel better or give me some insight into my condition, but I didn't want to make anything. Time was past or had flown or passed me by or hid under a mountain where it grew a beard, waiting. I didn't have any hair on my chin, I couldn't get used to the limbs, which felt awkward for the height of my attic apartment ceiling, it required me to bend over to get to the kitchen to make a cup of coffee. I made the coffee, and felt I needed to call somebody, to tell someone about my condition, but who, I could only think of him. I could write him and he could never answer. My dealer would be pleased, but I didn't want to talk to her. I stared at the phone lying on the bedside table. It didn't ring.

It was difficult to pinpoint the exact moment in which I had become obsessed. Obsession isn't instantaneous: it accumulates. At the time I hadn't known much about his work beyond what everyone knew. But I began my life as him one day when I found a t-shirt on sale at H&M for five euros; it was boat-necked and striped and reminded me of the shirts he'd worn around the time he was becoming a great artist, this was long before I had found myself in the predicament I was in now. Already I knew I had no chance of becoming a great artist. My work was too derivative, and I lacked delusional belief in my own genius, or was it talent, or was it dedication, or was it something else, whatever it was, the ability to persist long enough to make something of it. But he insisted himself upon me in small, incremental ways, ways I didn't register until they came at me all at once.

I knew the rhetoric was as important as the product and that my paper doll paintings didn't amount to much, so I decided I would make myself into a work of art. I would become him. I also wanted to understand him. The crass impulse hid a more sincere one. There was a video of him getting dressed in drag from the early Eighties, done in preparation, I think, for some photos to be taken by his assistant, and in the video he looked so forlorn. Forlorn. Critics were always pointing cocksure fingers at him and making judgments one way or

another, but they seemed to miss the point entirely. I wasn't sure that I could get at it myself, but I wanted to try. I began reading everything about him I could get my hands on, watching him and trying to imitate his voice. My dealer was thrilled, knowing that the provocation, regardless of the depth of the content, would generate some attention, would guarantee, if she was lucky, a few sales, at least. So I bought a few wigs and the boots and the pants. I already had my big nose and my Americanness, and my skin, though not as pale or mottled as his, didn't need much by way of modification. I got to work. Made videos where I dressed up like the artist and made art, mediocre paper bag paintings made of paper dolls and plaster. I enjoyed working with the gesso, there was something like comfort in laying down the chalky paste and smoothing it over the canvas and sanding it down. I didn't know how to make myself into a machine, so I would make a machine take my pictures. Cutting out the dolls relaxed me, and wearing the suit made me feel relieved. Always the process was under surveillance by the insistent red eye of my video machine.

I checked the time on my phone: already it was past noon. I had signed up for a workshop at La Casa Encendida, the contemporary arts foundation down the street; it involved four afternoons with an artist from Lisbon studying video and dance-related performance art. I wondered if I should still go, I worried that if I went to the workshop someone would detect my condition and detain me, but then I would be found out eventually, wouldn't I, and being found out would bring a kind of relief, and I was tired of ruminating, so I decided I would brave the heat. First the surgical corset then the striped shirt, then some black spandex pants that also worked, I noticed, for stretching to contain this new appendage. I put on my white running shoes, the only pair big enough to contain the feet, and a scarf and oversized shades, thinking that if I tried to look ridiculous, I might, on balance, blend in.

When I got to the rehearsal space reserved for the workshop it was already populated by a dozen or so young Europeans stretching and rolling about on the studio floor. I looked to have thirty years on many of them though the presiding artist was also middle-aged, a woman with short burgundy hair in a black pantsuit who peered at me silently through her Coke-bottle glasses as I walked in. A few people looked up to register my entrance, but no one seemed to recognize me. I went to the farthest corner of the room, and, afraid that any unanticipated movement might expose my scars, carefully adjusted my surgical corset and began to stretch. After a half an hour of stretching we gathered in a

circle to discuss what was going to happen. The artist spoke about distance and *emisor* and *receptor*, and though most business was conducted in dry, international English, she occasionally reverted to her mother tongue. Her Portuguese sounded as if it were being swallowed as it was spoken, all those vowels hidden away and contained at the top of the nose, the back of the throat. When I spoke I wasn't sure if it was with his voice or my own, I had been trying to sound like him for so long I no longer knew if I was still trying really or really couldn't not try. I ran the hands nervously over the torso, fingering the scars and veiny stitches like worry beads.

We were told to make these things the artist called 'choreogramas,' a term the artist said she invented, it was like a photograma but posing in a dance move, freezing, and then moving again. I wanted to tell her it was impossible to invent anything because everything already exists. Contemporary art is so easy to make fun of because it's so serious. This woman was so serious. It was August 6, 2012; the day they dropped the atomic bomb in '45, she said. She called it an anniversary. It was the day before my anniversary, too, I wanted to tell her that I was supposed to be thirty years old in twenty-four hours, though I didn't know anymore. I wanted to tell her he was there the day they dropped it, too, it was his first day at the Carnegie Institute and also his birthday, today he would be fifty-something or eighty-four, I didn't know anymore. If I can't stroke the scars when I get nervous I put my fingers over the mouth so that they can't hear me breathing and it relaxes me. She talked about the bomb and the people who died and then a few months later there would be more disasters on the same island, it was hard to know who to blame, she said, a butterfly, a wave, a god, a man. We were supposed to take our clothes on and off in fragments and perform the choreograma, the artist had a camera turned on us that recorded everything and an assistant who walked about the room zooming in on our hungry, earnest faces, and I wanted to say, I didn't know you were in a serious relationship, too. My beard—that's what I called the video machine I kept in the corner of my studio apartment to record me sleeping—had fallen from the beam I'd taped it to the night before, this was after my friends had come and gone and we'd all had too much wine and just before I fell asleep, but I was too drunk or tired or both to get up and do anything about it; it was there, lying on the floor impotently, and here I was, in this body. But here was her camera watching all of us, and the atmosphere in the air wasn't of sex, and it wasn't the desexualized nudity of fat Germans on Mediterranean beaches, it was somewhere in between, and I had to think she liked watching all these bodies undress, most of them not quite thirty but here she and I were starting to sag, nothing but droop

droop droop, we were both really up there, although I was still hopeful that I would wake up the next morning and turn thirty. We had to partner up, and my partner was from Lyon and named Alphonse and had dark eyes and long hair, which he would grab at and pull furiously when he wasn't expounding in a way I couldn't understand, or putting overturned houseplants onto his head. Everyone there loved him because he had charisma, although his energy and wild gestures were more than a bit phony. He wasn't crazy, he just liked to imagine he was creative enough he could be.

The artist put some music on and I felt uncomfortable there in my clothes with Alphonse watching me. I didn't want to take my clothes off, and wasn't sure what Alphonse would say when he saw the scars or the discolorations or what I now possessed, just hanging there, a small, terrified little being, and how would I take my shirt off without having problems with my wig. Other people had already begun to undress, and many of them were making faces and moving slowly, they all looked like they were in a very serious fashion magazine, and I was the only one not in on the joke.

I began, but I didn't want to do that, if I tried I knew I would feel phony. Usually, to get to the right thing the best way to do it is go straight through the wrong thing. So I started moving very quickly, thinking that the act of undressing is usually one of two things, either a performance, or something you have to do to get to something else, shower, sleep, change clothes, have sex, it was too much like work work work, here we weren't changing our clothes for any reason, it was a performance. You couldn't pretend it was to do something else and if you performed you were just doing what you were supposed to, which seemed like a reenactment of the expectation and not the occupation of it, so I thought what if I didn't pretend to do something I was already doing, which would have been faking it, but just tried to do something else, and then I wouldn't feel so self-conscious about being naked, I didn't want anyone to look at me, though I did want to look at everyone else. I tried to take my clothes off to get to my other body, a body which didn't have such a hold on my mind as his did, to get back to my own body, even though my own body was holding onto his like it mattered, now I just wanted to let it all go, to try and get around what I wasn't sure I was. I stretched my arms wide and hunched my shoulders so that the striped shirt rode up a few inches and my flesh was exposed. Then I moved my arms from side to side to release it further, releasing the fabric the way I wanted to release the rest of myself, and it made me nervous but I felt I was getting somewhere, so I moved more insistently and found myself doing the same with my pants and also with my underwear, so that they were not clothes so much

as circumstances shaped as sculptures I found confining. It seemed like a good thing to do to your clothes, to make them into twin sets of circumstances you divide by your body's halves, and my underwear was around my knees and I was bent over, ass in the air, trying to remove the wrinkled shirt without messing up my wig, the artist's camera always watching, and then the artist approached me. She surprised me, approaching me from behind, and on her face she wore a twin set of anger and disgust. I'm going to have to ask you to stop, she told me in English. You're very nervous, why don't you let your partner go, I don't think you understand the objective of the exercise. I thought she could have chosen a moment other than the one she did to expose me. I thought that if she were a real artist she wouldn't be trying to dictate the results, but she chastised me in that way avant-garde artists like to do, they are always the most papal in their desire for control. It seemed phony to me, but I couldn't think of anything to say in my defense and didn't have to, she was already walking away while my partner sat in the corner, watching impassively. I lowered the exposed, pale ass from the air and flopped the shirt back on and with the left hand yanked up the underwear. Alphonse said nothing of the scars or the exchange or the wig. I wanted to disappear, but it seemed I could only disappoint. He stood up and began to take off his clothes, moving slowly and pausing to look at me for effect, creating a moving portrait with his posture of certitude and beauty, and I sat there in the corner, ashamed, watching.

I left the workshop early and started back toward my studio but didn't know what to do with myself, I wanted to meet Gabi or Marco for drinks, I thought that maybe if I texted they would understand, but I didn't text them, for I knew in my current state that my friends would not recognize me. The mouth said things my mind did not abide, and try as I did to form small lines of connection through what I thought I knew to be another tongue, it always came out as a meal eaten sideways, the *ums* and *ahs* of his insistent mouth: I could think in Spanish, but no longer speak the words. It was really, really *peculiar*. I climbed the stairs to my apartment and opened the windows to let the outside heat of the evening mix with the inside calor. It was hard to say which was more stifling. I returned to my position on the low bed and tried to sleep, the sounds of the city dozing around me.

In late August there is hardly anyone in Madrid, and Madrid, depending on whom you ask, feels either desolate or remarkably, peaceably quiet. Perhaps you can tell a person's philosophy by plumbing her perspective on the matter. Those who see the city as abandoned are themselves a bit hopeless, and those who find the quietude a comfort carry an enviable kind of stillness within.

I couldn't sleep, so I thought about the artwork scattered about the attic studio, canvases with so many characters glued in papery flatness onto the finely ground chalk. I didn't know where my work would come from now. I didn't want to make my bullshit art, a so-called commentary on my anxiety of influence, I couldn't, not anymore, not since that influence had become my anxiety. When I had been faking it I was serious but now that this was serious I couldn't fake it.

Why did we do it? Why did we dedicate our lives to making things? Were we, as some accused us, trying to get around our own mortality? Or did we simply want to create for ourselves meanings as beautiful as the world we wished to inhabit, to protect ourselves from other realities? It certainly felt necessary—an obligation—or compulsion: as a famous writer once said to a 'nobody' who was struggling with her poetry and asked him what to do, he said: *try quitting*. Behind the tacit arrogance of the statement lay the admission that if you make things it is because you cannot *not* make things. Maybe our efforts were designed to redress the balance by filling out the episodic with the momentary, these works of creation were a reflection or a repudiation of the divine, it depended on whom you asked, we stood in locations that moved beneath us all the while, everything always in motion, but such episodes we hoped would guard against the rest, there had been too much misery, the balance was off, the artists were so many malevolent or benevolent beings working to work the balance off. We weren't going for posterity because it wasn't for us to decide, we were simply trying to prolong the moment, to safeguard against loss, and it didn't matter that it was a fool's errand, what we wanted and needed was to document all the things that delighted and disturbed us. We gestured, we made sounds with our throats and raised our eyebrows, we threw up our hands and adjusted our wigs.

I was looking for what we all looked for: understanding. If I wanted to be understood it was so that someone could recognize that what was within me was not necessarily the same as without. I understood that part of the problem was that I didn't understand what had happened to myself. I pulled a bar receipt from my pocket and overturned it. On the back of it was written in his hand: *People need to be made more aware of the need to work at learning how to live, because life is so quick and sometimes it goes away too quickly*. Somehow, in spite of the hour and the heat, after several hours of fretful pacing around the tiny space of my apartment, I fell asleep.

The next morning it was still too hot to do anything and the world still felt too abstract. The grackles grackled overhead, and I thought I would get a pizza in

the plaza or sit on the rooftop terrace of the Gaudeamus bar held up by the crumbling church. But I wasn't hungry and I wasn't thirsty and the surgical corset itched and made me sweaty and I didn't have the head to go to the kind of store I'd need to visit to buy another, to do so would be to admit my fate. I rinsed the lime green band with water and lay down again on my bed and tried to will the little electric A/C unit into working its cool air into the corner of the room where I lay. Clouds swam overhead and I stared at them through the attic skylight. For a brief period the moon in its fullness had been framed by this very glass, it spotlit the fake veneer floor for a few days in the first months of my living here. Having never had a skylight before I didn't think about the moonlight's movement; being in the attic apartment made me aware that I rotated along with the rest of the world. It is hard to record the earth's movement when the earth seems to submit so readily to our confident feet, hard to remember harder even to conceive.

My hands in their absence of color seemed to bleed into the sheets, and I felt as though there was nothing I could do about any of it, but then I thought maybe I should paint or go look at some art, I had been worried about going to museums and getting recognized, but after the workshop I knew my awkwardness would keep the spotlight of recognition from switching on, and besides, people had their heads in their technologies, their handheld families, it was unlikely they would even notice me. Or maybe people were just foolish and assumed that since he was dead all this existed outside the realm of possibility, although was that any more foolish than going about your business on the flat ground and saluting the sun as though it fixed itself according to your disposition.

It was Saturday and entrance to the Reina Sofia museum was free and later the Prado would be, too, it wasn't far to walk and I could always stop on Argumosa for a drink. Yoli had her tables out and since it was August I could actually get a seat, what was nearly impossible in June was so easy come late summer, the city had emptied of the people who could afford to leave and had left me and the rest of the abandoned to enjoy this small if bittersweet victory, an easily vanquished café seat. Yoli was a short but robust Peruvian woman who had been running her lemon ice and drink stand in Lavapiés for over twenty years, she wintered in Lima when it was summer there, it seemed like a smart way to make a living and though her skin looked the age of my body or maybe a few years older her disposition was much younger, she could easily whip out an extra table or chair if the place was crowded and the cops weren't around. Even if life felt too hard, even if getting out of bed felt like pushing against a weight

which never diminished, I would continue to love this neighborhood, even the *perro flauta* teenagers with their dirty dogs and their grating shouts of *pues y nada*, and the local drunk we had dubbed Moneditas for her singsong pleas for euro coins, who was nervy enough in her Spanish sense of entitlement to hit up even the West Africans who banked at the Caja Madrid, and the Ecuadorian man, another cast member from the Plaza Lavapiés Boozers, who was dancing one morning to music playing from the boombox on his shoulder, 80s style, the song was Ladies Night, and it was raining, and was it the rain or was it the song that made the scene absurdly funny and not absurdly tragic, or was it both, and the Bangladeshi and Indian and Pakistani men who owned the middle part of calle Lavapiés, and called out to you to stop and eat as you climbed the hill of Washfeet, and the woman from Sri Lanka who owned the frutería around the corner, whose husband tended to their baby while she weighed the vegetables and counted out your change, and the Spanish woman who washed the wooden stairs of the old corrala building where you lived, whose cat always ran underneath your legs as you ascended the five flights to your attic apartment, but here is Yoli coming toward you now, inviting you to sit down, so sit and order a tinto de verano with lemon ice, the lazy man's sangria, thinking this is all you need, in certain moments, to be happy.

The drink comes to me in a plastic stein, the limonada shavings floating over the cold red wine served alongside a small bowl of patatas fritas, and I take a sip and munch on one of the potato chips. The crumbled flakes land in my lap more than in my mouth, but no matter. The Lavapiés Twins lumber by and it is when I see them that I know this day is perfect in spite of my condition and the condition of the world and the relentless heat. They are wearing their appliquéd jeans and walking as they always do, very slowly, arms linked, and are positioned strategically so that each puff-painted cartoon dog is showing itself off on the light blue denim of each sister's outer thigh. I brought nothing with me to record the moment so I click them with the eyes. They are not really twins, these two little old ladies, their faces look nothing alike, although their outfits and gait are always perfectly matched, your friends say they're lovers but most likely they're widows, sisters maybe, who have each other and who dress alike because that was how their mother did it, and it never occurred to them to do it differently, even if they both look to be not a day younger than seventy. Each is wearing a blue plastic bracelet and pink blouse the same color as the cartoon dog's tongue. Their arms are crooked like questions which they answer for each other, and their backs curve forward into their rocking gait. Everybody, everybody loves the Gemelas de Lavapiés, and I wonder if they are privy to the

neighborhood's curiosity and goodwill. Curiously, they sell postcards of the twins at the sex shop behind the theater just a block from Yoli's bar. I wonder if they've ever been inside.

My drink empty and my legs itchy I get up and head toward the Reina Sofia, a museum whose air conditioning I like better than its paintings, but at least I can spend a few hours there without sweating too much. Walking up the calle Doctor Fouquet past the Librería de Lavapiés, I catch my reflection in a small gallery window and see the wig hairs sticking up in the middle of the head giving my disheveled appearance the finger. The window has sticky vinyl letters across it which seem ready to peel off, the art galleries of real importance are in the Barrio de Salamanca near Franquista furriers and fashion boutiques, this one has the contemporary sheen of a Chelsea space but is ten times smaller and the silver letters on the window say PUMA QUACKENBUSH — WORLD TRADE, and I think this is news to me or I had forgotten but the Reina can wait, I guess, I go inside. The bespectacled assistant hiding in a glass-walled office in one corner ignores my entrance, as gallery assistants do. The walls of the space are painted straightjacket white, and from them hang so many photographs, a record of someone else's time. In one of the pictures, an artist stands in front of a painting with the fingers against the lips, obviously mimicking the image on the canvas of a man wearing what was obviously a wig on the head, one young then gone, the other dead or close to dying. New York. There is no checklist, just a photocopied press release, which I ignore, and a projection against one wall. The info card says: WORLD TRADE, 11 SEPT 2011 (DVD, 24 HORAS, EDICIÓN 4 DE 11.

I sit on the bench and look at the video before me: images of the absence of buildings. That is my interpretation, anyway, you could also say it was a very slow film about the sky. But it didn't bother me when things were boring, especially when so much of life was made up of the dreary: waiting in lines, stamping forms, waiting in cells, trapped inside these bodies, these containers which would continue to betray us. It was nice to clear your head before an artwork that wasn't too insistent about how you looked at things, I always thought Beckett would have made a good dictator of some small European principality like Andorra, with his fussiness and precise insistence on a certain kind of reception, as if that were something you could control, as if you would want to. Oh, but we wanted to, of course. The image was in color but the color was almost drained from it, as if color were an afterthought to the viewing. A voice whispered so low I almost couldn't hear what it was saying. I took out my recorder and recorded it to get it back. This is some of what was said:

I remember once my dad was giving me a ride to the airport in New Orleans. I don't remember where I was flying to, maybe it was Madrid, my parents lived only a mile or two from the airport and it was summer, which meant everything was full and green and hot and humid to the point of being sticky. There were these tiny green lizards that were always around and they would eat whatever bugs they could get. In the blue minivan my father drove me to the airport in we were only a block from the house when I looked out the passenger-side window to see a tiny lizard, a baby really, clinging there. The car was still going pretty slow so it seemed to stay on the glass without too much trouble, but it wasn't a gecko, it was one of those brown lizards that change color from green to brown to green, just enough change to make you love them, with those throats that open out to lusty pinks when they breathe, this lizard must have found itself a little lost on its journey and I didn't know what to do. Seeing that little lizard there, trapped, clinging to the van window, and knowing that once the car sped up, it likely wouldn't make it, made me so sad for the creature's fate. I thought maybe when we got to the airport I could save it and then it could be an airport lizard and help people check their bags or hand out peanuts to disgruntled customers who were sick of waiting, the ones who line up hours before their designated boarding time, this little guy would be friendly in spite of his predicament, though I think he would have missed the green of our backyard. He hung on for most of the journey and I wondered what he was thinking, I watched him the whole way. It was only as we drove under the I-10 overpass that something in him ceded, we weren't going that fast, in fact my father was decelerating to a red-light intersection, but his webbed feet couldn't stick to the glass any longer and he blew away. I knew then, I understood in that moment, that our experience of Death would come for us in that same way, without mercy, although there was mercy, perhaps, in Death's insistence on the unexpected, in that her arrival and our departure times were forever a mystery.

The enemy is dead, long live the enemy. The image a projection of blue sky the color of blue sky with white clouds which do what white clouds do, they are drifting. They seem to drift more slowly than they should, as in a silent movie,

the sky the absence is what you would say if you had written the press release. I think about bodies lying in beds, sleeping, buildings shining like the superstars they outlast, collapsing, bodies in oceans, bodies trapped in rooms, bodies dead, drifting. A body could never outlive our aspirations the way clouds do. The video had left me far too pensive and the concept seemed better than the content and what kind of cracked-out name was Quackenbush, anyway.

I decided I needed to work, so I went back home and took some gesso and laid it on a small canvas and spread it around, and cut out paper dolls while the chalk dried. With my black marker in letters running up the canvas I wrote the necessary words: YOU DISAPPOINT ME. I cut out the faces of the dolls and glued the backs of the bodies onto the canvas. I thought about signing the work but what would I put there, so I signed nothing. I didn't know whether I liked the finished product, but at least it was done. Through the skylight so many birds could be heard crying out.

MIKE CROSSLEY

Predictive text

Nighttime in Ojai. I drank from the Casitas & shapeshifted into what who knows. An out of body experience. Brunch in Santa Rosa sounds like the worst. *Non je ne regrette rien mais regrette.* Next thing you know you self destruct 6–10 PM every other day. Thispanic attack starter pack. Thin air clean water good food & other supplies. Woke shit. Oak view sulphur mountains—the way the borders light up. Some of my friends sell drugs unincorporated w/ a certain stoicism. We don't have to unpack that.

R&B

A small battery powered tv in Manchester Square
I'm going to tell you some things you may already know
Urban blight's the criminalization of mental illness
Sometimes it's hard to make it work
& that's what this is: swaying palm trees,
idling traffic, a 67% increase in foreclosures
2015, Main & Spring, the 101 FWY
Remember Pam? You didn't know her but she died
Your staunched expression
The evergreen mercado

"I died and came back." —KRAIG GOINS

This space is late 1970s south central
No social security or health insurance but we are destined for change
The aerospace industry in the mid 90s, a Hawaiian chocolate factory
King-Drew Medical; fatal confrontations with police, this covert war
Some days we die and come back to life
It didn't used to be like this, the rain, the shear in two

RAQUEL GUTIÉRREZ

The Bar In My Neighborhood

has a mural on its wall where fantastical eggs boiled hard come home to wives with rolling pins leaving their lives, livers and lovers behind; they ensured a lively crowd tonight. Everyone is crackling and we take it upon ourselves you and me her and I for everyone mapping the pronouns thinking even pronouns can stop in at the local dive bar for a stiff one without ass grab beer back Tucson notorium. Through the storied doors the eau du jour of bleach and urinal cake bleaching out ghosts. There was nothing to step over but we did. We go inside and mind you I love a dive bar but the ersatz of disinfectant and even the heavy handed dissonance in the way disinfectant already signals its killable prowess weirds me out, its disinfectant cloud spray from the rafters is a nasal drip heralding the dirtiest place in the world clogging my esophagus. Oh The Buffet. I could eat my dinner there but all to say my life has taken an unexpected turn and that can be satisfying in the ways posthumous forgiveness or fame can possibly be satisfying but I guess I'll never know and you don't agree anyway because you argue that someone is bound to remember your flaws when you're no longer here to provide an overestimation of accomplishment. We walk into the bar and I am flooded with punchlines as well as gratitude that you're wearing pants at this Soul Train line of unwanted wayward hands that wander indisciminantly or would have had we stayed but the smell alone. My god, the smell. I could die in my tracks, stopped by the charge of cliché a well worn groove so lubricated I can not help but get into. I have said and have been held to this declarative utterance that I will get hammered here when I have a monumental event to celebrate as now I live next door to the dive bar you and I once tried to have a drink at. The cruelty of that memory now seared into skin each time I walk by every morning making its rounds for the graveyard shifts. This dive bar is around the corner from one of our Airbnb haunts where we holed up in for a week and I paid the whole things a month's rent in 2001 Los Angeles for eight days in Tucson. You didn't offer to pay half and being with you was not just that kind of expensive. I'd rather write you these devastating poems of meander and melancholy then have to wait for the train to decide its way South and West or keep its sorry caboose in the

Middle North. The Sephoras are better here. Southwest your way back to me the middle seat longing for the aisle. You called my poems crass and my anger crass and you say they startle you with their charge. And I read about Benjamin and Brecht because that is what I do now in your absence, I keep myself read at the ready thinking crudely together as a way to inhabit meaning because everyone could use a drink. The Buffet is one of the oldest bars built to serve the workers of the nearby railroad depot in the Iron Horse district of Tucson. Deference is the preference so I will take my crudeness and keep it a gorgeous mode of theorizing my bad behavior, a code of flesh.

Wounded Deserter

Thorn the stud finder
all the way down

you had no
idea of this
frontier

how its skin was
trapped in my own skin

you soothed my sentinal
and met my refusal to
register touch with cognizant
dog star

passed and dignified
my fugitivity, new planets

one winter broken in two
as neon spring awaits

I deserve your kyanite
finger upside down

Momentum

Semi-expectedly
I run into her
outside the pub and
on the periphery
I note
as I enter the group
with regular strokes
she zips and unzips her jacket

I thought
(therapy
and pills
three years)
you were in America
she says/I didn't
know you were back
(since May)

she: assisting a film
two months in London
doesn't say if
it's an internship
(paid or unpaid)
I don't say
I live with my rich girlfriend
whose wallet photo I hide
while I pay for a Guinness
at the bar
rent free
unspeaking inside
we sit almost conjoined/

speaking with others/
I sat
by her side expecting
to speak with her speak
with Carl instead
about creative writing
and class (socioeconomic)
student debt
his mean prospects and
the many dogs he walks
one of his three jobs
his episodes of homelessness

humbled
and bored
I hold back
our common complaints
incase

(comment
on the bar's kitsch
Carl dislikes
grandeur/cosy
chalkboard, leather, taxidermy)

all of this is borrowed
I should say
of my new material ease
this optimism has been loaned
to me
ask her

I wanted to speak to you/
I really wanted to speak to you
she says
(not with)

a cigarette
outside
after a swollen pause
of passing cars
I say, how come? ('just did') I'm

I can't
say I still can't
can't even say
I blocked your emails
rarely googled your name

argued
with you almost everyday
in bed/commute to work/in class I'm I can't
can't even this
is a different brain from
the one that pursued you
with its sincerity
the metaphors
of crises are materially true:
now scientists show depression scars
the brain and shrinks
its faculties

trenches
I imagine
thoughts unable
to scale tall smooth walls
of narrow trenches
pacing lengths
and outside differences
so forgotten
the trench feels true
an unyieldable
comfort
longed for
like a cruel home

the world shrunk tight
around shrunken faculties
enjoying few friends
for example yours
entrenched
is still the name
I repeat to withdraw myself
in stressful situations/
preempt laughing
a mantra addressed
to myself in the second person:
'*your name* left you, *your name* left you'

I tell her of my research
on mental illness and identity
her friend
who has a trust fund
more valuable than my father's house
has begun a magazine
whose most recent theme
was the mind
she says
I should send them
something
no she says
when I ask if it pays
it was only a suggestion
I hold my

tongue
shrinking window cigarette
and cringe I—Carl
resented me some
my ease
I sensed
I've climbed

Care

In Walworth public library, London
a black woman with neurological difference
better call her perhaps anguished or ill, or stray
for hours stiffly paced the shelves
arm outstretched, tracing the spines
with fingertips slack as if enraptured
in a film running through sunlit meadowgrass
or a field of tall corn

I once passed her, swaying within herself
on the high street
sweats puddled around her Nikes
knickerless, unshaven
no one stopped, nor myself
except to stare

some bush
athwart the poundshop
window display's bogof deals
and a beatific and uncanny face
maybe misremembered
maybe petrified

many slept—slept in Walworth library (9–5)
narcoleptic trade off
of their meds
I guessed

one white alcoholic also
oracle of ochre jelly, marbled livid red
face down always in a splayed novel
prop or portal

unejected
staff rapped only
near sleepers' ears knuckles
on the regular desks
and pointed to the no sleeping sign

so long as they feigned reading
or dazedly fixed on the middle distance
everyone was tolerated

Magnificent, She Said
(January part 1)

Friday January 20
Toxic city.
Magnificent, she said.
Mantra. Fidelity. Shalom.
Just another California.
Plane waiting game, break apart.
Air, watch the stars.
Born. Future. Lithium.
Don't wait; keep it simple.
War in the valleys.
Qui es? Message personnel.
Stranger. Wow. Rainbow.
Singers on hold for the soul.
Amazing moments like these.
Cherry. Enter. Fin de siècle.
Will, dear velvet, new song.
Hands in your pockets you said goodbye.
Howlin' for you, Leslie.
Audition, whatever, wherever, looking for something.
Bye. Alone. Him.
Expectations.

Monday January 23
Essence. Toxic. Sleeping.
Romantic new song.
Love story: Debra.
Darkside, grown up kids.
Trying to believe.
Respect. Melancholy. Honey.
No one knows me, la femme.
Walking requests disarm; I dare you.
Old blues, bruises, withers.
Drive, infinite king.
Join hands, knock me off my feet.
Lost sky, I don't know you.
Quit tomorrow transmission.
All drifting, she said told you.
Everything reminds me.
Traveling echo, a new life.
Clean. Take a walk. Just break apart.
Winter ditch singers gambling.

Tuesday January 24
Get out. Other lives. We were.
Letter to the editor.
After the disco.
Forty five dog years.
Wonderland man.
Break apart. Key to life. Bold arrow.
Write. Keyboard. Storm.
Answer. Echo. Rattling.
Still moves in secret ways.
Hungry heart won't go away.
Lost hold up, mistakes.
Just say goodbye in your turnaround.
As if ambassadors, almost smiling now.
Fruit fever, gunpowder cry.
Nobody other, things to come.
Breath in; go back home.
Numb. Broke. Lifer.

Wednesday January 25
My love in the silence flies.
Picture the valley, go back home.
Little jungle alien, tune revival.
Dark river, firewood, forwardness.
All my dreams, king, mister monument.
Love is the drug. Self control, may it last.
People mover, she said.
It seemed the better way.
Lost sky, gun, noise.
Hiatus, shade under the factory.
Letter. Affair. Simple things.
Don't be shy when you know where you stand.
Guest, break apart, dead can dance.
Remix. Rich. Rewind.
Project.

No Echo

I thought you just got off
talking about my cum,
but you're stretching me out
with my spot in your hand
when it comes to me, clear
and slick—I see. It's
because I said I wished
I could shoot. I said so
a few times. It's true—
I only know how much
so once I say it.
Most of the time cis people just walk around,
fucking everybody with their huge stuff
and either cannot or choose
not to see the dark liquid
making cave noise
between the body and an
answer to its question.
Another body, everyone
has that, a moonlike body
in another world.
Most of the time living people just walk around
pretending only transsexuals do,
because we're better at it
and for much worse reasons.
But could you ever
have another body? God,
I hope not. I remember
thinking, I can't forget
the freckles resting

on his shoulders,
like an avant garde scarf,
the second time. No echo
in the cave. What could
improve? But I'm sure,
in there, you reach its end
somehow, dodging cars
on a bike, some arduous
activity like that. How hot.
The shady beach with still pools
and the overhang. The afternoon
dark from some quirk
of the land and the sun.
The water dark and cool and a relief
to my God-given hot body,
shaking while you say,
"I wanna bathe in your cum."
Why does anything I say sound
like I don't like it? I like it.

Room

All the time! I try to conceive of us,
not planning but settled, and close—
say, within groping distance. I'm trans,
I can't walk across rooms. I'm trans,
all the houses I've lived in have numberless
rooms. Someone told me once, one of my teachers,
that I said I too much. I made sentences.
I started them each time with I. Chris,
I try all the time. I imagine worlds
with us in them but in all those worlds,
I'm thinking; I'm alone. No one else presses
the stalk of their thought on my thought. Chris,
come wherever I am right now—I can't see the walls,
I cannot feel the molding on the ornate doors.

Psalm XXIII
Every flesh looks better

lacking it   unclothed like how my Father will
never look at how I am finally good enough

for His heaven. If I jump
to how this ends—let's

begin again. I slide into
the ritual bath of sand

& its salt laps my illness
calls it of-the-flesh   sloughs

it clean as grass until I lay or lie
or snore   the word for halo

rimming me   its burn
I tell you again:

I am good enough
for your heaven. I just finally found out

how to make my own   strawberry seeds
between my teeth sticking to it

like poppy seeds on fresh-buttered
buns   like freckles on His flesh

I wear this ritual:
sweet almond oil anoint me

into the land of the valley of the
shadow of death, for I fear no evil.

You are with me—
your rod and this staph do comfort

me as I dwell low in the tick
of it: hair & skin & muscle & instruments

fashion a cup for this   my heaven
you enter only unclothed & let me feel

each table of a leg set before me.
Even the enemies in my war

torn body pull back
when the bath

water baptizes me   its lavenders filling
my cup   running over you as the goodness

& mercy releases me
here: this watered-down dwelling where

prayer can expand between us
that holy slick that confuses five

years ago & five years from now—
Or was it for the sake of naming love?

Let's begin again. I see I AM
good enough now but what are the odds

I choose any heaven other than mine
own set before me?

ISAAC PICKELL

the stories (that) aren't told

he said there's nothing about us   *a psalm*
without us, dissolution as in:
stagnation, intransigence in black
life, pure force undiluted by
reparation, an unfamilial beauty
indebted to pale reflections whose
possibility for neutral remains
undiagnosed: it's too easy to say
white is neutral, splintered i:
dentities and emergent modes re:
defining oppression as a poetry
prompt, free use and always fair
trade, leaves only the purposeful
discontents disconnected. blackness

not neutral, the shape of the back of
my head is not neutral, the ways mother
names each of her grandparents in the blur:
red quadrants where my hair grows against
its best interests are not neutral, questioning
when I should apply what product, that part
behind your cowlicks, isn't that funny, I don't
see a lot of regular people with hair like that an:

other forms of mimicry: can a caricature resist
the smooth charcoal scratches darkening our own
outlines [prerecorded bodies poorly painted by ex:
pensive pencils rosying cheeks of toy soldiers] mimicry

are prerecorded bodies, [mimicry]
are masks, [mimicry] are pressed onto
postcards and offered free for museum
opening weekends, [mimicry] are now available
for purchase, [mimicry] are silhouettes of enslaved
bodies with intimate trans-Atlantic travel plans and
[mimicry] dreams of the rising white pillar of Washington's
monument you can't help but see when leaving the gift
shop where you're told all proceeds contribute to curating

the archives, [mimicry] are assumptions my body will be
curated, mocking blank blue screens after presentation
endings, read close enough every white text about black
text feels guilty for the open ocean, the water's only blue
in recreation, the earliest paintings, how poorly they capture
live bodies projected onto prerecorded bodies in the complex:
ions of masks I wear: what does my body feel when it touches
skin: outrageously magical things happen when you play around
without the semblance of a symbol

lesser homilies

discourse! the provenance of whiteness deserves more
working through, demands reprocessing language
past thought into instinct into the common idea:
logical heritages of man into every good philosopher
must once contend with kant into the theological
roots of hermeneutics demand we recall the sacred
responsibility unto King Kunta with a Black Jesus
hanging in his hut, framed with switches grand:
mother found behind the great house into the Other

should be capitalized, every retelling of Icarus
performed as an homage to our ancestors
drowning, unable to afford a plane ticket.

Icarus need not be a cautionary tale; learning
to read demands we draw very close to its

light, eyes and skin acclimate to abduction, all
our gods' children can have wings, in youth's
speculative poetics, line breaks don't fall into the sea.

In the hands of a black poet, what becomes of the oldest myths?
Can they stack or pool or bend, are they passed between bodies, slip
through fingers, soothe in slippage, break into creases, accelerate into
opacity, divination, the inevitable of warping what's left in common:

we are stoic, not silenced; we are laying lucidity
to rest; we are buying stock in the intractable Other.

the bad man's prophet ≡ the world's gone to hell

vulnerability to the unsanctioned premature
death is a birthright speculative and soluble

manifest as double sided reprinted slave
holds, our bodies always been match sticks.

we were printed in the same weight and shade
as the half-height walls and the rounded hull
smooth and human meant for a return voyage

we weren't offered our own reproductions were
not built for. enough of us drown becoming a pronoun.

The Language of a Perfect Woman

selected for the Summer Literary Seminars Prize

My mother told me about her ALS diagnosis in an email. The text was in pink. She said she had lost some mobility in her hands. She ended the email with the following postscript: "I feel pretty good day to day. I have trouble with zippers, but can dress myself. It's hard to turn a key, but it can be done. Please don't feel bad for me. I'm giving you this information because I want you to know. There is nothing you need to do for me." I was two towns over when I got it. The subject of the email asked me not to come over.

John was zipping up his pants in the back of his Subaru as I stared into the dull light from my phone.

"Are you okay?" he asked, rubbing my back.

He squeezed my spine between his fingers. The gesture was so intimate and so uniquely John that I thought about telling him. Then his phone vibrated. He texted Christine back, and the intimacy was redirected.

"Oh, yes, of course." I said, and scrolled through every social media app on my phone in a stab at casualness. He dropped me off at my old apartment next to the Chinese Supermarket that smelled like pickled kimchi, and he drove home.

I googled how to feel. People say that you can feel however you want to, but they're wrong, there is definitely a right and wrong way to feel, especially when it comes to dying mothers. Even saying the word "dying" is not okay. It's "passed away" or "lost" like we would find these dead people under a couch cushion one day. I wanted to feel the way that people wanted me to feel. I didn't want anyone to get mad at me for some unsaid social norm I wasn't fulfilling. The internet said it was okay to feel angry (as long as you weren't angry for very long) and the internet also said "get ready to accommodate your loved one!" and that is when I realized that ALS was going to be an expensive way to die. Wheelchairs, handicapped bathrooms, treatments that may work but probably wouldn't, doctor's appointments where stern doctors would report that "yes, you're still dying" and live-in nurses and, Jesus, many, many other things that

my mother, a public school teacher, would never be able to afford. I had to move in with her. It was the only way this was going to work.

"You can't do that, people will think I'm dying," my mother said, when I showed up uninvited the next day.

I told her that she was, in fact, dying.

"Nobody likes dying people," she said. "We're not telling anybody except your aunts."

I told her that I googled a wheelchair that she would need and it was nearly three thousand dollars and that we should start an online fundraiser like what normal dying people do in order to pay to die comfortably.

"This is why I didn't want to tell you," she said. "Lost. Season Two. Episode Three." She diverted her attention back to the television. She had gotten a Smart TV that recognized her voice. The remote control sat unused on the coffee table. A talisman to show me that she could use it when I could see by the way she moved her hands that she couldn't. She had been dealing with this longer than she was letting on, and I didn't know. We hadn't talked regularly since I moved out of John's house and moved two towns over. She had screamed at me then. She told me that I was giving up on a good life, and that I was giving up on John. I said that I wasn't like her. She said I was more like her than I thought.

"I'm telling John," I said. She closed her eyes for a long time and spoke in a voice that she used to speak to her special ed first graders.

"If you tell him, I will kill myself." This is the exact kind of dramatic proclamation she thrived on, like when I was four and she told me if I didn't say three Hail Mary's before the plane took off that it would crash into the side of a mountain. Something about this statement in particular struck me as more than just dramatic forewarning. She said it like somebody who had looked up exactly how to kill herself and was going to do it right. After that I packed up my stuff, broke my lease, and moved into the guest room.

I did not tell John, which was easy, because he was a new father and a new husband. John talked to her, though. Once a week on the phone. John's mother had died when he was seven and my mother became his de facto mother. She took him shopping for back-to-school clothes. She invited him over for taco casserole when his father worked late, which was often. She spoke at his wedding to Christine, even though it hurt for her to do it, just because he asked. She loved him.

I kept thinking that John would notice the way her hand gestures had deflated or that the wheelchair wasn't because of a road rage incident in the Sam's Club parking lot, but so far he hadn't questioned her flimsy excuses. Perhaps he had noticed, but didn't want to. I told myself that it was a good thing, because when I was with him I didn't want to think about this new life of mine: helping my mother in the bathroom, endless seasons of procedural television (my mother only likes television that she can predict the third act of), and nursing night school.

I had meandered through my twenties doing odd jobs, from farm work in Bakersfield (never again) to working at Starbucks (latte art can go to hell). I didn't have a burning passion for any specific career, but my mother believed in that American "Live Your Dream!" mentality and I knew deep down if I didn't pick something soon, my life would only get smaller. Nursing seemed like a stable, somewhat dignified career that didn't make me want to puke (unlike Marketing: age 23) and I knew it would help us out with hospice bills down the road. It didn't hurt how thrilled everyone was that I chose such a Practical Career. My aunts were delighted, mostly because they sidestepped my mother's illness completely, as if they would catch it by doing too many favors for her. They figured if I was a nurse, and it was literally my job to take care of my mother, that they could continue being supportive from a distance.

The only person who didn't approve was John, who, whenever I got some aspect of my life together, took it as a personal affront that I hadn't done it when we were together (actually together, before he married someone else and starting meeting me in parking lots).

Six months later, it was my mother who said we had to go to the baby's first birthday party.

"I'll drop you off for sure," I said, painting my toenails light purple.

"We should both go." I stopped mid toenail and looked up at her. She was feigning being casual, pretending to concentrate on the newspaper in front of her.

"The baby won't even remember it," I said finally. John's wife Christine had made a video, set to a string-quartet version of a contemporary rock song, of the baby looking confused at various points in his first year of life. The baby, confused at the hospital. The baby, confused in a swimming pool. The baby, confused at a Chinese restaurant. "The baby will just be confused," I concluded.

"It's not about the baby," my mother reprimanded me. I glared at her. I was pretty sure John had only invited me out of obligation and to avoid any suspi-

cion he would raise by *not* inviting me. We had known each other since birth, and try as we might, there was no disentangling our lives. We grew up in the same apartment complex before my mother had finally saved up for a house. My aunt did his aunt's hair. His cousin did my taxes during my "freelance artist" phase. Our families were intrinsically linked. Under other circumstances, I would have said no, but she was dying, so I said yes.

I helped her take her pills, fed her some homemade cabbage salad with her fork, listened to her tell me the cabbage salad was not that good, which was true; strapped her in the wheelchair and followed her down the plywood ramp our handyman neighbor built, secured her wheelchair to the back of the van that I was struggling to make the payments for, stopped for two gifts, and drove to John's baby's first birthday party.

John and Christine lived in the nice part of town in the new-style McMansion—modern with big windows and polished concrete floors, identical to every house around it. My aunts greeted me warmly. My nice-but-anxious aunt told me they would be on bathroom duty for my mother during the party, much to my bitchy aunt's chagrin. I think they did it so they could remind me of it years later when I asked them to take my mother to a doctor's appointment. *Oh, Sophie, remember that time we were on bathroom duty at John's baby's first birthday?* I also thought, though, that they felt bad for me. As many times as I have told them that I broke up with John, they don't seem to believe me. They think he dumped me for Christine and that she took the life I wanted.

John greeted me cooly, and my mother very warmly, which she loved. We arrived late (my fault, on purpose) and were already on the gift-giving segment of the party.

I could tell by the look on Christine's face that the shovel was a huge mistake. The baby was delirious, with food smeared all over its fat little face. Christine held the full-sized shovel with a constipated look, as John watched through the camera app on his iPhone, cycling through facial expressions, trying to find one that would make everyone happy. My mother shook her head, and used the joystick on her wheelchair to wheel herself over to the Sauvignon Blanc. Christine was trying to salvage the situation. Christine's parents looked furious. Everybody else was drunk.

"It's a joke," I tried to explain. "When John and I were kids we used to joke about getting babies shovels at their first birthday party so they could be good Marxists who took pride in their work." I laughed, but nobody else did. "It's like an anti-Capitalist thing, we were dumb teenagers." I could see now that I should have gotten a smaller shovel, or maybe a shovel actually meant for babies, instead of the full-sized one from the dollar store.

"Oh, how adorable," Christine said, trying to understand.

"Ha-ha," John said and patted me on the back very hard. "What's next, babe?" he said to Christine. The air of relief was palpable when John, on the baby's behalf, opened my mother's gift, which was a $17 book about field mice that talked. I took that as an opportunity to back away and stand next to the hunk of marble John and Christine used as a cheese plate. My mom navigated her ALS by using both hands to gulp wine from her stemless glass. The doctor said she shouldn't drink, that she should really be on the paleo diet; she said, "I think early man would want to get wasted too, if he'd had ALS."

"How expensive do you think this is?" I glanced at the marble, then ate four pieces of cheese. She examined it, nudged it with her elbow to get a feel for its weight. It was dyed bright blue and shaped like a wine bottle.

"$700," she said, returning her attention back to the present parade. One of John's colleagues' wives had knit a hat. Christine was squealing and hugging the woman tightly.

"How?" I asked hopelessly. I couldn't afford supermarkets; for the last three months I'd lived off strange cuts of chicken and Jasmine rice from the corner store. My money went to my mother's medication, and her diet, which I was purchasing from a chef in the rich part of town who had an uncle with ALS. John and Christine had clean counters, and expensive cheese, and a high chair that connected to an iPad.

"This all could have been yours, you know," she said, and motioned for me to pour her another glass of wine.

I poured her wine and tried, very fixedly, to appraise an abstract painting over the fireplace. So, *that's* why we were at this stupid party, to remind me that I dumped John, and that he was now rich and married, to a beautiful, poised woman, and I was just me. She still resented me for taking this away from her.

Christine placed a nicely-wrapped gift onto the high chair. The baby grabbed at the package, unsure what to do with it, and then threw it on the floor. Everybody roared with laughter. Christine looked towards the heavens. John noticed and put a reassuring hand on her back. She tensed her shoulders and pivoted away from him.

A toddler waddled between the grown-up legs. He had drool all over his red cheeks; a bubble of spit pulsated and exploded at regular intervals. His hand clutched a pair of car keys that he was using to whack at people's shins. They chuckled awkwardly, looking side to side for the child's keeper, but too afraid to actually discipline him. Finally, a flustered blonde woman in an expensive look-ing blouse confiscated the car keys, scooped the boy up in her arms, wiped his

mouth off with a handkerchief and set him back down to continue his rampage. He promptly went up to John's baby's high chair and started shaking it like a coconut tree.

"Oh my!" Christine said cheerfully, the spaces around her eyes hollowed out. She seemed unable to move. John began to talk very fast and authoritatively, with an erect back, as though he were giving a speech. That was a sign that John was panicking.

"Oy," my bitchy aunt said, spitting out a kalamata olive pit onto her black plastic party plate. The boy's mother was nowhere to be found. I supposed she was weeping in the bathroom. Meanwhile, the high chair was wobbling violently. Nobody was doing anything.

I marched towards the high chair and lifted John's baby awkwardly out of it, balancing him on my forearm, with his wet mouth burrowing into my purple sweater. I bounced him a few times, which was much harder than I thought it would be. I was proud of myself. The single woman with no child-rearing aspirations saves the day.

The toddler on the ground promptly sunk his newly formed teeth into my shin. I yelped and piled the baby into Christine's arms, refrained from kicking the toddler, and steadied myself with the kitchen island. It took a moment for the blood to flow. Then it started to gush. The blood made the toddler aware that he'd done something wrong. To hide his guilt, he began to scream.

"What have you done?" The blonde, glassy eyed and fresh from the bathroom, rushed over to the toddler and scooped him up. The parents gathered around her and cooed reassurances. I exited to the backyard, leaving a trail of blood on the nice concrete floor.

There is something repulsive to me about having children, and how obsessed everyone in the world seems to be about having children. It's like they can't fall in love properly with other people, and need to create a little copy of themselves that they can fall in love with and care about. They believe, I think, that a little blob of like-minded flesh will deliver them meaning. I tried to explain this to John once, but he didn't understand.

"That's not what it's about," he said, taking my hand urgently in his, as if the gesture would change my entire point of view. "It's about creating life," he said, robotically. Creating life was exactly what I *didn't* want to do. There was too much life already. I even brought up adoption, but he wouldn't have it. He wanted *our* child.

My mother said I was just afraid. I had started to wonder if she was right.

I was more staunch about my beliefs before she had gotten sick. I wanted to believe that the idea of marriage and creating a family was some bizarre construct we had codified into a social norm. My life had become so difficult since then though. If I stayed with John at least I would have had a partner to help me through all this.

"Here." John appeared, carrying a small lunch box with a first aid sign on it. The kit looked small in his big hands. He reached for my leg and examined it. He wiped the blood away with a linen napkin. Two puncture wounds, like a vampire. He smeared the cuts with an antibiotic cream.

"Aren't you glad I'm not the mother of your children?" I intended for this to be a joke.

"You would be a great mother," John said quietly, and tied the the gauze around my leg in a neat bow. I could have stopped him from bandaging me. I was in nursing school after all, but I liked the feel of John's hand on my leg. I slid down to the patio next to him and rested my head on his shoulder even though I knew it was dangerous to do so. I stared at the little creek that some developer built behind John's house. It was nice.

I told him that I was sorry about the shovel.

"I can't believe you remember that," he said, shaking his head, but smiling.

"I remember all our idiotic teenage philosophies." John used to be different. He was handsome. He had color in his face. He ran five miles every morning. He sometimes would pick me up in the middle of the night to take spontaneous trips to the coast, to watch the sun rise over the ocean. It made me sad to see him now. He had bags under his eyes. His skin had a gray pallor to it and hung limply from his jaw. He had started to get a gut that bulged out over his stained khaki pants. He had a cell phone holder attached to his belt. He had nervous lines around his mouth. He looked sad. Every parent looked so sad.

"I'm glad you came anyway," he said, and looked deeply into my eyes, like I was the best and most beautiful girl in the world. At that moment, I wanted to tell him about my mother, about how scared I was. I wasn't ready for her to die. I wasn't ready to watch her die. I wasn't ready for the world without her, because even though she was difficult, and mean, and stubborn, she was my mother and when she died I would have nobody who actually loved me, which was selfish and made me feel even worse. I knew he would be kind. He would hold these things in his hands, and hold me in his arms, and it would be all right. Instead, I said nothing and he stroked my hair, letting his hand linger near the nape of my neck. I closed my eyes and wished I was different. I would be with John in a house similar to this one and we would have a pound of flesh

cuter than his current baby and people would be nicer to me, because I'd be normal.

"John, it's time for cake." Christine appeared in the doorway with a spatter of apple sauce on her collar. The color drained from her face as she watched John leap to his feet, almost pulling my hair out in the process. I stayed on the ground.

"Yes, cake, of course! It's a Star Wars one," he said in a very high pitched voice and rushed out. Christine stared at me, motionless.

"How are you feeling, Sophie?" she asked.

"Totally fine, just a flesh wound, but I totally might head out. Blood plus the wine is getting to my head!" Whenever I talked to Christine I tried to speak some other language, one spoken by perfect women, but I always got it wrong and sounded broken. Before I could try to flee, she kneeled on the concrete next to me and folded her hands in her lap. She tried to start a sentence a few times. I braced myself. This is the moment she tells me that she knows that her husband sees me every Wednesday and fucks me in his Subaru Forester, at the park where we used to mess around as teenagers. She knows that he calls me most nights and talks to me after my mother goes to sleep. She knows that he still tells me he loves me. She knows all this because the wife always knows. She wants me gone forever. I am a slut, and a terrible person, who will never be happy.

"I am so sorry about your mother," is what she said instead, and it took me a minute to really understand. "ALS?" she asked.

"Yes," I said, finally, bowing my head.

"John doesn't know." Christine said.

"No," I said. "My mother doesn't want anybody to know."

"I don't think he likes to notice when other people need him, " she said. She reached for my hand and held it for a moment. "I know he spends a lot of time with her." I tried to take my hand away, but she squeezed it harder. "I think that's good. I think at some level he knows." The baby started crying and she released my hand. She stood, brushed off her dress, and smiled. "Your secret is safe with me," she said, and then she walked back inside to a chorus of excited voices.

I ended up staying for cake. The baby knocked it off the table.

"Let's go," my mother said, and I followed behind her as she wheeled down the front path to the van. John stopped me at the door.

He looked around like a cartoon adulterer and said in a low voice, "So, I'll see you Wednesday?"

"I don't know, I had to change my Microbiology class to Wednesdays."
This wasn't true, and as I said it, I had no idea why I said it. Inside the house,
Christine was looking at us. She caught my eye, then continued cleaning off
the cheeseboard with a towel.

"Oh, okay, call me then," he said. I hugged him, not really caring what
anyone would say. I could smell the John I remembered, faintly—it was under-
neath the new John smell, but it was still there. I closed my eyes and focused on
it, the cigarettes, and arroyo willows on the street we grew up on, and sweat. He
was startled and only patted my back a few times. I released him, and turned to
open the back of the truck for my mother.

"What was that all about?" my mother asked, as she wheeled past me into
the truck.

"I am not going to this kid's second birthday party," I said. I buckled her
chair into the van and slammed the door shut.

Later that night, my mother was sprawled out on the hospital bed in her
bedroom. I sat in a chair next to her and lay my head down on the white sheets
that smelled like her rose lotion. A doctor show was on the television; a hand-
some doctor was talking about an "experimental surgery" to correct someone's
amnesia.

"That is not what real life is like," my mother observed.

I agreed with her. Nobody got miracle surgeries. Doctors were not in the
miracle business.

"I'm glad you're here, Sophia," she said, and suddenly her hand was tangled
in my hair. She couldn't use it to stroke my head the way she had when I was a
child, but she flopped it onto my head. It was warm and moist from the lotion.

"You know, goose?" That was a pet name she hadn't used in a long time.
"Not many people would do this."

"Watch old episodes of *ER*?" I asked.

She didn't laugh. "You were brave today." She let her hand linger for a
while in the nest of my hair. I looked up at her but she was staring at the screen.
Yesterday, I would have panicked at that statement. I would have wondered if
she knew about John and me. Today, I just believed her.

"I know this is not what we wanted," she said. "but maybe it's good. Maybe
it'll give us time to say goodbye." I thought about how this illness had been the
worst thing that has ever happened to me. At least that's what I'd been telling
myself for the past six months in order to cope. My mother is dying and I am
the only person who wants to take care of her. I had never thought that maybe
watching a parent die slowly is a gift in a strange way. We could say goodbye to

each other in small ways every day. I pushed my head into her arm and she bent over to kiss me.

"Now put me to bed," she said. We were back to our regularly scheduled programming: I recline the hospital bed flat. I place the mask of her Bipap machine on her face and pull the strings so it fits snugly; she makes a noise, and I adjust the straps until she nods. I flip the switch, and the machine whirs to life, and then I untwist the tubing so it doesn't catch on the drapes. She catches my wrist with her hand and squeezes.

DONG LI

the army dreamer

the river rolled patiently
                                        the crossing ceased quietly
she would gaze for hours beating clothes on the bank
                                        warily her years
if she spilled soup on the table she had to stand in the courtyard
                                        she would fall asleep against lichened wall
she stole family identity papers from her mothers wardrobe
                                        the threshold crossed
no turning back
                                        family disappearing in her mind
her travels her
                                        life was to begin
no traveler brought a good name to the family
                                        a dark green truck was waiting for her
started on horse engine
                                        noise overriding the river
falling prey to winter
                                        she startled in the back of the truck
the dark grey fabric illuminated by the moon
                                        waning inside herself
complete darkness of the interior
                        the orange tree in the family courtyard shined through frost
her mind went black
                                                                        ✳

oranges dropped in the faraway orchard
                                        light was turned on
she would cross the river
                                        she would join the army
she was not married off
                                        she was free
behind her ears she thought of happiness

                                                    ✳
                              from yangtze river to yellow plateau
a loose strand of hair
                                 an owl asleep on the stiff branch
she went away
                                            eventually
prairie in the foreground of her mind
                                        the river rolled
crossing quietly
                                                    ✳
the maid of honor has been dead for a long time
                  han dynasty receded into unnamed graveyards outside the wall
bones picked by birds
                                        in whipping sandstorms
only teeth glittered
                                        when light shone
when rain
                                        she was crossing
the dry river
                                        the grass high
sheep flashed over the paling moon
                                        she was ready
the emperor saw her off
                                     marriage sealed her red veil
she joined the hun parade against the picking wind
                                 her hun husband was by her side
he built her a yurt in a faraway place
                 the middle kingdom culture she passed onto the barbarians
the han emperor died a year after she was gone
                      she died sixty years before han dynasty crumbled to ashes
before barbarians tore apart the great wall
                                                    ✳
                                            come
easy to come
                                        go so difficult
to go
                              years laundered in the long long river
easy to part

                                        difficult to see you again
grief of love and hate runs deep in the grain
                                whispers dwindled between sand and stars
outside the wall
                                        smell of tumbleweeds
long pavilion by the ancient route
                                grass green to the edge of the sky
wind fingered willows
                                        flute died out
sunset mountain over mountain
                                the han dynasty went under
the hun crossed the ying mountain
                                the maid of honor has been dead for a long time
she could not find her step in the river

                                        ✳

                                as she herded sheep and meshed with grass
her sister was sent to the north to plant rice
                                up to the mountains down to the villages
maos slogans flapped in her face
                                        she also joined the army
daydreamed in her brown pupils
                                her hands bloated in rice paddies
she shaved her head and dumped her hair in campfire
                                her mind was never clear again
she dreamed
                                        on a night train
she crossed
                                she shuffled over the threshold
come easy
                                                come
go
                                        so difficult to go
years laundered in the long long river
                                        part easy to part
difficult to see you again
                                grief of love and hate runs deep in the grain
smell of dead husbands dead parents

*

the cultural revolution was over
the rustication movement was over

*

time changes

                                        economic prosperity
one way ticket to hell

                                        for parents
happiness

                                        deng opened china
the river rolled like a hand about to touch

                        quickly morning and evening on the other bank
years in the middle

                        the eyes could fixate on a point and see
remember

                                        after a long walk
from besieged city to river town

                she was beaten when the water bucket was not full
she would rather spend the night with stray dogs in the street

                        one day she left without moving her hands
the threshold still fired in her mind

                                        time past the river
disappearing

                                        covered
mutely

                                        she married herself off
family ties severed

                                        the town was small
she was laid off by the job assigned to

                                        she went to sea
business not for the respectable

                                        divorced
forced

                                        she opened a food stall
by the railway station

                                                    her legs became strong

running away from the police

                                                            permitless

years rivered on the side

                                        in her mind the threshold still

she made ends meet

                                                        under a new roof

the food stall moved into the station

                                                she hired helping hands

fell in love with one of them

                                                            never married

marriage was never in her mind again

                                                she traveled far and foreign

rivers and shores

                                                train ride jumped on her

she went almost blind

                                                                came home

her parents dead for a long time

                                        before their graves in the countryside

she spit fire

                                                                        ✳

                                                        light across the river

flooded the banks

                        wave of skin shield of blood gushing through bare prairie

wind howled through rice fields

                                                    sweeping ears of fragrance

from river town to hill country

                                                from rice paddies to wheat field

the crossing again

                                                    the crossing never again

day slides against the anguish of night

                                                    time shredding the mind

fog and rain in the mountains

                                                army dreamer on a white horse

a sleeve of twilight pierced the prairie waters

day slides against night anguish time shredding the mind when
her parents grabbed her hand to leave the family garden she
screamed their hands were heavy weighing on the throat like a
tub of water everything poured

a chain of events a single catastrophe wreckage upon wreckage
before her bare feet dead log of bodies floated and lapped against
long shores of the yangtze north of nanjing more bodies burned
in dripping fat men women young old

someone stood up from the ditch and tore up his smeared white
shirt a white flag waved japanese soldiers signaled him to jump
back his hands behind his head he waited and when he looked
up liquids from his eyeballs squirted

thirty japanese soldiers broke into his house he opened the door
holes from head to toe they shot him his neighbor dropped his
knees on the ground and begged they shot him and stomped on
his crushed flesh his bones cracked the first man's wife hid under
the table with a one year old in her arms they dragged her out
snatched her baby screaming they chopped the baby up started
a fire ready to grill in the yard the mother gang raped her breasts
sheared off a beer bottle in her vagina

five japanese soldiers flung themselves into a room a father
and two daughters were having porridge gone bad smell
forced japanese soldiers to hold their noses bowls dropped jaws
opened they bound the father to a chair gang raped his teenage
daughters before him inserted bundles of chopsticks into their
vaginas hammering them in with bayonets then hacked off his
daughters heads and smashed their brains on his face

a fifteen year old girl sought shelter in an american school in
the safe zone carrying her six month old child a japanese soldier
teased his bayonet on her buttocks she spit he stabbed her slit
open her belly yakking at a bloody lump he yelled

someone jumped into the river with his brother japanese soldiers
threw grenades his brother shredded to pieces he floated on
his brothers body parts under the cover of night when japanese
soldiers were gone he swam ashore leaving pieces of his brother
behind he took clothes off a headless man and put them on
found his way to the nunnery under the roof in the eastern city
the nuns gave him a rice bowl

in a neighboring village four brothers ran a farm japanese
soldiers found them put the eldest in a canvas bag and ordered
the other three to set fire in a well they sank the other three and
dumped the charred bag and lit cigarettes

inside the city walls people were driven to the central square with
their bayonets and rifles japanese soldiers stripped them whipped
them to crawl on top of each other drove their tanks back and
forth left and right until the ground flattened dragged out those
still alive and forced them to dig a big ditch and throw in their
dead the alive piled hay then threw themselves into the ditch

she felt quiet the city intact for six dynasties a relic she looked
away fixtures and fittings of everything rags and rubbles rough
stones naked beams shattered masonry inaudible invisible
washing off the fatigue of days no question of botany no grass not
a blade in sight upon days parcels and sacks crates and cartons
shoulders bent under their burdens people looked small no eyes
could be seen

the world shifts the yangtze meanders people were sleeping she
did not look she would fly them to foreign shores then storm
fired in the back of her mind bluing candlelit like ghosts like
ravens like something flying back to night

{she was caught up}
{days}
{she was pushed to walk the long road}
{before her}
{the walk}
{they were flying}
{skyward}
{river to shore}
{like ghosts}
{like ravens}
{like something flying back}
{to night}
{look away}
{no shade out of the darkness}
{there was no time}
{to think}
{to act}
{time shreds}
{she was flying jellyfish like}
{no difference}
{float}
{lightly}
{lighter}
{lightest}

from Comfort

is lining the interior with unbleached muslin. is tacking a line of pockets inside. is freshening feather pillows : without wringing, they are exactly right. is treating chapped hands with a thick salve of lard & flour applied at night. is confusing brining with burning. was afraid the dog had been killed but toward morning he was heard scratching at the door : a halo of silt in the sink : watered-silk in the attic : the need to wax : the cylinder itself. is mottled, is beetles killed with dish soap, diluted. is skirting the melting snow that clings to the house-sides, as if cold lived there alone. is wall studs : either mold or a spirit collecting : is what is the meaning of : ownership, full, or nothing at all : is staying because sometimes a body doesn't know when to stop :

is making a morning of wrong moves. is heather hung out to dry. is sleeping in the same room as the stove. is putting a wet finger to the wind. is wiping sirup from small but growing hands. is growing eyes in the back of her head. is the outer eye opening inner. up with the sun : hedge fence about the black cherries. is patterned planting. is herself the orchard quincunx. is stopping after the second form : coming home to be married : troweling a circle of sprouts from a heart-rotted oak. is accused of killing her own :

you were standing there : holding my hand to the wax : i was holding in my other : multiple hands a range of remedies and chemicals : the liquids eating away their containers : artifice dropping into the natural : blending there : something forming and i was still standing : toe cramping : doling out advice (you transcribing it with a hunk of lead) : bucket-handles rutting my forearms : red lines : divots : standing in sleep like a horse : milk pouring down from the eaves : and i said (or was it she) :

beware this warm grip
          between generations

for i live in the brown space
where all is resolved

PACO MÁRQUEZ

a petrel …

nada
    nada importa
        nothing matters
evil has won
the worst did happen
but we survived
and hide happily
trying to find the others
find a way to peace and life
for future generations out
of sheer love
find the others
web a web
against the forces of the violent
and beautiful nature itself
pulling us back to the soil we are
nothing matters
but those are just words
a conscience is the most secret bird
housed next to a quiet window in the back
of our body
evil won
so we are forgiven
for our idiocy as mother nature
will hold us in outer space one day
away from gravity and earth
her bosom as to a baby

nada en un río tibio
swim like a petrel flying underwater

Leaf on Water

we nap in grass while birds chirp.
     later we lounge to rain at the open window
with incense, wax, and lime rinds
     at sunset, descend the trapdoor
into the colonnade chamber
     through which a river flows,
wade the shallow water—
     carp rest above the mosaic
of no God's face.
the last sunlight fills the chamber
     and sinks into the river.
we are so quiet we
blend with the walls

MATTHEW KOSINSKI

A Coin Purse of Króna

this thick cube of sharks
                   meat / hot exhale tinted sulfurous

     not the color blue
     but its milk
     against the vista

     & the volcano that shattered itself

     my wife slits the cream of an auks egg / a birch twig sexes the liquor
                   / static shot of the parliament building 24/7

            when a whale corpse wound up ashore
            the entire village feasted

            for days /
            now the boats pilot closer

            / like the sudden appearance of an obelisk
             designed to vanish continuously

An Hurtful Angel
With a line from Austin Osman Spare

How long
have we stood in line
for this
peepshow? In a
waste
-land of
ecstasy, each
tepid atom
in its cocoon of self
-love. Mutated
fruit flies
with eyes for legs.
Rows and rows
of clean
unopened
boxes on the
shelves. A truly
inspired use of
sacred geometry:
The floor plan
channels all
psychic
energy
through the
cash register.
How to keep
a people
hungry and
hidebound.
Cross-
legged at
the center
emitting a low
and steady *aum*
is a pig in his tie
and tails.

Who is the slayer of your gods but a god? Kingdoms are their own despoilers.

Dire straits
direct the
eye and the
ear
toward the public
square. You cannot
turn a poem
into a
protest.
All differences are
reconciled
through
body language.
People keep
climbing the
stairs but at the
top
a man shoves
them back
down.
The papers
treat it like a fall.
Think: reaching
for that baddest
apple. Think: Old
Scratch,
who ultimately
lost his privileges
because he
demanded a little
more slop for the
cosmic dog bowl.
Solidarity
means you get
one
and you get one.

                                 ma, I'm looking
                                        for silver—

                              to want to rise
                                    but you

                        [beggar]

                    regard the wine
                    while hoarding filth in your gown

           'you have nice teeth
           and such fine hands'

as if someone
placed bouquets in our junkyard

                  imitation bells carol while this—

                  a distant church

Approaching sleep

I.   *I acquiesce*

by way of the blue light machine for insomniacs, projecting from the foot of my bed,
                                                                    the twenty-minute mode
                                                                    expanding and contracting
                                                                    my ceiling.

                              Only when I am naked,

the blue light says to me   I like that you believe in souls
that you drink tea
that you are not so smart

                              due to your feelings.

I say   blue light
                    breathing with you   exhales furniture

                                        beyond margins of the room.

My lower abdomen rises and falls

A lighthouse sinks in caramel

Crows ascend from fitted sheets

Goodbye gravel in driveways   Goodbye rain-blessed frogs

Up blue stairs
                                        and farther—
what are bad dreams?

          I've been waiting my whole life to be invisible.

Not enough oxygen to burn a candle, then

                                    all air   from breath

               to tornado

                       rushes   to leer at my newness.

I am a viscous child.

                   Breezes tendril

       too much.

                 Dear wireless apparatus

     dear LEDs

        I cannot sleep   while you lead me to sleep.

        I carry myself

               under covers.   Comforter, where

   will you lead me?   The future's a bed on my back.

II.   *I resist.*

                   Out of the blue — what are dreams
  but humming dangerous to follow?   It's impossible to guard against a piano,
or rooms locked from outside.

                 The place — underwater

   in a stately library.

           The time — magazines scream

   periodical panic on the hour.

      Who could be drowsy?   Flamingos twine
      pinks on the roof.

Sorry I forgot to build an elevator.

I'm not what I should be.

Sharks

cower   when approaching
                                      pillows.
                                                  Books fall overboard
                                                  if I put them down.

Some bodies drop off.

My last appeal to a woman etched in marble—her arms
wrapped around her torso—   I am attracted to her,   but she is only a relief.

Algae collects and crevices can't be reached.

I draw her out limb by limb
into a statue
                            so untouchable
                  she no longer holds herself.

III.   *I'm already there.*

Dear reader   you are welcome to the blue sofa,
                                              its accent clouds

are not raining now.

                                                  I am kissing you

but don't worry

you are a placeholder.
                            Be anyone else
                  if it's more comfortable.
                                                      I struggle so

not to lounge.
                            I brought parrots
                  to cacophony the dictionary.

You brought rampant lion eyes.
When you stare,   my reflection in the mirror
                                        shifts against my body's stillness.

                                    I don't trust the camels.
                        Anyone I kiss will want to sleep with me.
                                    Dominos topple,   but where's
        the first tile?
Egrets click their bills lightly—
                                I enjoy it.
                                    I would be a word
            in your mouth,   but what if
                                    you make only

slipping sounds.
                            I haven't decided if you smell nice   then
                    a fish stares and dies.

                                        So I sharpen my pencil:
                                        note the pain in your thigh.
Ogled hips   visit cubists.   I wouldn't dream this,   so I placed mirrors
        proactively,   watching for
                            HELP ME—   Sirens

            and gorgons

                                                wave

from opposite sides.
                                    Roses   clutch rosaries,
                        as if the beads   were brutes or infants.
            Who will carry the pillows?
                                    Enter amphibians

                    to erase you,   reader,   with ribbits.

I am sorry

        but if I leave

                I will leave them in charge.

IV.   *Nowhere*

           and tired of kissing,
          I build a nest of pillows
           to be in the middle.

      I swim under the umbrella of a large medusa.

    My Medusa,

you are perimeter.   Since I could speak,
  I sleep with still-fluid lava, your lightless universe.
    Tonight I wait for your serpents to spoon my bark.

    So near the wind   you fill sails without shaking them,
  I have never been anything more than a pail of water.

                I curl within your ear. You ladle

                    syllables.

             Your hands scan ribs—meticulously—

                 no lines are missing.

             Without turning, I tilt my hips

               so you can read the rest of it.

             Moat about me.   Throw on

             some mountains.

             I'll mouth dunes.

We are never two persons at a table.
Reptile fangs nuzzle shoulders

till they relax into cursive—my actual skin
bares every word.

V.   *In Paris*   *emphatic men*   *trance their manifestos.*

I receive them in dreams—kerosene, pleas. I did not
ask to be a beautiful animal. They burn their pages past
reading. They could just jewel the trunks of elephants.
I suggest they drink their words.

Visitor,

I am becoming more abstract
the longer you touch me.

A thousand pastel mouths

follow me into the dark.

Visitor,   you snuck in
with the Italian men
who were tourists.

I had also been a tourist,
but then the city broke me in:

between the cathedral
and the brothel,

I sprained an ankle;   catcalls

and bilingual cobblestone   rushed   *BELLA*
toward me;
I tripped over them.
I did not intend for my dress to be a nude.

Eclair towers tilted

into see-through slips.   A word may also twist:

my knees hit the ground,

body crumbled

into multiples: can triple-women

fend off the frames of art?   Sphinx fountains and graffiti

slide down my monstrous ledges.

I grimace:

art deco subways

uncork their bottles   as crutches worry malleable flesh.   Some

lace-top thigh-highs   grow me a red dress.   A balcony tumbles

into my balconette.

There—

how delighted I am
to remain intact.

A park bench.   A warm baguette.

Even in stillness,

ardent padlocks   coo   drunk fragrance.

Look:
words flea the open book.

We are not dogs today.

Visitor,   I cannot lock out

your shadows,   so I'll massage

your temples   toward our pillow.

The painter's brush-stroke

presses my skeleton: a bridge collapses on my fingers

when I trace my bones back to him.

I confront you

because you followed me into my body.   Haven't I done enough,
granting asylum in my mind?

VI.   *Tonight*   *I am a ticker-tape tragedy:*   *a woman transforms into weeds*

to dodge a predator dressed as a suitor. It happens in New Jersey as well as
Greece. I disappear into the marsh with a spray of oil (cranberry bogs by
the parkway). He says he'll take you dancing, but he is hunting:

paralysis.

Swampy floor-length skirts

need drugs

to thrive in dirt.

I grow herbaceous.

Hunter, you chase me

into wind-blown,

hollow bodies.

I am splintered terse.

Move, you fragments.

All we do

is fall properly.

Vegetation is a fortress defended by girls.

I am my children.

Basket-woven.   Ribbit-quivering.   The baby Moses
floats by.
          Make paper, be pressed by letters.   Dandelions,
    saplings,   Walt Whitman lounging.

No more shepherds.   Weeds

waft past minotaurs, pizzerias, dance floors
  bordered by snakes. In every remix, our robes disintegrate.

No one wishes to run new stockings the very first time.

Scarecrows conduct us off-key. Pollution
    serrates horizon   while satyrs recall a virgin,
        neon rivers licking every surface.

I go to seed
and wake to insects feeding on me.

Pursued   by jeeps,

mechanical teeth,   notes

pressed   by a myth's breath—

each morning   what I am dies again,

and what I am rises around me.

VII.   *Conservatory of flowers but also a conservatory—*

blue violets take up violins.   Trumpets vine
into orchids. Over the bed, rhododendrons pine for syllables,

the eyebrows of a funeral.
What if this circling bought me a ring,

a knot garden,   catkins radiating out.

Bouquets play for pleasure and for pyres:
red and white dragon-breaths
torch body sounds
to confetti
then to smoky ground.

Heavy footing. A daisy trying.
I could be color.

Seven shades in the musical scale made me love my underground parts—
                                              where blunders run hands over.

I am a net. I am a cloud forest when others think I sleep.

I could wake myself with laughing.

                        The nightmare is a fern,
                    tucking photosynthesis around clanging.

                  My mouth takes up color
                    to be an instrument.

        Tongue, do you promise to wake with me?

VIII.   *Sudden background beauty—is it frogs or snow?*

        Sloshing.
                        The bed lurches
            seasick,   but it was only a 4.6.

        If I want rest, do I get up or lie down?

    Baggy with blackout curtains.   Salt-mouth.
    The dungeon of coming to.

        Somewhere a squid improved itself while I held on in limbo.

                        My Medusa presses my back.
                          She would like to bend me in
                      to where she carried me last:

    sandy debris   stuttering dial tones
            a shiny hallway papered with amphibians.

                Legs stretch and ripple flesh.

There's no one else here, desolate lady.

A witch or no, this pillow sinks through briny leagues.

An ignition switch cascades my arteries
till hunger pangs capsize the blanket.

Violet on the inside,   I haven't grown tall yet.   I live for

a dolphin,   the visible spectrum. Breakfast.   Oolong.   No envelope to hold me.

My limbs are dipped in
   garbled prism, draped in seaweed.   Words I can't yet read—dewy,
      pliable color—

      rake my fingers through leaves of tea.

DAVID SCHUMAN

Small Best Man

Christopher is just a sixteen-month-old baby in a tux, the groom's half brother. The groom keeps referring to Christopher as his *best friend*, which doesn't say much for the groom. During the ceremony, Christopher's mommy must repeatedly rush the altar to keep Christopher from putting the rings in his mouth and when it is finally time for the rings to be presented the bride's must be forcibly extracted from under the baby's tongue. As the groom slips the ring onto the bride's finger, he proclaims, "It's pre-lubricated!" which nobody laughs at. Christopher is not allowed to ride along with the rest of the wedding party in the Hummer limousine because nobody can figure out a way to install his car seat. At the reception, however, he is allowed to sit in his high chair at the dais with all of the ushers and bridesmaids and their dates, having a royal time, smashing every food item into paste and attempting to put the paste in the Maid of Honor's hair. At a certain point, one of the ushers thinks it would be funny to give Christopher a sip of champagne, so he instructs his date to tip a little bubbly down the baby's throat, which she does. Christopher seems to like it, he cries out and inflates his cheeks and says something like *walla-walla* and licks his lips, so someone else gets the idea that they should dump out the contents of his sippy-cup and fill it instead with bubbly. Baby likes bubbly, doesn't he? Yes! Yes he does! Christopher's parents, the groom's father and his wife, who is much younger and also less dead than his former wife, the groom's mother, have been seated somewhere far away because the bride does not like them. She has told the groom that when he isn't looking, his father and young stepmother sneer at her. The groom, Christopher's half-brother and best friend, is in the bathroom throwing up and has been for a while. The baby is subject to the whims and fancies of a bridal party in full celebratory mode. Christopher finishes his sippy cup full of champagne, which was, truth be told, only half full, so they give him some more. *Walla-walla!* Christopher still really wants to put food paste in the Maid of Honor's hair, but his movements have become even more wildly erratic than they had been, and he just can't seem to reach the locks that swing, so tantalizingly clean, out of reach. Somewhere along the line, another of the ushers

thinks wouldn't it be funny to take a picture of Christopher smoking one of the celebratory cigars he's brought along? The gesture of the cigars was semi-ironic, he didn't think anyone was really going to smoke one of the disgusting things, but now that Christopher's got one between his lips and their phones are all out ready to snap a pic, it doesn't seem to make any sense not to have it lit. It's not like the kid's going to know how to take a puff, but then he does take a puff, and suddenly he's smoked the whole thing, somehow, and he cries, *walla-walla!* for another, only the usher doesn't think another cigar is a good idea, so one of the other usher's dates pulls out a pack of American Spirit Yellows—*the lightest kind*—she assures the group, but within fifteen minutes Christopher's smoked what was left of the pack, plus drained the sippy cup and moved on to gin and tonics, which are produced one after another by a banquet waiter who's worked three shifts in a row and has taken a molly and thinks this whole thing is ador- able and horrible. A little time passes and then suddenly one of the bridesmaids thinks, *Wouldn't it be funny to see a baby paying bills?* And so she draws a utility bill from her purse, it's in one of those blue envelopes they send when a bill is overdue, someone else has a checkbook, and suddenly Christopher is paying bills, everyone has one—cable, phone, medical, even mortgage payments— Christopher pays them all, drinking and smoking whatever the party can throw at him, and then the Maid of Honor speaks up and says wouldn't it be funny if Christopher and I got married, after all I am pregnant with his child! And so they get married—the minister is there at the reception and agrees to do it for a small fee—and then later they get divorced, because if watching a baby get married is funny, just try watching a baby get divorced! Meanwhile, Christo- pher is drinking—just straight gin by now—and smoking Marlboro Reds, not to mention the pills, they're for the pain from a workplace injury, but at this point there's little difference between pain and consciousness, and he's behind on the credit cards and the car payments and thank god the mortgage company gives a fifteen day grace period because maybe that insurance settlement will arrive by then, but also there's the child support payments and if that isn't enough there's this cough, a troublesome dry cough he can't seem to get rid of, though he guzzles Robitussin like it was breast milk, and he keeps wanting more, *wal- la-walla*, more smokes, more drinks, more pills, sometimes he'll see a woman stopped at a traffic light in a stylish haircut and imagine the life he might have with her, not to mention the girl at the office with the short skirts who seems to spend more time than she needs to fidgeting with the copy machine in front

of his cubicle, and once he's married to her there are two more kids to support, the youngest with cerebral palsy but he loves this one most of all, loves him more than any of it, it's the kind of love that galaxies burst out of. The kind of love that serves as the answer to the question he's had all his life. And suddenly Christopher clutches his heart—it appears as if he wants to tear it out of his chest and present it to the party, *walla-walla*—and slumps face first into the glop on the tray of his high chair, dead. And so here we are, the whole wedding party at a funeral for a baby and nobody thinks it's funny at all, not one bit.

"She's not a leash dog," Tom explains after you've asked him for one twice. He insists she'll come when you call. Tom's golden retriever is named Skye, which you insist on pronouncing Sky-ee just to hear him patiently correct you again and again. Tom's not the worst guy your sister's ever been with, which is a plus considering she's marrying him in a few hours. He's just a little slow to recognize when you're kidding around.

"Walk her at least two miles," Hannah says. "Otherwise she'll be all jumpy later."

Meanwhile, the dog is going nuts in your room because she heard the w-word, wagging her chunky tail and knocking half your skin care products off the nightstand. Hannah and Tom are foregoing the traditional bridal party, but since you arrived at the lodge yesterday, they've been asking for little favors. "So you can feel like a part of things," Hannah says. Last night it was untangling a stubborn knot in the lace of one of Tom's dress shoes before the rehearsal dinner. At six this morning your sister had asked you to proofread the vows they'd written. "I want them to be sweet," she'd said, shoving two loose-leaf pages and a cup of coffee at you, "But not corny."

And now the dog. Skye is going to walk with Tom and Hannah as they descend the aisle together, with a little satin pouch containing the rings tied around her neck, but she needs her exercise first.

"Don't let her come back without pooping," Tom says. "Sometimes if she's over-excited by a new place, it takes her a while."

You catch your sister's slight wince. Hannah's never been one for the prosaic side of pet ownership. When your dad brought a kitten home one Christmas when you were kids, Hannah had chosen the name—Phoenix—and crocheted an array of tiny sweaters the poor thing was forced to endure through endless photo-sessions, but she'd balked at the idea of opening the smelly cans of food or cleaning the litter box. Those chores had fallen entirely on you.

And so here you are, bulked out in thirty layers of Hannah's North Face, making your way through the lobby of the lodge. Half of the Main Line is here for the wedding, it seems. You raise a mitten at a group of your mother's skinny, batty friends then leave them to whisper about you. The lobby has these columns that look as if they were cut straight out of a redwood forest going up about a hundred feet, and the floor is composed of flat river stones. Tom's family—his parents are both some kind of million-dollar-a-month lobbyists for the

fossil fuel industry—owns a part of this place, which is why you've all flown out to Wyoming. "When I'm here, I'm home," you heard Tom's dad tell a table full of gin-blossomed bankers last night, and there he is now in a—wait for it—honest-to-goodness cowboy hat.

You're almost out the door when you hear your mother's voice above the breakfasty din of the café off the lobby. She gets up from the table where she's sitting with your dad, leaving her plate of egg whites to cool.

"It's nice to see you pitching in on the big day," she says, reaching out to brush a wisp of hair off your forehead. It's one of those micro-edits you've always read as her attempts to make you just a bit more like your sister, gestures you've been flinching from since you were twelve. You don't disappoint this time around.

"Christ," she says, as she always does. "You'd think I was going to pluck out your eye."

Skye, meanwhile, has nuzzled your mother's crotch, leaving a streak of saliva in precisely the spot nobody wants to see a moist patch on a lady's skirt. Your mother's so buoyant with the excitement of the day, she doesn't even notice.

"Will you at least give your father a little wave? He's convinced you hate him."

"I do," you say.

"Well I thought we'd agreed to a truce this weekend. For your sister's sake?"

You raise your hand and wiggle your fingers in your dad's direction, a pantomime of civility. He's too busy stuffing his face with elk steak and eggs, or whatever version of manly breakfast they serve here, to notice.

You raise your eyebrows at your mother.

"How's that?"

She offers her weariest look, waving you away.

It *is* beautiful here, you admit, once you're outside and away from all the bullshit, what with the range slashing at the sky and cumulus clouds piled so high and thick it seems like a person could climb them into heaven. Skye noses her way to the creek, dripping yellow splatters into the snow in excitement.

After fifteen minutes or so you get into a nice walking rhythm, puffing white steam, over a rise and then you can't see the lodge behind you anymore. The water under the ice in the creek crackles in a delightful way, and if your phone wasn't stuffed inside all the microfiber and fleece you'd take it out and make a recording for Gin back home in Philly. Gin creates sound installations, layering mundane things like the drone of an office copier with the screams of mating alley cats. More and more, they rely on you to bounce ideas off of, and you've

spent hours listening to them talk across the fifties dinette table in the middle of your loft in Fishtown. Sometimes you just focus on one part of their face as they talk—the way their eyebrows bob when they get onto a subject they're really excited about, or the tiny mole that disappears into the crease at the corner of their mouth when they smile. They're only your roommate for now but you've got a five-month plan.

A few times you get a little too close to the edge of the creek and the ground beneath you creaks—a creaky creek!—and you realize there are pockets under the snow, places where you might fall in up to your knees or worse, a real "To Build a Fire" situation. So you stomp about twenty yards up the bank where the ground is solid and monitor Skye from there.

The dog is having the time of her life, burying her snout in the snow and unearthing pinecones and branches, and probably moose turds, which she tosses into the air in pure ecstasy. You find yourself hating her a little less, and even try out a couple of those kiss-kiss sounds to get her to bound up and nuzzle your hand, your knees, before she dashes back to the creek's edge where the really cool dog-stuff is.

It can't have already been a mile, but there's the narrow section of the creek Tom mentioned as a good turn-back point, just up ahead where a fallen tree has dammed up one bend and dried another so with a good leap a person could get across. You make a few more of the noises to get Skye to come back, and she does start to make her way up to you, until she stops in her tracks and turns.

On the other side of the creek is something you can't see but Skye can, or more likely she hears it, as her floppy ears have gone all rigid and quivery. And then, abandoning all her goofy ragdoll capering, she's off like a flaming arrow across the creek and after whatever has got her attention.

Shit.

Fuck!

You call after her, but the cold air gets into your throat and it's hard to yell as loud as you want to. A rooster tail shoots up in the snow about a hundred yards away as whatever was hiding there—a rabbit or whatever—takes off toward the expanse of tundra. Is it *tundra*? It suddenly seems important to know what things are called.

You shimmy your way down to the creek—the banks are steeper here than they were, and the creek doesn't look as traversable from this angle as Skye made it seem, so the best you can do is stand there on the crust of ice and lift the binoculars Tom had strung around your neck like a medal as you were on your way out. "I spotted a golden eagle with these yesterday," he told you. "I

could count the feathers in its tail." The things are so high-powered it takes you a full minute to fumble Skye into view, already a few football field lengths from where you stand, still streaming after the rabbit or fox or squirrel and there's nothing you can do about it except hope she gives up and turns around.

You lose focus after raising a mitten to rub at the tip of your nose, which is starting to go numb, and by the time you catch sight of Skye she's probably a mile away but finally stopped, thank Christ, and gone rigid, like she's looking at something again, so you wiggle the binoculars a little further up.

That's when you see them, just black shapes, a line of about seven or eight emerging from the tree line, fanning out in a semicircle.

It's a story you'll tell differently the further you get from it. In forty minutes, back at the lodge, exhausted and soaked from having run the entire mile back through the snow, you'll gasp it out in three lines, a panicked haiku, to the first person you collide with. That person, a teenage bellboy whose eyes, you can't fail to notice, light up when you get to the gory part, will run for Tom, who, before the elevator doors have fully opened, will rush to you and grab you by the shoulders so violently that bruises will form a day later. Back in Philly, you will draw the narrative out as long as you can, enraptured to be the object of Gin's undivided attention, for once, basking in the steady cool regard of their gray eyes as you try to describe how at first Skye thought it was a game, how she hopped around the way dogs do, stuck her butt in the air in a "play bow," and then, in that terrible after, what appeared in the binoculars like red ribbons, endless red ribbons, drawn from Skye's body, tugged across the whiteness of the snow. Five years from now, seated with your sister on the primly upholstered sofa in her living room in Bryn Mawr, taking little nibbles of a shortbread cook-ie she's offered from a porcelain plate as she weeps over her third miscarriage, and about the suspicions she has that the senior partner Tom keeps mentioning over dinner is more than just a *mentor*, you will offer the story as sort of meta-phor, a prophecy in reverse. Fifteen years from now, having resolved to finally weed a garden that's gone untended in your yard since a lover left three years before, you will tell the story to yourself. Ivy has taken over, and you spend the morning outside in a sunhat and a pair of cutoffs, yanking it from the ground. It is satisfying to get your fist around a cord of vines and pull, watching the ivy rise from the ground for yards on either side of yourself, releasing clumps of black earth. You wear a pair of leather gloves your lover left behind. Stiff, they still bear the curves of her fingers. The neighbor's dog has gotten its nose stuck under the fence again, digging, and begins to scream, and this reminds you. And long, long from now—so long that conceiving of it at this moment would

be impossible—when your youth is gone and the great loves, adventures, and disappointments of your life have crusted over into a stiff shape you recognize as you, your father, with only hours left in his own existence, will ask again for the story you have told him many times before. And you, having long ago forgiven him, will bend down and whisper it into his ear.

But now, here, this isn't a story. Not yet. You are witnessing something tiny through an instrument.

For a millisecond, like you're Wonder Woman, you get this impulse to go to Skye, to try to save her, but even nudging your foot a fraction of an inch forward unleashes the creaking sound, and you're not going to die today, not for a dog you only just decided was good people. All you can do—what you must do, it seems—is to watch unflinchingly through the lenses as the killers approach.

JOHN MARADIK

The Gibber

all of us have read The Gibber
it is a fairytale
about old men
sex fishing baseball
it's the kind of book you keep
I love The Gibber
I just want to get in there
my teacher told me
I'm going nuts
but I can't wait
for all The Gibbers
to come to life
my teacher said "we're
done with The Gibber"
but there were so many
coming off the page
the other night one talked
to me real loud
he said "I'm so glad to be alive"
then he climbed into my bed

bob dylan

married the other
bob dylan
they gave birth
to a little
shrunken one
who sang backwards

Suspense

Teaser Sequence

[Wind howling] [Bell clanging] [Owl hooting] [Train horn blowing] [Scream-
ing, panting] [Shrieking] [Panting] [Whimpering] [Shrieks] [Flies buzzing]
[Bell clanging] [Cell phone rings, beeps] [Thunder rumbles]

Oh, snap.

Episode 1

For sixty minutes, two damaged detectives

move their faces in the ballpark of feeling.

The investigation won't turn out. Those who had power

still do. Predictably the weatherman predicts more rain.

Another day another dead

chick. They're naïve the way elk were

before the state brought back the wolves

…

Memory's a drawing you keep drawing till

there's an image there.

At the bottom of the drawn pond: body body body body body body body.

Cue haunting instrumental melody

…

The person most likely to be the killer absolutely

isn't. The leads seldom speak.

Conversation isn't cheap

…

Memory's a series of low-res film stills pinned

to a cheap cork board. Faces look like each other

but recognizable. In the secret room, perpetually

dreary weather

...

Every killer must long for the long

caress of the long hard look

...

The dead girl's the only one who's herself.

Episode 3

At this point, it's an elimination game:

any day now, DNA in red flannel

will wash ashore and crack

the case quick as the missing girl's

mother cracks a Coor's. Everyone's ful

filling their stereotype.

Torn caution tape, graffiti, a flashlight in broad daylight.

No one's lived here since the murder. No one's

ever lived here. It's a set-up

…

The closet sky glows in the dark.

The detective sees what

the boy might have seen. Another scene

inside a car. Another heavy metaphor

…

Days pass in no clear order.

The man waiting to hang isn't guile

less but the detective's finally figured

he didn't do it. "It took this long…?"

…

On death row, outside's only a glimpse

through dirty windows, the larch faintly

attaching the sky to the earth

The hostage attempts to humanize itself—

> I understand, you can talk
> to me, I lost my son, I'm having
> a cigarette, I lied to you before
> about my son, he left…

—to establish a believable bond

the hostage-taker will only unwillingly

break. I know what you're trying to do, he says

into the rearview, and it won't work

…

But it works: twice he fails

to shoot. The gun falls

into the bay, sirens shriek, hands

where we can see them, it'll be on the news later.

He is a criminal—just not the one

she's after

When we finally arrive, it's like

like really?

Like pulling into a gas station

and being told we're here! Like what the

huh

…

In this version, the boy only sees his dad

once behind glass

before the state…

There's no universe in which

this hasn't happened.

The state's motives remain obscure

…

Up until the very unlikely last

last second, we believed the phone would ring, just under

under the wire. Even a light man drops like

like a stone.

With its wires cut, a piano

is just piano-

shaped

A pinkish swirl, a steamy fug, all evidence (even that

trademark sweater) burned. Only a detective can execute

a perfect murder. Not this one. Her face impossible

in a mirror. But wait. The smell of blood's here still

…

Is killing necessarily

criminal? She just chose just

ice for one at

the price of

the others

…

It's a delightfully torrential day, every occurrence absolutely

unlikely.

An old phobia has placed us perfectly in

our places.

Episode 9

The rest of the story drags rapidly along:

convenient localized amnesia, a mother's brutal tendresse, a dull detective

turned curiously sharp

…

In the end, all the characters are finally naked

in their pants: the good guys get away
with murder and the bad guys

aren't really so bad

…

Sometimes the killer simply is

the one all the clues point to.

Series Finale

At the very, very end, we get what we wanted:

sun, a smile, some blue silk. "You were my best friend."

Breath

Each day when he wakes up he wants to fill the bedroom with a tone

Each day when he wakes up he wants to fill the bedroom with a tone. He imagines the tone before he gets out of bed. A tone that feels full. That resonates his small body. That seems to gain intensity from its surroundings. A tone that seems endless. But instead of playing the tone he usually goes to the kitchen to make coffee. The tone stays in mind even as the radio comes on announcing things that have nothing to do with the tone. That are in fact anti-tone because they are closer to noise. Can become background. Can transmit thoughts but cannot fill a room with an endless well of sound. A tone that becomes content. That becomes inhabitable space.

Certain experiences exist only in writing. They are composed of the sound and weight of words. They are related to an irredeemable loneliness. When you know that no one else is there and maybe no one ever will be. For him it is hard to read when someone is watching. The tone of the book cannot take over because the tone in the room is too strong. There is life in the words and there is life outside of the words but both are dependent on a certain relationship with silence.

You cannot read when your house is burning down. Nor can you write. Writing and reading have their own tones. The tone cannot be played in a book. The tone is composed of more than words. And yet when the tone happens. When it emerges like a fragrance in a bedroom. When it rears its pony head. In these moments it is best recorded in the sound of thoughts meeting silence and turning into words. This morning he announces in the silent room that he is writing the tone into words.

Because it is true that the tone is also an experience of writing. Like an experience of moving. Like when he arrived in a basement venue and walked closer to the music and the sound became a room within a room with only a bare red lightbulb around which all the musicians were arranged. They were tightly

wound around the center of a tone that seemed also lodged in the intestines of each of them. The tone had a throb that came both too quickly and too slowly. Everyone swayed with the tone and some people shouted phrases over it. They shouted these phrases because if they didn't they would be forced to move the tone out of their bodies through a different orifice or through the destruction of something around them which was the opposite of the tone. They would have to possess something or be possessed. And maybe this is why everyone is smoking too. He thinks. Smoking has to happen around this throbbing tone. In order to be possessed by the tone we have to burn things and put the burning ashes in our bodies like food.

☦

This morning he tries to play the tone in his bedroom:

A tone emerges. He tries to hear it. It has different parts that almost coalesce into a tone of depth. But they don't. He has to take another breath. The pause is insurmountable. He cannot play another tone yet. He must wait until the tone in the room is audible and he can play a tone that mixes with that other tone. He waits looking out the window at the rain and the dead leaves. He watches someone walk by with an umbrella. He begins to hear something. The tone emerges but it is not the right one and no one walking by notices it. He tries to see it but he only notices the white walls and a soft hunger in his stomach. Instead he plays a variety of tones that he hopes will become the tone as they accumulate. They have weight and depth. They are composed of air and thought. His body follows the regular accumulation of tones that seem to say something in the room about the tone but aren't exactly the tone. One tone should be enough. But it rarely is. As soon as a tone is followed by another tone then we already have the story that takes over from the tone. A story like a key that lets you into a door which is the home you return to. But with the tone you can leave and it follows you. There is a silence in the room that is pleasant and reminds him of the tone. He leaves for he is hungry and the tone that will not come is not food.

At night he goes to a basement where someone is playing a variety of tones and someone else is turning them on and off. Louder here and softer there. Someone is typing on a computer and then speaking on a phone. Someone is fidgeting with their hands. Someone is asking how he is doing. Someone is

alone sitting horribly upright in anticipation. Later another person comes and sits across from the upright person. He imagines that they are meeting to speak about the tone. Perhaps they—like he—had come to the basement to hear the tone.

The man playing tones is bent over in concentration. He presses different buttons and tones come out. It seems that they are never the right tone. Sometimes high tones emerge. Sometimes lower tones. Sometimes the man playing looks around to see if he can judge the looks on people's faces. The man would say under his breath: "There." "Ah." "Okay." And he would wince sometimes. One person drinks a beer and nods. As if he knows that the tone would soon come that would allow all the other tones to stop. Eventually the man stops pressing buttons and the tones subside. He stands up and says "I'm going to stop." Everyone seems surprised. The other man keeps nodding.

‡

The following day he finds himself standing and listening. Waiting for the tone to come. He is swaying in the almost-silence facing a wall. His weight moves from one foot to the other. His hips tilt. His shoulders sway. His arm rotates. It occurs to him that he is dancing. He is dancing but there is no tone and no rhythm. He is swaying in homage to the tone. It's a summons. And an invitation. With his whole body. His hands are in lose fists—elbows out. He closes his eyes. Before he can hear the tone he can see it. It looks like guitar strings. He imagines the sound of a major third. But rather than hearing it he sees it which means that he sees the strings and knows they are resonating as a major third. Soon he can hear it. As usual the major third is complex. It is just-barely-in-tune. It wants to change into a perfect fourth. He thinks maybe this is the tone he has wanted to fill the room with. He feels his back muscles loosen. Now his body is swaying and the sway itself is providing the momentum. He is not doing anything but his body is moving. The tone that he sees in his mind is making him sway. If he were to stop the tone would disappear. Some minutes pass. His eyes open and he is facing a different direction. He listens. There is no tone. Only the almost-silence of the room. Only the diffuse light coming through the window.

That evening he goes to a basement where someone has suggested that he may hear the tone. It has to do with the moon and the tides. The volume of water in

the river. The correct proportion of cloud cover. A crowd has gathered to hear the tone presumably. They walk into a large room that is a basement but doesn't feel like a basement. There are bright lights. Everyone sits. Someone tells him he must remove his shoes if he is to hear the tone. He waits while people talk. The anticipation mounts. The lights go down and there is a tone. It is opaque. It wavers. It seems to come from high up in the room. It weighs on him and feels cool on his skin. It is like a buzz. But it is lower in pitch. It begins to fill the room. It reminds him of being at the dentist. But it is artistic. There are people moving towards the front. The lights change and the cool feeling on his skin becomes more intense. He can't see what the people who are moving are doing and he can't discern why. The tone is becoming less audible but the lights are getting brighter and they keep changing. What do the lights have to do with the tone? They seem to be related. And yet their relation is fabulated. He begins to think that the tone would be more full if the lights stopped changing. Unless the lights are the source of the tone.

Afterwards someone is explaining what happened in the basement. They are standing in another room. There are lights and some soft music that someone is trying to hide in the background. The man is explaining that the lights were the source of the tone. But also there were other tones. Other sources. The people moving were not the tone. The lights were important. The man seems to be teaching him about the tone. He is trying to learn what he is supposed to learn about the tone. The man says: The tone is an apparition. The man says: The source is unknown. The man says: The tone is always there just like the moon. The man says: Did you hear it? The man says: I heard it. I want to sit down. He says.

‡

A few days later he wakes up thinking about the tone. He thinks that maybe the tone he had considered the previous evening in yet another basement was not the right tone. Or that it wasn't really a tone at all. Worry presses into his abdomen creating a pang of something. In a state between dream and wakefulness he begins to consider that maybe the tone has been an illusion the whole time. What he had thought was the tone was in reality nothing more than a base desire. A fool's errand. His experiences with the tone seem unverifiable now. (While it's true that he remembers seeing the tone – seeing it light up and dance in the night – this experience feels no longer relevant.) Few other people

in the world seem as concerned with the tone as he is. There are men who have militantly shaven faces and wear stripped suits and seem to extract something from the tone. And there are others who talk about the tone with wide eyes and language that is jumbled. There are some that bob their heads while drinking beers and smiling ambiently. But he has never related to these people. This morning it is clear: he hasn't really produced the tone. He has never seen the tone. It remains as elusive as ever. No matter how many basements he finds himself in he doesn't usually find the tone or even something that you could say resembles the tone. Aspects of the tone perhaps. Or certain layers of it. But he has yet to encounter the tone in its richness. Like a saucepan of gravy that you dip some bread into. Like a pound of butter that you pass a warm knife through. Like a cool foggy night that envelopes you when you leave a dusty basement. Like having enough money for a little while. Like the unsayable becoming audible.

Nevermind all that. This morning he is sure that the tone has never been real. And the feeling leaves him with a hole in his center.

‡

Interlude for assembling the instrument

He is assembling the instrument while the sun is going down. He lies the case on the floor in front of the chair. He unclasps the metal pieces that keep it closed. He opens the lid. The smell is strong. He knows this but he can't smell it anymore. This makes him think that the instrument is like his home which he also can't smell anymore. He lifts the body of the instrument. He feels the cool metal. His fingers curl over the finger parts. He depresses the keys and they spring back. They feel oiled and smooth. They move silently but forcefully. His fingers know the grooves and they produce pleasant clacks. He rests the body of the instrument on his lap vertically so that his face is close to the keys. He looks at them all. He depresses each finger part and each one springs back. It feels good. This close to his face the smell is faint but he knows for others it would be very strong. He rests the body of the instrument on his lap. He pulls the long curved part out of its velvet pouch. The dull metal of the curved part fits into the top of the body of the instrument. He reaches into the case by bending forward over the instrument and feels it pressing into his abdomen. He pulls the grease out. He applies the grease like a lip stick to the cork. He rubs it in

with his index finger and his thumb. Then he takes the mouth part out. He puts some of it in his mouth to cover it in saliva. It tastes sweet and old in his mouth. He feels his mouth fill with saliva. He moves it around in his mouth. He puts the whole thing in his mouth so it is all wet now. He used to be afraid to do that because he thought maybe he would swallow it by accident. But now he does it each time. And the gentle pressure on the top of the throat is how he knows that it is completely wet. He takes it out of his mouth. Using the screw he screws it onto the mouth part making sure all the lines are lining up and the pressure is just right so the screw makes an indent into his skin. He looks again at the attunement of the various mouth parts. He makes an adjustment. He twists the mouth part over the greasy cork. With the instrument on his lap he bends over to get the strap. He unfolds the strap and puts it around his head. It hangs down like a necklace. He lifts the instrument to affix it to the strap. Now the instrument falls into his two hands. The fingers move into place unthinkingly. He brings the instrument to his mouth. Some of it goes into his mouth. His tongue touches part of it. He stops here and begins thinking about the tone. His eyes are closed. There is the time before any tone has been produced when the tone is still silent and he imagines how the air in the room will be disrupted and will vibrate with the tone. He thinks about how all the space in the room is inside of the instrument that he holds with his fingers and his mouth.

‡

The next day he is standing in his bedroom and the sun has fallen so a cool black night stares back at him from outside the window. He is holding the instrument and he is preparing to play it. He is considering the beginning of the tone. There is the time before any tone has been produced when the tone is still silent and he imagines how the air in the room will be disrupted and will vibrate with the tone. And then there is the time after the tone begins. Once the tone begins everything has changed and you cannot go back to the time before. The tone orders the world when it comes into being. It has a moment of impact. The beginning of the tone sets up the conditions of its life. A tone that begins in the middle of the instrument with a plaintive and incisive call will not seduce with an invitation to warmth. It will cut the room in half. It will enter the stomach and move up to the throat. It is marked by its pressure. Like a strong tap that you turn on and it sprays you accidently. A tone that begins in the bottom part of the instrument will come out twisted on itself looking like rumpled velvet and will seduce into its folds. It enters the stomach and moves

down through the pelvis. It opens space rather than cutting it. It is a bucket of warm water you put your feet into. A tone that begins high up on the instrument can go unnoticed. It can be shy. It can miss the body altogether. But if it starts out right then it can leak down like water pouring over your head. The moment before you are able to perceive if it is very cold or very hot. The high tone has the closest relationship to silence of all the tones. It is woven with silence. Silence is its engine and its friction.

The most important thing is that before the tone is played anything is possible. You can walk to into the corner of the bedroom. You can walk onto a stage with a thousand tired faces looking at you. You can sit in your chair facing out the window at the damp night. You can stand in the middle of a circle. And before you begin everything is possible. The tone could be a flood or a bright light. It could be a machine that has many different parts that all start moving in unison creating a great noise. It could be a bomb or a fire that rips through the room. Before it has begun it is all of these things. People sometimes ask him about improvisation. They ask if the tone is like improvisation. And he replies that the tone only has a beginning. Once it has begun it begins to dance and yell. It chooses its own directions and inclinations. Its eyes roll into the back of its head. There is no improvising or composing. The tone lives in a possessed state. And yet the terms of that possession are what is important. If the tone doesn't start right then it can become a mere posture. It can go through the motions hitting all the important moves but in the wrong order and with the wrong temperature. Many people mistake the life of the tone for some kind of destiny or else some wet dream of freedom. But in fact there is only the impact. Sure you still have to listen to where the tone is going. Sure you still have to have your feet square to your hips in case of surprises. But the important thing is to get the tone right in the beginning and this has everything to do with being in the silence and picking the tone out of the silence.

Today the tone has not yet come. He is scanning the silence waiting for a layer to open up where he can fit the tone in. He begins to create silence that becomes breath and soon he slides a tone into the room it looks like a lopsided ball of green mass with hair on one side. He holds it. It moves. Another part of it falls off and rolls away up the wall that he is now facing. The tone is two and he is struggling to understand their relationship. But as sometimes happens the tones get larger and start trembling until he is no longer in the room. They are trembling and expanding and pushing him out of the room. They begin touch-

ing all the surfaces and getting under the bed. They wait there shining lights and trembling softly in the silence that is now completely rearranged.

‡

The tone comes up as a melody written by Albert Ayler on this Wednesday evening. He takes the notes and carefully arranges them in order in his bedroom. He wants to suspend them in the room somewhere between the ceiling and the floor. Hanging each tone in the air is complicated. You have to start the tone and work it until it is weightless. You have to make it shiny and smooth like a hard candy. You have to find the place it resonates. When it is resonating the light changes. Then you know that you can go to the next note. When all the tones are hanging you can go back to the beginning and make them spin. Then the light really starts to go. The song is called Ghosts and he sees that each note is a hovering spinning ghost. The ghosts each have stories that are in the notes but are also more than notes. Each note means something terrible and true. Waiting until all the notes are hanging takes a long time and renders the melody unrecognizable. So he wonders at the efficacy of his strategy. When all the notes are there: is that the melody? Or is it the melody only if you play them all in the time they have been allotted? He thinks it is more important to allow the notes to transform into the ghosts they were obviously intended to be. These ghosts are not happy but it is nevertheless a beautiful site to see them hovering there spinning. Reflecting the light. He tries to keep them going. When the notes are all hovering then a tone starts to come above and below the notes. The tone is not the notes. But without the notes the tone would not come. The tone is beautiful and frightening. Hearing it means that he is not working. Hearing it means that he is not writing. The tone is not his job. He shudders to think. The tone is not food. The tone is not the expectations he had. The tone cannot protect him except from silence. Thinking this he stops holding things and they begin to fall away.

Later that night he is in a basement and someone is asking him about the tone. He thinks he doesn't have much to say but the person is pausing to allow him to speak. So he is speaking. He talks about different strategies for producing the tone. He begins to list them. Waking up. Standing. Thinking. Coffee. Listening. Shaking. Sitting. Spacing. Stopping. Looking. Touching surfaces. Waiting. He starts to wax poetic about the different strategies he has employed in his bedroom. But the person stops him and says: what about the tone? And he says oh

yes the tone. The tone is a feeling that you have when you are not hungry. You can write about it in fits and starts. It is not a thing nor even a feeling but rather a fact of life at certain moments. Working is the opposite of it. Sleeping is a close analogy. You cannot dream about the tone but the tone is of the same substance. The tone is defined by direction and intensity. Like a river perhaps. But the tone is not a river nor is it water or even wet in any way. It is dry. Mostly it is air. Often it is warm. If the tone were weather it would be rain on dry pavement. If the tone were a cloud you would be inside it. If the tone were a car it would be rolling down a hill in neutral.

‡

Today a number of people gather in a basement to play the tone. At the agreed upon hour they converge and begin assembling different instruments. They all have coffees in their hands. They have paper too. And little stands to put the paper on. They arrange themselves in the room using chairs and stools. They get closer to some and further from others. Someone is saying how the tone will sound. Someone is saying that the tone will begin and go through a middle section and then it will end profoundly. Everyone is talking about the tone. And also they are talking about airplanes landlords taxes shopping food. The sound of the talking is beautiful because of the room which is big and has high ceilings. There is the tone of the talking and then there is a decrescendo of talking and slowly there is a crescendo of tone as the instruments begin to vibrate. Someone is saying that the tone is not in tune. (How could it be?) Someone is saying that the tone is too fast. Everyone is in a line waiting their turn. Everyone is considering how the tone should be and they are taking turns playing it and listening to it. Soon the tone gets going. It's like sandpaper. It has grain and it changes the air as it moves. It appears like a solid line in front of them. They rest things on it. Everyone takes valuable things that they have and they rest these things on the tone. The tone is getting weighed down. It begins sagging on one side so someone has to hold the tone. The tone is strong but also feels that it could give way at any moment. There is a tension in the room due to this fact. Everyone is divided between people in charge of holding the tone and people in charge of producing beautiful things to rest on top of it. But these roles keep changing according to a logic that no one fully understands. It seems that there is a balance that everyone is acutely aware of and yet not able to predict.

Then someone begins telling a story about the tone. They are telling the story also in tones that they are resting on the tone and weighing it down. The story is beautiful and sad. They are yelling the story and the tone is full and sandpapery. The story doesn't so much have a beginning and an end. It doesn't so much have characters or actions. It doesn't so much happen over time. It is a tone like all other tones. A tone that means something because of the way it started and hung there. It becomes another solid line in the basement. There are two lines that are vibrating subtly. Everyone is happy about the lines. There are only a few sips of coffee left.

Later on in the cold night he hears someone talking about how bats have a different reality than us. They exist in a world of smell and sound. He stands at the window of his bedroom with the instrument. He sees: His reflection. A stationary car. Someone walking by. He tries to move the car with the tone. He tries to move the car in the darkness. The parked car that is not the tone. A reality of sound. He has yet to raise the instrument to his mouth.

NANCY KLEPSCH

"Writing is like sex. First you do it for love, then you do it
for your friends, and then you do it for money." **VIRGINIA WOOLF**

I wrote this poem thinking of G K too
& whatever writer was featured today:
Is 23 died of TB wasn't a likeable boy
Stuttered was unhappy & forlorn
He did miserably in school had parents
That beat him published his first novel
About a white girl & a white boy
It was a huge success enough to meet
The TB prognosis with almost jocular
Hilarity A different she needed the countryside often
To recover there she met a woman
Not much is known but what is known
Is on a scrap of burned paper
Scribbled I want to lick the north portico
of your…
No one knows what the ellipses mean—
Other em dashes go unexplained too—
She wrote an essay about sisters
But never had one & then
The doctors told her she was cured
She started writing she was terrified
She kept in touch she did good work
We all did
For the love of it for our friends
& then for money

Matthew Broaddus "Recently, I've been reading and re-reading a book called *Scandinavians* by Robert Ferguson. It's fantastic because it doesn't purport to be one thing; it's part history, part travelogue, part memoir, and also just a really fascinating cultural study. Perhaps inspired by Ferguson's book, I've also been reading a lot of Tomas Tranströmer, both Patty Crane's translation of his selected poems called *Bright Scythe* and Robin Fulton's translation of Tranströmer's new and collected poems entitled *The Great Enigma*. I appreciate that Crane's translation provides the original Swedish, which I can't read but still enjoy comparing side by side to her English translations of the poems. Aside from all the Nordic stuff, Tomaž Šalamun's collection *Andes* has been a huge inspiration to me poetically in the last year. My poems in this issue definitely take a cue from his couplet form in that book. In terms of all-time favorites, CLR James's book about so much more than cricket, *Beyond a Boundary*, continues to inspire me for how it goes against the grain of colonial logic in such a sophisticated way. Similarly, Jamaica Kincaid's *My Garden (Book):* is another favorite of mine for its humor, quiet outrage, intelligence, and its unique perspective on gardening as both personal hobby and colonial project. I admire these books by James and Kincaid because they connect leisure, taste, and pleasure to the history of black subjectivity, which has largely overlooked these issues. My first chapbook, *Space Station*, is available from Letter [R] Press."

David Buuck is reading/re-reading Sean Bonney, Gloria Anzaldzúa, Tove Ditlevsen's memoir trilogy, Gerarld Murnane, the new issues of *Commune* and *Pinko*, texts on place and space for a course he's co-teaching at San Quentin Prison's College program, and with co-editor Ted Rees, Kevin Killian's Amazon reviews, for a forthcoming *Tripwire* pamphlet. He lives in Oakland, where he edits *Tripwire*, a journal of poetics.

Jackie Clark Author of *Aphoria* (Brooklyn Arts Press) and the chapbooks *Office Work* (Greying Ghost), *I Live Here Now* (Lame House Press), *Sympathetic Nervous System* (Bloof Books), and *Depression Parts* (dancing girl press). Recently read and enjoyed *A Life's Work* and *The Outline Trilogy*, both by Rachel Cusk.

Mike Crossley On the Non-fiction turntable: *Six Easy Pieces* and *Six not so easy pieces* by Richard Feynman—On poetry: *There are more beautiful things than Beyonce* by Morgan Parker— On fiction: *In the rogue blood* by James Carlos Blake.

Adam Day "I'm currently reading Jillian Weise's collection *Cyborg Detective* and really engaged by it, as well as *Two Serious Ladies*, by Jane Bowles, *The Essential Rosa Luxemburg*, and Derrida's book about accepting death, *The Gift of Death*. I've recently re-watched, and highly suggest the phenomenal film *Theeb* (1914; Jordan, UAE, Qatar, UK) featuring the Bedouin community in the Wadi Rum desert, and about the Great Arab Revolt against the ruling Ottoman Empire. My sense is that everyone should at some point read Mark Danner's book *El Mozote*, about the December 1981 massacre of the village of El Mozote by the Salvadoran Army's select, American-trained Atlacatl Battalion. I'm dipping in and out of Edmund White's funny, strange bio of Jean Genet and just finished Will Eno's play *The Realistic Joneses*. I'm looking forward to *The Look of the Book: Jackets, Covers, and Art at the Edges of Literature* by Peter Mendelsund and David J. Alworth."

Brandon Downing "It's history season, you all. I've been tripping on Richard Zack's *Island of Vice*, which explores Teddy Roosevelt's time as NYC Police Commissioner in the 1880s; like, the wickedest urban era ever ever. The image of him going on DL night patrols and busting sleeping-on-the-job cops and feral taverns with Jacob Riis is so rich and strange. Simon Schama has also taken hold, and I re-read *Landscape and Memory*, was blown away again, god what a poet, then moved onto *An Embarrassment of Riches*, his look into the social phenomenon of Dutch identity during its golden age, which got more slog-y, sadly...so I read his catalog piece on Damien Hirst's completely fake *Treasures from the Wreck of the Unreal* wondering, how is this man's mind going to process everybody's favorite art villain? Well, surprise, the art's totally great. I can honestly say I almost convinced a very very rich person last year to buy the entire collection. Long story. Oh, but you want to know about poetry. I don't know. I've been kind of devouring Jana Prikryl's poems. She's teaching me to be louder when I'm quiet? If that makes any sense."

Makmak Faunlagui | *Calling A Wolf A Wolf*; Vittorio Aurelli | *The Project of Autonomy*; Florencia Castellano | *Monitored Properties*; Todd Colby | *Splash State*; Nicolas Destino | *Heartwrecks*; Charles Fourier | *The Hierarchies of Cuckoldry + Bankruptcy*; Thom Gunn | *New Selected Poems*; Ibn Khalawayh | *Names of the Lion*; Manuel de Landa | *A Thousand Years of Nonlinear History*; Robert Lax | *Poems 1962–1997*; Geoffrey Nutter | *The Rose of January*; Frank O'Hara | *Meditations In An Emergency*; *The Penguin Book of Haiku*; *Phaidon Atlas of Brutalist Architecture*; Trey Sager | *Dear Failures*; Waly Salomao | *Algaravia:Echo Chamber*; Christian Schlegel | *Honest James*; Li Shangyin | *a new translation* by Chloe Garcia Roberts, NYRB; Mónica de la Torre | *The Happy End/All Welcome*; *Toward A Concrete Utopia: Architecture in Yugoslavia 1948–1980*; Virgil | *The Eclogues*; *Pictures from Brueghel* | William Carlos Williams; Alejandro Zambra | *Bonsai*

Rachel Galvin's poetry collections include *Elevated Threat Level, Pulleys & Locomotion, Hitting the Streets* (translated from the French of Raymond Queneau), and *Decals: Complete Early Poems of Oliverio Girondo* (translated from the Spanish with Harris Feinsod). In 2019 she published a chapbook translated from the Spanish of Alejandro Albarrán Polanco, *Cowboy & Other Poems* (Ugly Duckling Presse). Rachel is currently reading Don Mee Choi's *Hardly War* and her translation of Kim Hyesoon's *Autobiography of Death*, Urayoán Noel's *Buzzing Hemispheres/Rumor hemisférico* and his translation of Wingston González, *No Budu Please*, and Raquel Salas Rivera's brilliant self-translation *The Tertiary/Lo terciario*.

Peter Giebel is Currently Reading: *Blue Laws* by Kevin Young; *Landmarks* by Robert Macfarlane. Currently Rereading: *The Book of Job*, a new translation by Edward L. Greenstein; *It* by Inger Christensen, translated by Susanna Nied

Alyssa Claire Greene is currently working on a book of short prose pieces about Sarah Winchester, the development of the modern gun, and American myth-making. She is currently reading Shirley Jackson's *We Have Always Lived in the Castle*, Yoko Ogawa's *Revenge*, and Greg Grandin's *Fordlandia*.

C. R. Grimmer "My current project, 'O (ezekiel's wife)' is just out from GASHER. The print manuscript features Colleen Burner's visual art series, "Hewn Fruit," alongside the poems. The audiobook edition is a fundraiser for The Florence Immigrant & Refugee Rights Project. For more info, visit crgrimmer.com. I'm currently reading, adoring, and teaching Prageeta Sharma's *Grief Sequence* and Larissa Lai's *Automaton Biographies*, among many, many others."

Raquel Gutiérrez "I'm reading Cherríe Moraga's *Native Country of the Heart*, her new, gorgeous memoir of growing up in the borderlands of Los Angeles' San Gabriel Valley and Sylvia Chan's elegiac *We Remain Traditional*. I find myself returning to my favorite prose: Helena María Viramontes' *The Moths* and Gaston Bachelard's *The Poetics of Space*.

Evan Harris is currently reading Lydia Davis, Cyrus Console, and Bruno Latour.

Sarah Heady is a poet, an essayist, and the librettist of *Halcyon*, a new documentary-style opera about the death and life of a women's college. She is also the author of *Corduroy Road* (forthcoming 2020), *Niagara Transnational* (2013), and *Tatted Insertion*, a letterpress collaboration with book artist Leah Virsik (2014). Currently reading: *Getting Back Into Place: Toward a Renewed Understanding of the Place-World* (Edward S. Casey). Recent loves: *River* (Esther Kinsky) and *Ongoingness: The End of a Diary* (Sarah Manguso). Perpetually haunted by: *The Descent of Alette* (Alice Notley), *Housekeeping* (Marilynne Robinson), and *The Rings of Saturn* (W. G. Sebald).

Kathleen Heil "Of the books knocking about in my head and heart, recent reads that resonate deeply include Bojana Kunst's *Artist at Work: Proximity of Art and Capitalism*, Elaine Scarry's *The Body in Pain*, Ocean Vuong's *On Earth We're Briefly Gorgeous*, Heike Geißler's *Saisonarbeit* (available in English from Semiotext(e), tr. Katy Derbyshire), and Olivia Laing's *The Lonely City*, which contains moving reflections on David Wojnarowicz's and Andy Warhol's work. Of the many books both by and about Andy, I'd also recommend his diaries along with David Bourdon's and Wayne Koestenbaum's biographies."

Ava Hofmann "I don't have any books published, but I'm currently rereading Jos Charles' *feeld* for the third time, as well as reading Robert Walser's *Microscripts*, Paul B. Preciado's *Testo Junkie*, Edie Fake's *Little Stranger*, and Jerika Marchan's *Swole*. My work is also heavily inspired by M. NourbeSe Philip's ZONG!, Hannah Wiener's *Clairvoyant Journal*, Armand Schwerner's *Tablets*, as well as large swaths of the oeuvres of Cecilia Vicuña and Douglas Kearney. If you want to read other poems I've written, my website is www.nothnx.com"

Zebulon Huset "*Sirens of Titan* was a turning point in my reading, but Kurt Vonnegut's *Bluebeard* remains my favorite of his many tremendous novels. I've read each one. Other books that made deep and lasting marks would be David Kirby's *The House of Blue Light*, Campbell McGrath's *American Noise*, Denise Duhamel's *Star Spangled Banner*, Yusef Komunyakaa's *Dien Cai Dau*, Brian Turner's *Phantom Noise*, Cormac McCarthy's *Blood Meridian*, Isaac Asimov's *Foundation* series, Kim Addonizio's *Tell Me*, Li-Young Lee's *Rose*, Bob Hicok's *Animal Soul*, and, oh, let's say *Watership Down* by Richard Adams. When other kids were freaked out by the murderous bunny cartoon I sought out the more visceral book, my first poem was even written in the spirit of a fatalistic rabbit. I'd also add Galen Rowell's coffeetable adventure photography book *Mountain Light: In Search of the Dynamic Landscape*, which isn't literature, but it certainly affected the way I view the world at large. Right now I'm re-reading Kai Carlson-Wee's debut collection *Rail* and I have noticed I've been using Charles Harper Webb's anthology *Stand Up Poetry* for my blog a lot lately, as well as for enjoyment."

Stephen Ira "I'm reading Aristilde Kirby's chapbook, *Sonnet Infinitéismal n°3 / Matérial Girl n°8*. I'm reading a novel, *Since I Laid My Burden Down*, by Brontez Purnell. I'm reading Diana Hamilton's new book of poems, *God Was Right*."

Gabrielle Jennings Current Reading: *Float*, Anne Carson; *A Call for Revolution: A Vision for the Future*, Dalai Lama and Sofia Stril-Rever. All-time Favorite: *The Ravishing of Lol Stein*, Marguerite Duras.

Kirsten Kaschock is the author of four poetry books—*Unfathoms, A Beautiful Name for a Girl, The Dottery, Confessional Science-fiction: A Primer*—and a novel, *Sleight*. Her book of poetry, *Explain This Corpse*, is forthcoming. She is currently reading Roberto Bolaño's *2666*, Sabrina Orah Mark's *Wild Milk*, and *The Letterbook of Eliza Lucas Pinckney*.

Adam Kinner *Calamities* (Renee Gladman), *Garments Against Women* (Anne Boyer), *My Paris* (Gail Scott), *Je Nathanaël* (Nathanaël), *I have to live.* (Aisha Sasha John).

Wayne Koestenbaum has published nineteen books of poetry, criticism, and fiction, including *Camp Marmalade, Notes on Glaze, The Pink Trance Notebooks, Circus*, and *My 1980s & Other Essays*. His new collection of essays, *Figure It Out*, comes out in May 2020 from Soft Skull Press. Right now he is reading Salka Viertel's *The Kindness of Strangers*. Recently he enjoyed Rachel Zucker's *SoundMachine*, Michael Harper's *Dear John, Dear Coltrane*, Yvette Siegert's translation of Alejandra Pizarnik's *Extracting the Stone of Madness: Poems 1962-1972*, Christine Pichini's translation of Michel Leiris's *The Ribbon at Olympia's Throat*, *We Both Laughed in Pleasure: The Selected Diaries of Lou Sullivan*, edited by Ellis Martin and Zach Ozma, and Wendy S. Walter's *Multiply/Divide: On the American Real and Surreal*.

Matthew Kosinski is currently reading Italo Calvino's *The Complete Cosmicomics*; Elaine Scarry's *The Body in Pain*; Ian Monk and Daniel Levin Becker's anthology of Oulipian works, *All That Is Evident Is Suspect*; and about three years' worth of *Black Warrior Review* back issues. Before that, it was CA Conrad's *While Standing in Line for Death*, Asad Haider's *Mistaken Identity*, and Tess Brown-Lavoie's *Lite Year*.

Charles Legere is currently reading Héctor Abad's *Oblivion*, René Girard's *Violence and the Sacred*, and the species accounts in Steven Hilty and William Brown's *A Guide to the Birds of Colombia*.

Dong Li is a poet of the lost world. He published the Chinese poet Zhu Zhu's collection *The Wild Great Wall* in English translation with Phoneme Media in 2018 and Zang Di's collection *Gesellschaft für Flugversuche* in German co-translation with Carl Hanser Verlag in 2019. He translates C. D. Wright, Forrest Gander, and Eliot Weinberger into Chinese at the moment and loves Cioran in this season.

Robert Lopez is the author of three novels, *Part of the World, Kamby Bolongo Mean River, All Back Full*, and two story collections, *Asunder* and *Good People*. A new book, *A Better Class Of People*, will be published in 2021. "What I've been re-reading .... Grace Paley's *The Collected Stories*, Barry Hannah's *Ray*, Peter Markus' *Bob or Man on Boat*, Juan Rulfo's *Pedro Paramo*."

Angie Sijun Lou "I recommend *Evening Oracle* by Brandon Shimoda, *Palm-of-the-Hand Stories* by Yasunari Kawabata, *Transverse* by Lindsay Choi, *Illuminations* by Walter Benjamin, and calling your mother."

John Maradik Reading and re-reading *Pee on Water* by Rachel B. Glaser.

Jose-Luis Moctezuma is a Mexican-American poet, translator, instructor, and editor. His poetry and criticism have been published widely. His chapbook, *Spring Tlaloc Seance*, was published by Projective Industries in 2016. His book *Place-Discipline* is published by Omnidawn. Born in San Gabriel, CA, he now lives in Chicago.

Paco Márquez is author of the chapbook *Portraits in G Minor* (Folded Word Press, 2017). More at pacomarquez.net. "Some of the books I'm currently reading include *Dissolve* by Sherwin Bitsui; *De umbral en umbral* by Paul Celan (Spanish edition); *Poesía Completa* by Pedro Mir; *A Drink of Red Mirror* by Kim Hyesoon; *El laberinto de la soledad* by Octavio Paz; *Creative Evolution* by Henri Bergson; *The Qur'an* translated by Tarif Khalidi; and *The Book of Delights* by Ross Gay. Less known but one of my favorites is Malagasy poet Jean-Joseph Rabearivelo's *Translated from the Night*. Robert Duncan is someone I always go back to."

John Patrick McShea's recent recommendations include Leah Poole Osowski's *hover over her*, Mary Ann Samyn's *My Life in Heaven*, Malena Morling's *Astoria*, and Michael Herr's *Dispatches*. He is currently reading Graham Greene's *Our Man in Havana*.

Damon Moore "In the countdown to my first introduction to Days of Poetry and Wine festival in Ptuj, Slovenia, and as a visitor only, I am looking forward to hearing live poetry read by international poets who do not suffer my sense of dread at the prospect of reading their poetry aloud. What is it exactly that draws people to listen to poets read? I am hoping to find some answers! I don't so much seek out books of poetry as read and re-read particular poems which I dwell on longer than I probably should. At the moment I am revisiting 'Les Collines', Guillaume Apollinaire's poem from his second and final collection, *Calligrammes*. I love the image of a writer looking up at the skies over Paris, watching two airplanes, a red and a black, one the symbol of his youth, the other of his adulthood. Who will emerge the victor from that encounter? I voraciously read and am intrigued by any novel featuring fictional poets or touching on poetry-related subjects, and have just added *The Necessary Angel* by C. K. Stead to my prose collection."

Anna Morrison "Books that have recently engaged me: *Flung Throne* by Cody-Rose Clevidence; *YEAH NO* by Jane Gregory; *To Float in the Space Between* by Terrance Hayes; *Reason and Other Women* by Alice Notley; *The Rose of January* by Geoffrey Nutter; *City Eclogue* and *To See the Earth Before the End of the World* by Ed Roberson; *Pictorialist Poetics: Poetry & the Visual Arts in Nineteenth Century France* by David H. T. Scott; *Supplication: Selected Poems of John Wieners*; *Vigilance is No Orchard* by Hazel White; *Casting Deep Shade* by C. D. Wright. And I'm always returning to Emily Dickinson, H.D., Robert Duncan, Barbara Guest, Brenda Hillman, Gerard Manley Hopkins; Audre Lorde, Lorine Niedecker, and more C. D. Wright."

JoAnna Novak is the author of the novel *I Must Have You* and the book-length poem *Noirmania*. Her second book of poetry *Abeyance, North America* will be published in 2020. Just finished-but-still-reeling-from Yoko Ogawa's *Revenge: Eleven Dark Tales*, Garrett Hongo's *The River of Heaven*, and Beth Ann Fennelly's *Great with Child*. "Two hardcovers I'm excited to crack open: *Doxology* by Nell Zink and *The Institute* by Stephen King."

Colleen O'Brien "I've published a chapbook, *Spool in the Maze* (DIAGRAM/New Michigan Press), and am currently reading *What Is Poetry? (Just Kidding, I Know You Know): Interviews from the Poetry Project Newsletter* (ed. Anselm Berrigan), Ann Beattie's *The New Yorker Stories*, and *The Xenofeminist Manifesto* (Laboria Cuboniks)."

Phyllis Peters is currently reading Yasmina Reza's *Babylon*, but she is always re-reading her faves: *The Deleted World* (Tomas Tranströmer); *The Anthologist* (Nicholson Baker); *Hard Child* (Natalie Shapero); *Communion* (bell hooks); *Aria da Capo* (Edna St. Vincent Millay); *The Alexandria Quartet* (Lawrence Durrell); *The Lichtenberg Figures* (Ben Lerner); *Lolita* (Vladimir Nabokov); *The Collected Poems* (Dylan Thomas); *Franny and Zooey* (J. D. Salinger); *By Night in Chile* (Roberto Bolano); *The Good Thief* (Marie Howe) . . . . All proceeds from her most recent novel, *Untethered: A Caregiver's Tale*, are being donated to Alzheimer's research. The story is pure cathartic fun aimed not at our seniors, but in praise of caregivers everywhere. Please visit www.phyllispeters.com.

Isaac Pickell "As a PhD student I read mostly what I'm told, save the hours set aside for my in-process project uncommissioned elegies, or the hours set aside for what's new, but occasionally I have time to stick on Dawn Lundy Martin's *Life in a Box is a Pretty Life*, Douglas Kearney's *Buck Studies*, John Wiener's collected *Supplication* [which always reads like love], Renee Gladman's *Ravicka* novels, Jonah Mixon-Webster's *Stereo(type)*, and cris cheek's *persistent whimsy*."

Robin Rahija "Books that have made me cry recently: *Extratransmission* by Andrea Abi-Karam, *River Hymns* by Tyree Daye, *Tunsiya/Amrikiya* by Leila Chatti."

Suzanne Scanlon "I am the author of *Her 37th Year, An Index* (Noemi) and *Promising Young Women* (Dorothy). I'm currently reading Enrique Vila-Matas' *Dublinesque* and Marguerite Duras' *Me and Other Writing*. I'm rereading Sylvia Plath's *The Bell Jar* and Lily Hoang's *A Bestiary*."

David Schuman Recent Reading: *Walking on Lava: Selected Works for Uncivilized Times* by The Dark Mountain Project; *The Need* by Helen Phillips; *The Stranger* by Albert Camus; *Hard Mouth* by Amanda Goldblatt; *Avery Colt is a Thief, a Snake, a Liar* by Ron Austin.

Kate Shapiro was born and raised in Dallas, TX. Her current reading list is *The Ghost Network* by Catie Disabato and *Cult X* by Fuminori Nakamura. Her all time favorite novels are *Bad News* by Edward St. Aubyn and *Lonesome Dove* by Larry McMurtry. The story published in this issue of *Fence* is dedicated to her wonderful, brave, and hilarious uncle Ben Stephens, who passed away from ALS earlier this year.

Chris Stroffolino lives in Oakland, CA. Recent books he's enjoyed are: *The End of Spectacle*, Virginia Konchan; *New Sutras*, Suzanne Stein; *A Little More Red Sun on The Human*, Gillian Conoley; *The Book of Scab*, Danielle Pafunda, and *Squeezed: Why Our Families Can't Afford America*, Alissa Quart.

Michelle Taransky is currently reading: *Blue Flame* by Emily Pettit, *Cover Songs Cover Songs Cover Songs Off Days* by Jordan Stempleman, and *Out of Nowhere Into Nothing* by Caryl Pagel. "My books: *Barn Burned, Then, Sorry Was In the Woods* & the forthcoming *Abromowitz-Grossberg*—where these poems are from!"

Jamie Thomson "I've been reading Tim Dlugos' collected (*A Fast Life*) and a selected of Rolf Dieter Brinkmann's poems (*An Unchanging Blue*, translated by Mark Terrill)."

Daniel Tiffany is the author of five volumes of literary criticism and five collections of poetry, including his most recent (with Blunt Research Group), *The Work-Shy* (Wesleyan Poetry Series, 2016). He is reading: *The Book of Margery Kempe*; Szilard Borbely, *Berlin. Hamlet*; Stacy Doris, *Fledge*; Kevin Holden, *Birch*; Renee Gladman, *The Ravickians*; Richard Greenfield, *Subterranean*; Michael Snediker, *The New York Editions*; Heriberto Yepez, *Transnational Battlefield*.

Erin Trapp Rachel Carson, *The Edge of the Sea*; Larissa Lai and Rita Wong, *Sybil Unrest*; Paula Heimann, *About Children* and *Children-No-Longer*; Jenni Fagan, *The Sunlight Pilgrims*; Ingeborg Bachmann, *Borrowed Time*.

Lloyd Wallace "Talking first about recent releases, both Aria Aber's debut *Hard Damage* and Christine Gosnay's latest chap *The Wanderer* are better than Christmas, and should be bought immediately. Also worth mentioning is the recent anthology put together by Robert Pinsky (titled *The Mind Has Cliffs of Fall*) concerning "poetry at the extremes of feeling" and including some of the strongest work by Emily Dickinson, Monica Youn, Major Jackson, and more—it was probably my best read of the year, and I would recommend it to anyone. Moving onto the older stuff, which I'm always revisiting, I'll name Yusef Komunyakaa's *Neon Vernacular* and Robin Fulton's translations of Tomas Tranströmer as two of my most-permanent favorites."

Adrienne Walser is reading *Indelicacy* by Amina Cain and *Three Women* by Lisa Taddeo. She just finished Robert K Massie's biography, *Catherine the Great* and just began Eli Clare's *Brilliant Imperfection: Grappling with Cure*. She has published writing in CARLA (Contemporary Art Review), *Pastelegram: Projects Exploring Archives and Artistic Process*, *Jacket 2*, *Art Book Review*, and *Film International*.

Emma Winsor Wood *A Failed Performance: Short Plays & Scenes* by Daniil Kharms, translated from the Russian by me and C Dylan Bassett; *A Time for Everything*, Karl Ove Knausgaard; *Poetic Notebooks: 1974–1977*, Eugenio Montale; *Baby, I Don't Care*, Chelsey Minnis; *A Timeshare*, Margaret Ross.